Shadow of the Dragon

Ray Williams

Shadow of the Dragon

by Ray Williams

Published by Aurelias Publishing

ISBN: 9798339656104

Dedication

This book is dedicated to my wife and dearest friend, Diane Williams. She is a woman of great courage, compassion, and kindness who has inspired me to be the best person I can be.

Acknowledgements

The making of a book is rarely a singular enterprise, although the author contributes the creative content. Many people have helped. I am grateful to those who have helped me bring *Shadow of the Dragon* to fruition.

First and foremost, I acknowledge my wife and best friend, Diane Williams, who contributed countless hours editing my manuscript and offering valuable insights for the book.

I also most appreciative of Stephanie Frank, and for her support, endorsement, and helpful feedback.

Table Of Contents

Preface

In recent years, the world has seen an alarming surge in the trafficking and abuse of fentanyl. This potent synthetic opioid has wrought havoc across communities and claimed countless lives. Despite relentless efforts by law enforcement agencies worldwide, the illicit fentanyl trade continues to flourish, evolving into an intricate and elusive web of crime that spans continents.

This fiction novel explores a shadowy conspiracy at the heart of this crisis, one that involves a formidable alliance between a Hong Kong Triad and a Mexican drug Cartel aided by the Central Intelligence Agency (CIA). It reveals the underbelly of the global drug trade, where ruthless criminal organizations operate with near impunity, facilitated by the complicity of big business, financial institutions, politicians, and even government bodies.

The story delves into the depths of corruption, examining how powerful interests perpetuate the drug trade for profit and influence. Banks turn a blind eye to money laundering activities, allowing vast sums of illicit money to flow seamlessly through the financial system. Corporations, eager to expand their reach and maximize profits, engage in clandestine dealings that bolster the capabilities of drug trafficking networks and allow shady drug money to buy up legitimate businesses. Politicians, driven by ambition or compromised by greed, offer protection and policy favors in exchange for kickbacks and campaign contributions.

At the core of this complex and perilous landscape is the CIA, an institution that, while tasked with safeguarding national security, has historically employed morally dubious tactics. Numerous investigations, reports and legal documents have shown that the CIA has broken many laws, used criminal enterprises and deceived and lied to government officials, including the President, since the Agency's inception to pursue geopolitical objectives and contain perceived threats. This dark side of the CIA's operations underscores a chilling truth: that in the global game of power and influence, the lines between right and wrong, ally and enemy, often blur beyond recognition. And that justification is a strong belief that "ends justify the means."

Amidst this turmoil, some refuse to be silenced. In this story, a tenacious DEA Special Intelligence Agent, Angela Torres and a determined Hong Kong police inspector, Blake Morgan, form an unlikely alliance, united by their shared commitment to justice. Their quest is bolstered by the support of Senator Bryce Connor, Chairman of the Senate Intelligence Committee, who leads an investigation into the CIA's clandestine activities. As an ally, Senator Connor uses his position of power to expose the hidden machinations of the intelligence community, providing a critical lifeline to those fighting on the front lines against the drug trade.

Through the intertwined stories of these courageous individuals and a cast of characters caught in the crossfire, this novel seeks to shed light on a shadow conspiracy of fentanyl trafficking that spans the globe. It is a tale of courage, betrayal, and the relentless pursuit of truth in a world where corruption runs deep, and the stakes are unimaginably high. The story will take you to Hong Kong, Mexico and the United States to illustrate the global nature of the fentanyl conspiracy.

As the battle against the fentanyl epidemic rages on, this story stands as a testament to the resilience of those who fight against the tide of criminality and corruption. It is a call to acknowledge and confront the uncomfortable realities that underpin the drug trade, and to demand accountability from those who exploit human suffering for their gain. It is a story calling out for light to be shone on the shadow of the dragon.

In reading this book, may you find not only a gripping tale of intrigue and suspense but also a deeper understanding of the forces perpetuating the global drug crisis. And perhaps a glimmer of hope that through awareness and action, the tide can be turned.

Chapter 1

Fall of the Dragon

Hong Kong, 1987

The neon-drenched streets of Hong Kong hummed with their perpetual symphony of chaos and order as dusk melted into the cloak of night.

Wan Chai, a district brimming with life and energy, was a dichotomy of tradition and modernity. The gritty industrial docks were evolving, bristling with the clanging symphony of cranes and forklifts as they danced around towering cargo stacks. Majestic container ships glided into the harbor, casting long shadows, while weather-beaten junks floated gently in the choppy waters, juxtaposing ancient silhouettes against the modern cityscape.

In 1987, Wan Chai was a meeting point between East and West, past and present. Neon signs jostled for space alongside older red lanterns, casting a soft, ethereal glow over the bustling streets. A torrential downpour swept the night sky, baptizing Hong Kong relentlessly. The southeast wind bared its teeth at the harbor, coercing tiny, bobbing boats to seek refuge and scattering city-dwellers from the labyrinthine streets.

In the heart of this frenetic cityscape, Tan Shui Kin Hospital in Wan Chai stood as a beacon of sterile calm amidst the urban frenzy. Under the indifferent glow of fluorescent lights, Simon Chan, Dragon Master of one of the most prominent criminal Triads in Hong Kong, the Wo Shing Ye, burst through the double doors and limped toward the stairs leading to the street below.

Senior Inspector Blake Morgan of the Royal Hong Kong Police Force walked beside Chan. Dressed in navy blue pants and a white shirt, Blake cut a striking figure. At forty-two, his Welsh and Mexican heritage sculpted him into rugged contrasts: piercing blue eyes framed by a mane of curly black hair against a tanned, angular face. Each line on his face spoke of years of hardship and determination; his lean, athletic form was a testament to a life of martial arts discipline and military rigor.

Blake's journey had been extraordinary. Born during WWII in Hong Kong, he was a prisoner of war of the Japanese along with his family. He inherited a survival instinct from his resilient father, a Chief Inspector of Sanitary Health Services. These formative experiences sculpted Blake into a man of unyielding resolve, courage, and strength. Fluent in Cantonese and Mandarin, Blake's deep understanding of Hong Kong's intricate cultural fabric was a testament to his dedication to the police force. He faced the mammoth task of navigating the dark waters of Hong Kong's Triads.

Blake had served in the British military early in his career, following his father's footsteps. He was recruited into the Special Air Service (SAS), the special forces predecessor of the US Navy Seals. The SAS training was grueling, including the famous long marches across the rugged terrain of the Brecon Beacons in Wales, carrying heavy rucksacks and navigating with maps and compasses. The final test was the Endurance March of forty miles within a strict time limit. In dense jungle conditions, candidates learned survival, navigation, weapons, and combat skills. The close-quarter battle training included urban room clearing, hostage rescue, and hand-to-hand combat. The attrition rate in SAS is ninety per cent, and Blake was one of the durable minorities that succeeded. That training and discipline had proven to be essential to his success as police officer.

Blake emerged from the sterile confines of Tan Shui Kin Hospital in Kowloon, the acrid smell of antiseptic still clinging to his clothes. He had just gone toe-to-toe with Simon Chan, the infamous Dragon Head of the Wo Shing Ye, whose very name sent shivers down the spines of criminals and business owners throughout Kowloon. Blake's interrogation of Chan regarding his attacker had been met with silence.

Chan's leg wrapped in a bandage, was a testament to the brutal dance of power that constantly threatened to tear the city apart. The bullet wound was a stark reminder of the fragile peace that existed between rival Triads, a peace that now teetered on the brink of all-out war.

Blake had hoped that Chan's vulnerability might finally crack the impenetrable wall of silence surrounding the Triads. But as the minutes ticked by, that hope had withered and died, replaced by a gnawing frustration that clawed at his insides.

Chan's eyes, cold and unyielding as steel, had revealed nothing. His lips, twisted in a mocking smirk, had offered only silence and contempt. With each evasion to Blake's questions, each calculated pause, Blake felt the answers he so desperately sought slipping further from his grasp. *"I have to remained centered and calm,"* Blake reminded himself. He was reminded of the wisdom of the Stoic philosopher Seneca: *"You may be sure that you are at peace with yourself, when no noise reaches you, when no word shakes you out of yourself."*

As he stalked out of the hospital with Chan, anger boiled within Blake. For a dark, terrible moment, he found himself wishing that Chan's attacker had aimed true, that the bullet had found a more vital mark. The thought was a stark reminder of how this endless war had eroded his optimism about controlling the Triads.

Simon Chan's gait was a torturous dance of agony and determination. His uneven steps betrayed the dark history etched into his soul, a visible echo of the violence he had both endured and inflicted. Once youthful and vigorous, his face had succumbed to time and the exertion of authority. Deep lines creased his countenance like battle scars, weaving a tale of age and dominion.

Chan was a name whispered with reverence and fear in the shadowy corridors of the criminal underworld. His reign as the

Dragon Head of the Wo Shing Ye Triad left an indelible mark on the city. Blake, hardened by encounters with the criminal world, reached out to gently halt Chan's unsteady walk, having calmed himself. "Although that gunshot wound in your leg didn't inflict grave damage, it might be prudent to spend a day or two recuperating in the hospital," he said to Chan. "We haven't finished discussing how you came to take that bullet."

Chan's head shook imperceptibly, his silence an unspoken declaration of defiance. With a predator's keen gaze, Chan surveyed the bustling street, his commanding presence subdued by the slow, painful steps he took. Unbeknownst to him, danger lurked in the patient malevolence concealed within the shadows.

A sleek, black sedan careened down the street, engines roaring like unleashed beasts. Before Chan could react, the vehicle screeched to a halt, disgorging two assailants cloaked in black sweatsuits. Their faces, covered with black masks, projected determination, their hands wielding meat cleavers that gleamed ominously under the flickering streetlights. The assailants descended upon Chan and Blake with a barbaric frenzy, their cleavers cutting through the air with deadly intent.

Blake's hand instinctively reached instinctively to his belt towards his service revolver that wasn't there. He cursed inwardly, regretting his decision to forgo his firearm. But as the glint of steel sliced through the air, Blake's body responded with a fluidity from countless hours of grueling martial arts training and meditation.

Years of the deadly Krav Maga martial arts had honed his reflexes to a razor's edge. Blake's forearm snapped up in a lightning-fast block, deflecting the cleaver. He pivoted on his heel, a move straight out of Shotokan Karate, narrowly avoiding a second attacker's wild swing.

The scene became a blur of motion. Blake's feet danced across the grimy pavement, his Taekwondo footwork keeping him one step ahead of his assailants.

These weren't street thugs – they moved with the coordinated precision of trained killers.

Blake's vision tinged red, not from blood loss but from a familiar darkness rising within him. Anger – old, deep, and terrible – had been his constant companion since childhood. Now, it surged through him like molten steel, sharpening his senses and numbing the pain.

With a guttural roar, Blake unleashed a flurry of Wing Chun strikes. His hands became blurred, raining precision blows on pressure points and nerve clusters. The assailant engaged with Blake crumpled, clutching a shattered collarbone.

The assailant, eyes wide with dawning fear, swung his cleaver in a desperate arc. Blake slipped inside the man's guard, years of muscle memory taking over. His left hand deflected the blade while his right formed a rigid spear-hand. In one fluid motion, Blake drove his fingertips into the attacker's throat, crushing the windpipe.

As the man gasped and staggered, Blake's fury took control. His fist rocketed forward, slamming into the attacker's sternum with bone-shattering force. The impact lifted the man off his feet, sending him crashing to the ground.

Blake pounced, straddling his fallen foe. His fists became pistons, driven by rage and adrenaline. Each blow landed with a sickening crunch, pulping flesh and shattering bone. Blood sprayed, coating Blake's knuckles and spattering his face.

A cold realization settled in Blake's gut as the red haze of battle faded. His perfectly placed strike to the heart – a killing blow he'd trained for but never truly intended to use – had ended the fight before it began. The savage beating that followed had been nothing more than a grim epilogue written in blood and fury.

Chan, despite his resilience, faltered under the relentless assault of the other assailant. Blood sprayed onto the pavement, mingling with flecks of flesh in a gruesome tableau. Chan's agonized grunts echoed through the night. Overwhelmed by the attacker's savagery, Chan lay crumpled on the ground, his body a canvas of gaping wounds and spilt blood.

Chan's assailant swiftly retreated before Blake could engage with him, disappearing like a spectre into the awaiting black car. Just as he fled, a hospital security guard burst through the doors, his shouts of alarm and outrage piercing the night.

"Get a doctor out here, fast," Blake barked at the guard.

As the assailants vanished, a car screeched to a halt at the hospital's curb. Burly men, members of Chan's Triad, leapt out and rushed to their fallen leader, uttering threats, screams of shock, and interrogative questions peppered at Blake. One of Chan's loyalists remained by the bloody body of their leader, while another sprinted back to the waiting car, which sped off in the direction of the escaping assailants.

This brutal assassination, executed with chilling efficiency, sent a clear and chilling message echoing through the city that night. It was a declaration of war, a seismic power shift. As the news of the Triad leader's death rippled through the labyrinthine streets of Hong Kong, it was understood by all that this was just the opening act of a darker, bloodier saga, one that would seep into the business community and even the hallowed halls of government.

As the adrenaline ebbed from his system, Blake found his mind drifting to the ancient wisdom of the *Tao Te Ching*, which had been an integral part of his martial arts training. The stark contrast between the violence he had just experienced, and the peaceful teachings of Lao Tzu struck him profoundly.

"Why do I get so angry and full of rage?" he thought. The hours of psychotherapy had helped, yet there was still a fiery blackness there that couldn't be calmed or extinguished.

But now, in the eerie calm following the storm of violence, words from the *Tao* echoed in his mind: *"The soft overcomes the hard; the gentle overcomes the rigid.*" Blake pondered this paradox. His training had made him hard; his experiences had made him rigid, yet here he stood, victorious but unsettled. Perhaps true strength lay not in his ability to fight. But in his capacity to remain centered amidst chaos swirling around him.

Another teaching in his training surfaced is his thoughts: "*The best fighter is never angry.*"

Blake wasn't lost on the irony. His anger had fueled his actions to the point where it made him formidable but at the cost of a man's life. The *Tao* taught that the sage acts without effort and achieves without striving. How different might this encounter have been if he had approached it with a calm mind and a soft strength?

As the sirens of approaching police cars filled the air, Blake closed his eyes and took a deep breath. He recalled one more line from the Tao: "*To know others is intelligence; to know yourself is true wisdom.*"

In this moment of reflection, Blake realized that his journey to understand the criminal underworld of Hong Kong blended with his journey to understand himself. The path ahead was unclear, but perhaps by embracing the principles of the *Tao*—balance, non-action, and the unity of opposites—he could navigate both the external conflicts of the city and the internal conflicts of his nature.

The calm that settled over him now was different. It wasn't the eye of the storm, waiting for more violence to erupt. Instead, it felt like the first step on a new path—one that might lead him to strength beyond mere physical prowess and a peace that could withstand the chaos of his chosen life.

Chapter 2

The Force Gathers

In his dimly lit office at Wan Chai's Royal Hong Kong Police Headquarters, Blake Morgan looked over the reports about Triad activity in the city. His thoughts swirled in frustration and disbelief. It had been over a week since Chan's murder, and they still had no substantial leads.

He forced himself to revisit the lesson he'd learned about himself at the hospital and took three deep breaths to center himself into calmness.

Police Inspector Dennis Wang glanced up from his desk, a knowing smile curling his lips. Years of working with Blake had made him familiar with his superior's mercurial temperament. Still, he'd noticed that Blake could instantaneously switch off his stormy visage and suddenly become calm. "Anything from the people interviewed on the street before the hospital?" he asked.

Blake shook his head. "Crickets," he said placidly.

Wang, a Hong Kong native and a seasoned veteran of the police force, was a decade older than Blake. His short black hair, now sprinkled with strands of grey, framed a youthful face with piercing black eyes that seemed to see through the very soul.

Their conversation was interrupted by Police Commissioner Jack Blair, a burly Scottish man with family ties to the British Foreign Office, which had helped him rise through the ranks. "Have Internal Affairs finished interviewing you about the assailant's death, Blake?" Blair asked.

"Yes," Blake replied, "and gave me the green light to return to work."

"Still, remind me never to take one of your punches," Blair said lightly.

Blake looked embarrassed. "If I had to do it over again, chief, I would have just subdued him."

David Smith, the beleaguered Senior Police Inspector, joined in. As head of the Criminal Investigation Division, Smith had weathered relentless public and media criticism for failing to quell the escalating gang violence in Kowloon. His worn expression spoke volumes about his twenty years of service.

"Simon Chan's death has sent shockwaves through the city," Smith intoned with a heavy heart.

Blake added, "The other assassin who escaped wore a black mask, and their car had no license plates. So, we still don't have any ID on them."

Smith nodded solemnly. "I'll assemble a team to take over the case ASAP," he began, a glimmer of hope in his eyes. "*This could be a chance to regain some respect,*" he thought.

Commissioner Blair shook his head firmly. "David, I want you and Blake to conduct this investigation personally and cooperatively. With Chan being the Triad Dragon Head, it naturally falls under Blake's jurisdiction. Dennis, you will provide a backup for Blake. I don't want junior officers handling this."

Smith's face fell, disappointment etched upon it, but he deferred to Blair's directive.

Blake nodded, acknowledging the collaboration ahead. "I'm sure David and I can work together cooperatively."

As the meeting continued, Blake watched Smith intently. Rumors of Smith's connections to the underworld had long shadowed his service, but no hard evidence was ever produced. Despite Smith's long years of service, Blake couldn't shake his gut-level mistrust of him.

Blair's voice broke through Blake's contemplation. "I don't have to tell you the scrutiny we're under. The Foreign Office has had us under a microscope since the scandals involving our eroded public confidence. And the Governor wants results yesterday. My job may in the balance."

The Independent Commission Against Corruption (ICAC) had made significant strides in cleansing the force, leading to the conviction of numerous tainted officers. Blair had played a pivotal role in the ICAC, which propelled him to become a commissioner. Morgan, too, had been seconded to the ICAC, tasked with bringing some of his fellow officers to justice. Later, he had been appointed to head the Triad Society Bureau, clashing with Smith, who had yet to participate in the ICAC investigations. Both Blair and Morgan recognized the perilous ground they trod, with Chan's assassination threatening to expose the police force to harsh scrutiny once again.

With a heavy sigh, Blair reiterated the gravity of the situation. "We've got a potential powder keg here, and I want it defused. Blake, David, I want daily updates, and let's move swiftly."

"Got it, Chief," Blake replied. Smith nodded in agreement. Together, they exited the office.

Back in Blake's office, he, Smith, and Wang regrouped. "David, can I suggest you have your team talk to as many of your informants as possible to find anything important? Dennis, head back to the hospital and interview the staff again. The clock is ticking, and we don't want it to be a time bomb," Blake said.

Wang and Smith nodded, though Blake could see the displeasure on Smith's face.

The three men dispersed, leaving behind the unusual quiet of police headquarters.

Chapter 3

The Shadow Conspiracy Begins

Raul Ramirez, the head of the Tijuana drug Cartel, lounged on the deck chair of the white-tiled terrace, overlooking the pool cantilevered on the hillside, seamlessly blending into the Pacific Ocean below in the Costa de Oro near Tijuana. Blazing red bougainvillea draped the ten-foot white stone walls surrounding the stately new home. Armed men in T-shirts, shorts, and sandals patrolled the perimeter, their AR-15s at the ready.

Ramirez, his pock-marked face a remnant of untreated chicken pox, was dressed in white cotton pants and a loose guayabera shirt. His thick moustache framed an angular face with black eyes that darted from side to side when he spoke. He prided himself on his athletic physique, which he maintained through daily workouts in his mansion's gym. He fancied himself irresistible to women, yet those around him were paid or "recruited" from poor families.

Clipping the end of a long, fat cigar, Ramirez lit it, taking deep drags before the smoke coiled around his head. He poured two glasses of smoky mezcal from an unmarked bottle, the liquid catching the harsh sunlight. As head of one of Mexico's fastest-growing drug Cartels, Ramirez was embroiled in a war with three other aggressive established Cartels.

Across from Ramirez sat his right-hand man and cousin, Raphael Salinez, a stylish, meticulous man in his thirties. Dressed in a white linen shirt and pants, Salinez had worked his way up in the Cartel to become Ramirez's most trusted advisor.

"A Hong Kong Triad is making a power play," Salinez said his eyes glinting with a predatory hunger. The words hung in the air, heavy with promise and danger. "They're looking to forge a partnership in

Fentanyl trafficking. Chinese production, Hong Kong distribution, and us." He paused, savoring the moment. "We'd be the pipeline to the hungry veins of America."

Ramirez's eyes narrowed to slits, his fingers tightening around the crystal tumbler of mezcal. The smoky liquor burned his throat, a fitting companion to the fire igniting in his belly. "Fentanyl," he mused, rolling the word on his tongue like a bitter candy. "It's a whole different monster. I thought the Triads were married to their precious heroin trade."

Salinez leaned forward, his voice dropping to a conspiratorial whisper. "They were, Raul. But times change, and so do empires. Think about it – we've got the routes carved in blood, the army of loyal *soldados*, the infrastructure built on bones and bullets. They've got a product that makes cocaine look like child's play. Together?" His smile was a shark's grin. "We could crush every other Cartel from here to Colombia."

Ramirez reclined, the antique chair groaning under the weight of his ambition. "We'd be not just moving mountains, Rafael. We would reshape the whole continent." He took another sip, letting the alcohol fuel his growing excitement. "Fentanyl isn't just another high – it's a goldmine wrapped in a body bag. Cheap to make, easy to hide, and the profits . . . ." He whistled low. "We'd be making money faster than the U.S. Treasury."

"Control the Fentanyl, control the country," Salinez declared, slamming back another shot. The glass hit the table with the finality of a judge's gavel.

The Mexican afternoon stretched around them, the air thick with potential. Distant coyotes howled as if sensing the shift in the underworld's tectonic plates. The breeze whispered through parched mesquite, carrying the scent of imminent change.

"Set it up," Ramirez commanded, his voice as dry and unforgiving as the Sonoran Desert. "I want to look these Hong Kong players in the eye."

Salinez's grin widened, a touch of nervousness creeping in. "It's already in motion, *jefe*. We're meeting their representative in Hong Kong next week."

Ramirez's gaze snapped to his lieutenant, sharp enough to draw blood. "Is that so?" The words dripped with icy disapproval.

Salinez stiffened, his earlier bravado evaporating. "*Sí*, Raul. I took the initiative. Their liaison reached out, and I couldn't let the opportunity slip."

Ramirez took a long, contemplative drag on his cigar, the ember flaring like a demon's eye. "Who's our dance partner in this tango?"

"Raymond Fung," Salinez replied, relief evident in his voice. "A high-ranking *capo* in the Min Ho Triad. They say he's got a mind like a computer and a heart of liquid nitrogen. Ruthless doesn't begin to cover it. But he's maintained an air of respectability as a mainstream businessman."

A low chuckle rumbled from Ramirez's chest. "Smart and ruthless, eh *Amigo*? So, are these Min Ho boys the top dogs in Hong Kong?"

Salinez leaned in, his voice dropping to a hush. "No, *jefe*. They're the hungry wolves nipping at the heels of the Wo Shing Ye Triad. Fung's got legitimate businesses, too – a shipping empire that'll move our product like ghosts on the tide. If we lock this down, we'll be untouchable." He paused, his expression grave. "But we tread carefully. The Triads are not like our South American cousins or the Mafia. Their world operates on different rules."

Intrigue flickered in Ramirez's eyes. "How so?"

"Honor and loyalty are their religion," Salinez explained, his tone deadly serious. "Cross them, and there's no hole deep enough to hide in. They'll paint the walls with your blood and use your bones for chopsticks. If you betray them, they'll kill your family as well. And their organizations are loosely run, not like the Mafia."

Ramirez nodded slowly, a cruel smile playing at his lips. "Then we show respect. We play their game. But we never forget who we are, Rafael. This isn't just a partnership – it's the birth of an empire that will make Escobar look like a street corner pusher."

Salinez raised his glass, firelight dancing off the crystal. "To our empire, then."

Ramirez met the toast with a resounding clink. "To absolute dominion."

As they drank, the sun bled crimson across the horizon as if nature recognized their ambition's magnitude. The future stretched before them, a canvas waiting to be painted in shades of power, profit, and violence. Raul Ramirez and his Tijuana empire stood poised to seize destiny by the throat, consequences be damned.

Chapter 4

The Enemy Within

In the cavernous depths of Drug Enforcement Agency (DEA) headquarters in Washington DC, shadows writhed on the walls like restless spirits, cloaking the assembled agents in an aura of clandestine urgency. The air hung heavy with unspoken tension, each breath laden with the weight of impending revelations.

Angela Torres, a Special Agent in the Intelligence Division of the DEA, stood at the head of the table, her large hazel bright eyes sweeping across the room. She silently recited a passage from Marcus Aurelius' *Meditations*: *"You have power over your mind—not outside events. Realize this, and you will find strength."* The weight of the impending revelations threatened to overwhelm her, but Angela centered herself, embodying the Stoic principle of focusing only on what was within her control.

Angela's rebellious strand of midnight hair cascaded across her flawless olive skin, a stark contrast that only accentuated the fierce determination etched into every line of her face. She was a study in contrasts - a vision of captivating beauty concealing a body and mind as brilliant as they were strong as steel.

Born into a legacy of power and wealth, Angela had spurned the gilded cage of her family's expectations. The untimely deaths of her parents - her father, a billionaire and respected Ambassador to Spain, and her mother, the iron-fisted matriarch of a cosmetics empire had only fueled her resolve. Despite inheriting a fortune that could sustain generations, Angela chose the treacherous path of justice, driven by an insatiable hunger to make the world a better place to live.

Her journey had been forged in the crucible of Georgetown University and tempered in the unforgiving fires of Quantico. There, she had honed herself into a weapon - precise, lethal, and utterly devoted to her cause. But it was more than mere training that set Angela apart. Her mastery of Krav Maga was legendary, a dance of violence that had saved her life countless times in the shadowy world she inhabited. Her marksmanship was spoken of in hushed, reverent tones, and her ability to read the souls of men through their eyes was nothing short of preternatural.

Despite the tumultuous path that led her here, Angela had found solace and strength in Stoic philosophy. The teachings of Seneca, Epictetus, and Marcus Aurelius had become her North Star, guiding her through the treacherous waters of her chosen profession. She often reminded herself of Epictetus' words: *"It's not what happens to you, but how you react to it that matters."* This philosophy had shaped her into a paragon of emotional resilience, a quality that would be tested to its limits in the coming days.

Yet, her discipline, physical prowess, and confidence were balanced by her humanity, her empathy, compassion, and kindness for others who were less fortunate and victims of circumstance or the cruelty of others.

As she gazed upon her hand-picked team, Angela felt the weight of their collective knowledge pressing down upon her. The air crackled with anticipation as she opened her notepad, her voice cutting through the silence like a blade. "Alright," she commanded, her tone brooking no argument, "I want to hear everything. Hold nothing back."

Agent Juan Moreno, his face a roadmap of scars and hard-earned wisdom, was the first to speak. His voice, gravelly from years of shouting orders and inhaling desert dust, carried the weight of grim tidings. "The Cartel war," he began, each word dripping with foreboding, "it's spiraling into madness. Assassinations have become as common as breathing in Juárez, Acapulco, Cancún -- Christ, even tourist havens like Tijuana aren't safe anymore."

Angela's eyes narrowed, her mind racing to connect the bloody dots. "Who's behind this carnage?" she demanded, her voice a mixture of steel and barely contained fury.

Moreno's response painted a portrait of chaos and violence that uncommonly surprised Angela. "It's open warfare among the Cartels turning some cities into war zones. The Guadalajara Cartel, the Sinaloa Empire under the infamous 'El Chapo', the rising tide of violence from the Jalisco New Generation and the Tijuana Cartel, it's a hydra of evil, each head more vicious than the other."

But Moreno's final revelation sent a shockwave through the room. "One of our most trusted assets," he said, his voice dropping to a whisper, "overheard a conversation at the table next to his in a cantina and had the foresight to record it on his device. It was a CIA operative talking with someone from the Tijuana Cartel. About fentanyl imports from Hong Kong."

As the shocking information about potential CIA involvement washed over her, Angela felt a momentary surge of despair. But years of Stoic practice kicked in, and she quickly regained her composure. "*I cannot control the actions of others, only my own,*" she reminded herself silently. With this thought, she channeled her emotional energy into a laser-like focus on the task.

Moreno's words hung in the air like a death sentence. "What?" Angela breathed, her usual composure shattered by the magnitude of this revelation.

Moreno placed an audio tape on the table, confirming the reliability of his source. Angela's mind raced through a labyrinth of possibilities, each more terrifying than the last. The CIA, an ally turned enemy? It was unthinkable, yet the evidence stood before her, undeniable and damning.

Agent Richard Hall's Mexican heritage evident in the fire that blazed in his eyes voiced the question that burned in all their minds: "Why? Why would the CIA dirty their hands with drug trafficking?"

The silence that followed was deafening. In that moment, Angela knew that the war they had been fighting was about to change dramatically. The enemy was no longer just across the border. It was within their own ranks, hidden behind badges and oaths of allegiance.

"Our assets' words chill me to the bone," Moreno continued his voice barely above a whisper. "The CIA operative spoke of a need for drastic action against the rising tide of Socialist and Communist groups in Mexico -- groups that the CIA thinks pose a threat to U.S. interests. And then, the unthinkable -- they suggested enlisting a Cartel's aid in this endeavor."

The air in the room seemed to thicken, each breath becoming a struggle as the implications of this revelation settled upon them. Angela's mind raced, her thoughts a maelstrom of shock, disbelief, and a growing sense of betrayal.

"Angela," Moreno pressed, his eyes boring into hers with an intensity that spoke volumes, "has the FBI given any hint, any whisper of CIA involvement with these Cartels?"

Angela's response came slowly, each word carefully measured. "Not to my knowledge," she admitted, her voice laced with a steely determination. "But I will unearth the truth, no matter how deeply it's buried."

Turning her razor-sharp focus to Richard Hall, Angela probed further. "Richard, what news from your end?"

Hall's lips curled into a sardonic smile, a mirthless chuckle escaping him. "It seems today is ripe with revelations that would shock anyone not hardened by our line of work," he mused darkly.

Angela waited, the tension in the room ratcheting up with each passing second.

"I was in Monterrey," Hall began, his words painting a vivid picture of clandestine meetings and whispered secrets. "My informants there spoke of a sight that sent shivers down their spines -

Raphael Salinez, the ruthless second-in-command of the Tijuana Cartel, locked in an intense discourse with a mysterious Chinese individual."

Angela leaned forward, her eyes gleaming with a predatory intensity. "And the subject of this tête-à-tête?"

Hall's response was like a thunderbolt. "Fentanyl," he said, the word hanging in the air like a death sentence. "The word was used repeatedly, unmistakable even to my informant's straining ears."

A suffocating silence descended upon the room, broken only by the sound of racing heartbeats and shallow breaths.

"Fentanyl," Angela repeated, her voice barely above a whisper. "Not cocaine, not heroin, not marijuana. But fentanyl?"

Hall's confirmation was solemn, weighted with the gravity of its implications.

Angela's mind whirred into action, her words sharp and precise as she issued her directives. "Richard, I need you to dig deeper. Leave no stone unturned. Juan, keep your finger on the pulse of these Cartel conflicts - I want to know about any tremor, any whisper. As for me, I'll be delving into this CIA matter and reaching out to our counterparts in the Mexican police. The moment either of you uncovers anything of substance, I want to know. We'll reconvene in two weeks or sooner if events dictate. Your dedication and hard work are our greatest weapons in this fight. I want to thank you for your dedication and commitment."

As Moreno and Hall filed out, Angela remained, the gentle rocking of her chair starkly contrasting the tumultuous thoughts swirling in her mind. An ominous feeling settled in the pit of her stomach, a premonition of the storm that was brewing. The specter of the Iran-Contra affair still loomed large over the nation, and now these whispers of CIA collusion with Mexican Cartels, possibly in league with Chinese criminal syndicates. It was a powder keg waiting to explode.

With a heavy heart but an iron resolve, Angela rose, her steps echoing through the hallway as she made her way to her boss Roger Jones' office. The brief walk felt like an eternity, each step carrying the weight of the world.

As Angela prepared to brief her superior, she took a moment to center herself. She recalled Seneca's words: "*We suffer more often in imagination than in reality.*" While the situation was undoubtedly grave, allowing fear or anxiety to cloud her judgment would serve no purpose. Instead, she steeled herself to face whatever challenges lay ahead with clear-eyed determination.

Jones looked up as she entered, his weathered face a map of years spent in the trenches of this never-ending war. "Sir," Angela began, her voice steady despite the turmoil within, "I've just concluded a briefing on Mexican Cartel activity. What I've learned is beyond anything we could have imagined."

Jones leaned forward, his eyes narrowing. "Go on, Angela. I can see this is serious."

Taking a deep breath, Angela plunged into the abyss. "We have credible intelligence suggesting CIA involvement with the Tijuana drug Cartel. Moreover, we've uncovered a potential connection between a high-ranking Ramirez lieutenant and a member of the Hong Kong Triads. The topic of their clandestine meeting? Fentanyl trafficking."

Jones' face paled, the gravity of the situation etched in every line. "Oh, great," he muttered sarcastically. "Are these sources reliable, Angela?"

"As reliable as they come, sir."

Jones' response was swift and decisive. "We're walking into a minefield here, especially if the CIA is involved. It wouldn't be the first time we've locked horns with them, but this... this is different. I want you to drop everything else. This is your sole focus now. Whatever resources you need, they're yours. Just say the word."

Relief washed over Angela, knowing she had Jones' unwavering support. "Thank you, sir. I have a team ready to move. With your approval, I'd like to reach out to our counterparts in Hong Kong and see what they know about these Triad and Mexican activities."

"You have *carte blanche*, Angela. Do whatever it takes. But remember, this stays between us for now. Your reports come directly to me, understood?"

"Crystal clear, sir. Thank you."

As Angela turned to leave, the weight of what lay ahead settled upon her shoulders. She knew that the coming days would test her like never before, pushing her to the very limits of her abilities and resolve. But as she stepped out of Jones' office, there was a fire in her eyes and steel in her spine. Whatever dark forces were at play, whatever sinister alliances were being forged in the shadows, Angela Torres was ready to face them head-on, come what may.

Chapter 5

Echoes of the Dead

The Hong Kong air hung heavy with the weight of history, thick with the echoes of a past that refused to fade. The ghosts of 1941 lingered, their whispers carried on the salty breeze that swept in from the South China Sea. In the wake of Pearl Harbor's infamy, the Japanese army had descended upon this land like a relentless tide, crushing resistance in mere weeks and condemning thousands to the cruel embrace of internment camps. Those camps had become crucibles of human suffering, where abuse, starvation, and death reigned supreme.

Near Stanley village, perched on a hill overlooking the vast expanse of the South China Sea, stood a somber memorial. Its weathered gravestones bore silent witness to the atrocities committed on this very soil where a prison camp once stood. Stretching out before it, two graveyards lay side by side - one adorned with stark white stones that gleamed in the sunlight, the other marked by traditional Chinese graves, their curved roofs like miniature temples housing the souls of the departed. Together, they formed a poignant tableau, a stark reminder of lives cut short, and dreams left unfulfilled.

Blake Morgan moved through this hallowed ground, his steps measured and purposeful. His lean frame, honed by years of grueling training in the British SAS and further tempered by his service in the Hong Kong police force, was clad in a loose linen shirt that rippled in the gentle breeze. Beige cotton pants completed his casual attire, a stark contrast to the gravity of his surroundings.

Despite his imposing physical presence, Blake strove to embody the Taoist ideal of *wu wei* - action through non-action. His piercing blue eyes, which seemed to hold the ocean's depths within them, reflected a calm that came from years of practicing this principle. In his work as a detective, he had learned the value of allowing events to unfold naturally, of not forcing outcomes but rather aligning himself with the flow of circumstances. It had been a battle against the deep rage that still dwelled in his soul, one born from his imprisonment in a Japanese WWII POW camp.

In his hand, Blake clutched several bauhinia flowers, Hong Kong's signature bloom, their purple petals a splash of life amidst the solemnity of the graveyard. He offered a few to Sabrina Fung, his longtime friend and confidante, who stood beside him like a pillar of quiet strength. Sabrina's jade green silk suit whispered with each movement, a testament to her refined taste and privileged upbringing. Yet her eyes truly captured one's attention - pools of deep emerald that sparkled with an intoxicating mixture of strength and vulnerability, wisdom beyond her years and a pain that time had failed to heal fully.

Sabrina's auburn hair cascaded down her back in gentle waves, catching the sunlight and setting it ablaze with hues of copper and gold. As the heir to the influential McDougal business dynasty, she carried herself with a regal bearing that belied the weight of her heritage. Her father, a hero who had fallen defending Hong Kong in the war, had instilled in her a fierce determination and business acumen that had transformed her into a prodigy in her own right. Yet beneath this polished exterior lay a heart still aching from the loss of both parents - her mother having succumbed to illness a few years after the war's end.

Together, Blake and Sabrina knelt before three gravestones, their fingers intertwining as they laid flowers in reverent silence. The cool touch of the marble beneath their hands served as a stark reminder of the finality of death, of lives cut short and futures stolen. Sabrina's grip tightened on Blake's hand, her voice barely above a whisper as she said, "I'm glad we're here together, Blake. It means more than you know."

Blake nodded, gently squeezing Sabrina's hand. As they knelt before the gravestones, he recalled another passage from the *Tao Te*

Ching: *"Being deeply loved by someone gives you strength, while loving someone deeply gives you courage."* The bond he shared with Sabrina, forged in the crucible of shared hardship, was a testament to this wisdom.

The air around them seemed to thicken with memories, the ghosts of Stanley Camp rising unbidden in their minds. Blake could almost hear the echoes of suffering, the harsh conditions that had forged an unbreakable bond between the survivors, and the white stone markers of young, inexperienced Canadian soldiers who had given their lives to defend Hong Kong from the Japanese invasion. His gaze drifted to the memorial, its weathered surface etched with names that had become a litany of loss. Sabrina, ever attuned to his moods, asked softly, "You still feel it, don't you? The weight of it all?"

Sabrina's eyes softened, a mix of compassion and shared pain swirling in their depths. "Sometimes," she mused, "I think those left behind suffer as much. We carry the burden of memory, of lives unlived."

Blake's shoulders sagged slightly, the weight of survivor's guilt pressing down upon him. "I wish I could have saved them," he admitted, his voice barely audible.

"You were just a child, Blake," Sabrina reminded him gently, her hand resting on his arm. "You did what you could. More than anyone could have expected."

"The nightmares" Blake began, then trailed off, his eyes distant. "They still come, once in a while."

Sabrina's voice was a balm, soothing yet tinged with her pain. "Their pain and suffering are in our DNA, Blake, and will be there all our lives. The best we can do is live a life worth living in honor of them."

"As always, you are very wise, Sabrina," Blake responded, kissing her hand.

As they stood, brushing grass from their knees, neither realized how prophetic those words would prove to be. The air between them grew thick with unspoken thoughts, years of shared history and suppressed emotions threatening to bubble to the surface. Blake, ever the detective, sensed the change in atmosphere and sought to navigate these treacherous waters.

The air between them grew thick with unspoken thoughts. Blake finally broke the silence. "How are things with Raymond?"

Sabrina's eyes clouded, a storm of emotions passing across her face before she managed to school her expression. "He's filed for divorce," she admitted, her voice barely above a whisper.

Blake couldn't hide his surprise, his eyebrows shooting up as he processed this information. "I didn't realize it had deteriorated so much," he said, his mind racing to reconcile this news with the couple he thought he knew. "You've been married, what, three years?"

"It was never easy," Sabrina sighed, her shoulders slumping slightly. "Raymond's father only agreed to our union with a prenup. It was a business arrangement as much as a marriage. What's ironic is that I should have insisted on a prenup. My wealth far exceeds Raymond's or his father's."

Blake, sensing the raw pain beneath her words, tried to redirect the conversation. "You don't need to elaborate," he said gently. "Not here, not now."

But Sabrina leaned in, her eyes searching his face with an intensity that made Blake's heart skip a beat. "You're the only one I can confide in, Blake," she said, her voice thick with emotion. "You've always been more than a brother to me. You understand me in a way no one else does."

Blake felt her pain acutely, his own heart constricting in compassion. "Do you want to salvage the marriage?" he asked, treading carefully.

"I thought I could win his acceptance," Sabrina admitted, a bitter laugh escaping her lips. "But Raymond wants me to abandon my businesses, to be nothing more than a trophy wife. I won't do that."

"Weren't these issues apparent before the wedding?" Blake asked gently, trying to understand.

Sabrina's eyes flashed with a mixture of anger and regret. "You know Raymond's struggle with directness," she retorted. "I suggested counseling, but he refused. Now he's closed off completely." She paused, her gaze dropping to the ground before rising to meet Blake's once more. "Truth is, I settled because I couldn't have the man I truly wanted."

Blake's brow furrowed in confusion. "Who?"

"How can you be so oblivious, Blake?" Sabrina exclaimed, frustration coloring her voice. "You! It's always been you!"

Blake felt as if the ground had shifted beneath his feet, his mind reeling from this revelation. Yet even in this emotional turmoil, he was drawn to the Taoist concept of yin and yang, the interconnectedness and interdependence of seemingly opposite forces. Perhaps his relationship with Sabrina had always contained this duality of friendship and more profound love, each aspect defining and complementing the other.

"You may read criminals well, Blake," Sabrina said, a sad smile playing at her lips, "but you're hopeless when it comes to women!"

Blake recognized the truth in what she said. He hesitated as Sabrina spoke. "Do you still love him?" he asked softly, almost afraid of the answer.

"I did once," Sabrina admitted, her voice barely above a whisper. "Not anymore."

As they neared the cemetery gate, lost in the swirling emotions of their conversation, a sleek black limousine pulled up with a quiet purr.

The door opened, and Tang, Raymond's father's assistant to Samuel Fung, Raymond's father, emerged. His face was ashen, his usually impeccable appearance disheveled. The gravity in his eyes sent a chill down Blake's spine even before the man spoke.

"My master Samuel has been killed," Tang said, his voice shaking with shock and barely contained grief.

Sabrina gasped, her hand flying to her mouth as the color drained from her face. Blake instinctively reached out to steady her, his mind already racing through the implications of this news.

"What happened?" Blake demanded, his voice sharp with urgency. "Has it been reported to the police?"

Tang's gaze dropped to the ground, unable to meet their eyes. "Not yet", he admitted. "I had stepped out briefly to run an errand for Master Fung. When I returned," His voice broke. "He was lying there in a pool of blood. Mutilated."

Blake's jaw clenched, his detective's instincts kicking into high gear. "Where was Raymond?"

"Meeting clients in Kowloon," Tang replied, his words coming faster now. "I informed him immediately. He directed me to find you here."

Blake nodded, his mind already formulating a plan of action. "Alright," he said, his voice steady and authoritative. "Sabrina and I will go to the Fung residence now. I need to preserve the crime scene. I'll contact police HQ as soon as we arrive." He turned to Sabrina, his eyes softening with concern. "Both of you will need to give a statement too. Are you up for that Sabrina?"

Sabrina nodded, her shock giving way to a steely resolve. "Of course," she said. "Whatever is necessary. But Blake," she hesitated, "I can't stay in that house now. Not after this."

"Is your family home still available?" Blake asked, already anticipating her needs.

"Yes," Sabrina confirmed. "I'll go there once we're done." She paused, a flicker of uncertainty crossing her face. "Should I disclose our marital issues to the police?"

Blake considered for a moment before responding. "Only if asked directly," he advised. "Just be truthful."

A chill ran down his spine as they walked to Blake's car. Near the entrance to the cemetery, a red dragon-shaped grave marker caught his eye. Its ruby eyes seemed to gleam with malevolent intent, an ominous presence that lingered long after they had driven away. Blake couldn't shake the feeling that this was only the beginning of the dragon's awakening heralding a storm that would shake Hong Kong to its very foundations.

Chapter 6

Second Strike

Blake and Sabrina departed the graveyard, their footsteps a solemn rhythm on the ancient stone path. Fifteen minutes later, the Fung mansion materialized before them, its imposing white columns gleaming like bones against the bruised twilight sky. Hong Kong's skyline sprawled below, a glittering tapestry of light and shadow that seemed to mock the colonial opulence perched atop The Peak.

As they ascended the marble steps, Sabrina's fingers dug into Blake's arm urgently. Her breath came in short, ragged gasps, each inhalation a battle against the rising panic within her. Blake could feel the tremors running through her body, a physical manifestation of the emotional storm brewing beneath her carefully composed exterior.

"Easy," Blake murmured, his voice a soothing balm in the growing tension. "One step at a time. You're stronger than you know." He silently willed his calm to envelop Sabrina, hoping to provide an anchor in the tempest of her emotions.

Tang materialized at the door, his usually impassive face now a canvas of worry and barely contained distress. The foyer's crystal chandelier cast a kaleidoscope of shadows across the marble floor, creating an unsettling dance of light and dark that seemed to mirror the turmoil within the house.

"Where are they, Tang?" Blake asked, his voice low and controlled. He allowed his question to hang in the air, neither pushing nor retreating.

Tang's eyes flicked towards the stairs, a fleeting gesture laden with unspoken dread. "The office, sir."

Blake nodded, then turned to Sabrina. Her face had drained of all color, her green eyes wide with a fear that seemed to consume her entire being. "Sit here," he said gently, guiding her to an antique chair with a tenderness that belied the gravity of the situation. "I need to assess the situation first."

"Blake," Sabrina whispered, her grip on his hand tightening to the point of pain. "I'm scared." The raw vulnerability in her voice pierced Blake's heart.

He squeezed back, channeling all his strength and reassurance into that simple gesture. "I know. You have the strength to get through this." As he spoke, Blake reflected again on a Taoist teaching: "*Being deeply loved by someone gives you strength, while loving someone deeply gives you courage.*" In this moment, he felt the truth of those words more profoundly than ever before.

The staircase curved away from the entrance, a sinuous path leading to the unknown. Blake's hand glided along the polished banister, its cool smoothness starkly contrasting with the air's heated tension. At the top, the office door stood slightly ajar, like a mouth frozen mid-scream. Blake pushed it open, the hinges releasing a soft, mournful creak.

The scene that greeted him was an assault on the senses, a tableau of violence that seemed to suck the air from his lungs. Samuel Fung lay sprawled on the Persian rug, his once-pristine linen suit now a macabre canvas of crimson. A bloodied cleaver, its blade gleaming with malevolent purpose, rested nearby in a slowly congealing pool of blood.

Raymond stood frozen, his gaze locked on his father's lifeless form. His hands trembled violently, clutching a blood-soaked handkerchief like a lifeline to sanity. The raw anguish etched on his face was almost unbearable to witness.

"Raymond," Blake said softly, approaching with the caution one might use with a wounded animal. "Have you called the police?"

Raymond's head snapped up, his eyes wild with a mixture of grief, shock, and something else, something Blake couldn't quite place. "Blake? Oh god, my father." His words dissolved into a choked sob as he stumbled backwards, collapsing into a chair. A smear of red stained the silk upholstery, a vivid testament to the horror unfolding.

As Blake pulled on a pair of latex gloves, he centered himself, drawing upon the Taoist principle of seeing the whole picture without trying to control it. "*The Master sees things as they are, without trying to control them*," he reminded himself silently. Aloud, he said, "I need you to focus, Raymond. Tell me exactly what happened."

Raymond swallowed hard, his Adam's apple bobbing like a buoy in a stormy sea. "I was in Kowloon at a meeting. When I got back, I found him lying on the floor in a pool of blood." His voice cracked, splintering under the weight of his emotions. "I tried to help him, but he was dead."

"The handkerchief," Blake nodded, his tone carefully neutral. "Is it yours?"

"Yes, I thought I could stop the bleeding." Raymond's words were saturated with a mixture of desperation and futility.

Blake's eyes narrowed imperceptibly. "Did you touch the cleaver?"

"No!" Raymond's voice rose sharply, a note of something akin to panic creeping in.

Blake held up a calming hand. "Alright. One more question, Raymond. Were your father's past associations with the Triads truly in the past?"

Raymond's face flushed, a storm of emotions playing across his features. "What are you implying? My father was a legitimate businessman!"

"You know as well as I do that it was rumored your father was associated with the Triads."

Raymond's face flushed with anger. "That's a malicious lie!"

Blake said evenly "I'm asking questions that need answers."

A commotion downstairs heralded the arrival of the police. Blake gently guided Raymond out of the office, his reassuring and authoritative touch. "Wait here."

Two police cars had arrived, their flashing lights casting an eerie blue glow over the manicured grounds. A group from the Organized Crime Division entered the mansion, led by David Smith. Blake watched as Smith briefly interacted with Sabrina and Tang, his face a mask of grim determination as Tang escorted him to the office.

Smith's dark expression spoke volumes as he emerged from the crime scene. He nodded tersely at Blake. "I'll take it from here, Blake."

"Right," Blake acknowledged, his mind already racing ahead. "But I'll have to tag along, as there are clear indications this might be connected to the Triads. Same murder MO as Simon Chan's assassination."

Smith's response was clipped, his demeanor unusually frosty. "Well, the boss has to okay it," he replied, "and by the way, he told me to tell you to see him back at headquarters ASAP."

A flicker of surprise crossed Blake's face. "Did he say what it was about?"

"No." Smith's flat tone brooked no further discussion. He then motioned to Sabrina to follow him to another room for questioning.

As Blake turned and walked down the stairs, he felt the weight of unseen eyes upon him. Climbing into his car, he cast one last glance toward Smith, a sense of unease settling in his gut. Smith's behavior was more irritating than usual, a departure from his typical professional demeanor.

Blake's mind whirred with unanswered questions as he drove away from the Fung mansion. *Something didn't smell right,* he thought. *Raymond had few answers, and his evasiveness about his father's past didn't ring true. On a personal level, I'm worried about Sabrina. I need to help her through this."*

Chapter 7

Agency Warfare

Angela Torres steered her nondescript sedan through the labyrinthine security checkpoints surrounding CIA headquarters, her mind as focused as a razor's edge. The weight of her mission—uncovering the truth about the alleged Mexican Cartel-Triad partnership—pressed upon her shoulders like an invisible titan. Yet, true to her Stoic principles, she kept an outward calm, her face a mask of professional detachment.

When she first joined the DEA, she was made keenly aware by veteran agents of the bad blood between the DEA and the CIA, not just about conflicts of jurisdiction but about outright interference in DEA investigations and prosecutions. And it was clear to her that the CIA was top dog in the pecking order from the White House's and Congress' perspective.

As she navigated the gauntlet of barricades and stern-faced guards, Angela reflected on the words of Marcus Aurelius: *"You have power over your mind—not outside events. Realize this, and you will find strength."* She drew a deep breath, centering herself. Whatever lay ahead in her confrontation with Jack Cross, the enigmatic Deputy Director of the CIA's Special Covert Operations Group, she would face it with equanimity and resolve.

The imposing edifice of CIA headquarters loomed before her, a monolith of glass and concrete that seemed to scrape the very sky. Angela's shoes clicked against the polished floor of the cavernous lobby, the sound echoing off marble walls that held secrets beyond imagining. Her gaze was drawn inexorably to the CIA seal embedded in the floor, its inscription now almost sardonic: *"And ye shall know the truth, and the truth shall make you free."* A wry smile tugged at the corner of her mouth. *"How much truth would I uncover today?"*

"Special Agent Torres?" A voice cut through her reverie. "Richard Helms at your service. Deputy Director Cross is expecting you."

Angela turned to face a middle-aged man whose impeccably tailored suit spoke of power and influence. She met his firm handshake with one of equal strength, a glimmer of surprise flickering in Helms' eyes at her grip.

"A pleasure, Mr. Helms," she replied, her voice steady despite the tumult of emotions roiling beneath her composed exterior.

As Helms led her through antiseptic hallways, each identical to the last in their bland, government-issue sterility, Angela's mind raced. The Political Action Group, under Cross's direction, dealt in shadowy realms of influence and manipulation in countries around the world. How could drug trafficking possibly align with U.S. foreign policy objectives? The very notion sent a chill down her spine, but she pushed the feeling aside, focusing instead on the task at hand.

"Make yourself at home," Helms said as he ushered her into a secluded meeting room, gesturing towards a sideboard laden with refreshments. The door closed behind him with a soft click, leaving Angela alone in the sterile space.

She poured herself a glass of water, the cool liquid a balm to her nerves. As the minutes ticked by— five, then ten, then twenty — Angela recognized the age-old tactic of making her wait. A power play, pure and simple. She allowed herself a small, humorless chuckle. *"The art of true living in this world,"* she murmured, recalling Epictetus, *"is more like a wrestler's than a dancer's practice."*

When Jack Cross finally deigned to enter the room, his presence seemed to suck the very air from the space. Tall and imposing, with a military bearing evident in every precise movement, he exuded an aura of authority that bordered on arrogance. His penetrating blue eyes swept over Angela, assessing her with a cold, calculating gaze that might have intimidated a lesser agent. Instantly his manner shifted into practiced charm.

"Angela, so glad to see you again," he said, his tone a study in false cordiality.

"Hello, Jack," Angela replied, matching his familiarity with a warm handshake that belied her inner steel. "It has been a while. I believe the last time we crossed paths was at the Smithsonian benefit."

"Oh, yes, I remember," Cross said, lying. He gestured for her to sit, his movements brusque and impatient. "You'll forgive me if we hurry our discussion. I have a meeting with my superior in half an hour." The unspoken implication hung in the air: *You're not as important as you think you are.*

Angela nodded, unfazed by his transparent attempt to rush her. "Of course, Jack. I'll be brief." She settled into her chair, her posture relaxed yet alert, starkly contrasting to Cross's rigid stance.

"And although this room is secure," Cross added, his gaze flicking to the camera mounted in the corner, "you know our conversations are recorded."

"I'm well aware of CIA protocols," Angela replied, a hint of steel creeping into her voice. She launched into her briefing, laying out the grim reality of the Cartel wars with clinical precision. As she spoke, she watched Cross's face for any flicker of reaction, any tell that might betray his knowledge or involvement. But his expression remained impassive, a mask of practiced neutrality that only fueled her suspicion.

"I'm here to ask you," Angela said, her tone direct and uncompromising, "if your division is involved in any way with Mexican drug Cartels or Hong Kong Triad drug traffickers."

The silence that followed was heavy, pregnant with unspoken tensions. Cross's face remained an inscrutable mask, but Angela caught the briefest tightening around his eyes. "Where did you get that information?" he inquired, his tone maddeningly even.

Angela recognized the deflection for what it was—an attempt to put her on the defensive by asking her questions. She'd learned how gas lighters worked a long time ago. "From our field agents in Mexico and their reliable informants," she replied coolly, waiting for any sign of recognition to flicker across Cross's features.

"I cannot confirm or deny what you described," Cross replied, his voice dripping with bureaucratic evasion. "National Security. Any information I have is classified above your pay grade."

Angela felt frustration mounting within her, a tide of anger threatening to overwhelm her carefully cultivated Stoic calm. She took a deep breath, centering herself. *"The obstacle is the way,"* she reminded herself silently, drawing strength from the Stoic teaching. Aloud, she pressed on, "I guess I'm saying on behalf of the Intelligence Division of the DEA, I need to know. Our mission and mandate are to pursue the war on drugs vigorously, and that includes identifying any government personnel who may be aiding or abetting—either purposefully or unknowingly—the Mexican Cartels and other drug syndicates."

Cross sat up straighter, his posture radiating irritation. "I understand all that, Angela. I've answered your question."

"Come on, Jack," Angela persisted, her tone a mixture of friendliness and steel. "We're on the same team here, trying to protect our country. Can you at least investigate the matter and seek permission to advise me of your findings so the DEA can follow up appropriately?"

For a moment, something like respect flickered in Cross's eyes, quickly replaced by his usual mask of indifference. "I can do that if I get clearance to do so." He glanced at his watch, the gesture a clear dismissal. "And I'm sorry, but I will have to run. Thank you, Angela, for bringing this to my attention."

As Cross stood to leave, he approached Angela, patting her arm in a patronizing gesture that set her teeth on edge. "Perhaps sometime soon, we can have lunch together and catch up on our personal lives."

"Thank you, Jack I'd look forward to it," Angela said tinged with sarcasm. "And I look forward to hearing from you soon about my inquiry." Angela replied, matching his false cordiality with her own, even as her mind raced with the implications of their conversation.

Cross nodded. "As I said, I can do that if I get clearance to do so." He looked at his watch and then walked briskly out of the room.

Left alone in the room after Cross's departure, Angela replayed the exchange in her mind. *"His evasiveness, the standard "National Security," and "classified information" responses, pointed to something bigger, something hidden beneath layers of bureaucracy and secrecy. How could he not know what was happening in his division? Or was he simply that adept at concealing the truth?* she thought.

As she made her way to the elevator, Angela's determination solidified. she needed to report to her boss, Roger Jones, to apprise him of her meeting with Cross and her team's new findings.

As the elevator descended, Angela drew strength from the words of Seneca: *"It's not because things are difficult that we dare not venture. It's because we dare not venture that they are difficult."* The path ahead would be challenging, fraught with danger and deception. But Angela Torres was ready to face it head-on, armed with her unwavering determination.

Chapter 8

A Debt Repaid

The late afternoon sun cast long shadows across Hong Kong's skyline as Blake strode purposefully towards police headquarters. The city's energy pulsed around him, a chaotic symphony of honking horns, chattering pedestrians, and the distant hum of construction. But beneath the surface vibrancy, Blake sensed an undercurrent of tension, as if the very air was charged with the portent of impending change.

Entering the precinct, Blake felt the weight of his responsibility settle more heavily on his shoulders. The bustling activity of the station – phones ringing, keyboards and typewriters clacking, hushed conversations between officers created a backdrop of organized chaos that mirrored his own tumultuous thoughts.

He made his way to Commissioner Jack Blair's office, each step measured and deliberate. The Triad's involvement, Raymond Fung's evasiveness, David Smith's hostility, and his own growing concern for Sabrina Fung churned in Blake's gut, making this one of the most challenging days of his career.

Blake knocked on Blair's door, took a deep breath to center himself, and entered at the commissioner's gruff invitation.

Blair's office was a study in organized clutter, case files and reports competing for space with family photos and commendations. The commissioner sat behind his imposing desk, his face etched with the lines of countless sleepless nights and difficult decisions.

"Report," Blair said in a businesslike tone, motioning for Blake to take a seat.

Blake settled into the chair, feeling the tension in the room like a physical presence. He began his briefing, his words clipped and urgent. "We've got a second Triad-style hit, sir. Samuel Fung, taken out in his own home office. No witnesses, just a bloody scene and a lot of questions."

"Any clues to a possible perpetrator?" Blair asked.

"Negative, Chief."

As Blake detailed his unsatisfying interview with Raymond Fung, he could see Blair's expression darkening. Raymond's apparent amnesia about his father's Triad connections and the unexpected complication of Sabrina Fung's ongoing divorce added layers of complexity to an already convoluted case.

"Then David Smith swoops in," Blake added, a hint of frustration coloring his voice, "acting like I'm treading on his turf. Something's not adding up here, Chief."

Blair leaned forward, his eyes narrowing. "Two Triad hits? This stinks of something bigger. I want you on this, Blake. Full steam ahead. Smith can keep digging, but you're to coordinate. This is your wheelhouse."

"Understood, sir, but could you remind him?" Blake nodded, feeling a surge of determination.

"There's more," Blair continued, his tone grave. "American DEA is sending a heavy hitter our way. Special Agent Angela Torres, head of their intelligence division. They've got wind of a Mexican Cartel-Hong Kong Triad connection. Fentanyl trafficking. This could be huge, Blake."

Blake's eyes widened, his mind racing to process this new information. "Fentanyl? Mexican Cartels? What hornets' nest have we kicked over?" The case's complexity was expanding exponentially, like ripples in a pond spreading outward from a thrown stone.

"You're my point man on this, Blake. Meet Torres, get me answers." Blair's words were both a command and a vote of confidence, and

Blake felt the weight of expectation settle on his shoulders. "Is there anything else, Blake?" Blair inquired tiredly, the strain of leadership evident in the slump of his shoulders.

Blake nodded, his mind already racing with possibilities. "One more thing, Chief. Chow Yung Zhou's resurfaced. Says he's got crucial Triad intel. I'm meeting him at the Hong Kong Club."

A flicker of recognition passed over Blair's face. "Zhou, the one who helped us shut down that prostitution ring a few years back, right? In exchange for reduced charges?"

"That's right," Blake confirmed. "He's become one of our best informants since then, and now has legitimate businesses here and in Macau. He contacted me, said he had important information about Triad activity. Given our current situation, I think it's worth hearing him out."

"Amazing how he landed on his feet. It sounds like he wants to pay the debt he owes you."

"I'm hoping he has something worthwhile."

Blair nodded slowly, processing the information. "Agreed. But watch yourself, Blake. Zhou may have gone straight, but old habits die hard."

As Blake turned to leave, he caught sight of the exhaustion etched on Blair's face. It was a stark reminder of the toll their work took, not just on themselves but on those around them. "Chief," he said softly, "take care of yourself. We need you fighting fit."

Blair managed a weary smile, the gesture softening the hard lines of his face. "You're right, Blake. I'll clock out early today."

Blake left the office, his steps purposeful. He had a report to file, a team to brief, and a potentially game-changing meeting with Zhou ahead.

As he headed for the Hong Kong Club, Blake's resolve hardened. With Blair's unwavering support behind him and his dogged determination, he'd unravel this web of corruption and violence. The Triads, the Cartels, the shadowy players pulling the strings were all in his crosshairs now.

In the face of this sprawling investigation, Blake knew that his greatest asset would be his ability to remain centered and true to himself. With this thought anchoring him, he set out into the bustling Hong Kong evening, ready to meet Zhou and uncover whatever truths awaited him at the Hong Kong Club.

The Hong Kong Club was an oasis of refined tranquility amidst the city's ceaseless cacophony. As Blake crossed the threshold, the chaotic symphony of the street faded, replaced by the soft murmur of discreet conversations and the gentle clink of a fine Chinese tea service. The air, heavy with the scents of aged leather, polished mahogany, and the faint aroma of premium cigars, seemed to whisper secrets of a bygone era.

Crystal chandeliers cast a warm, subdued light over the Members Club Bar, their glow dancing off meticulously polished brass fixtures. Paintings of Hong Kong's colonial past adorned the walls, silent witnesses to countless clandestine meetings and power plays. Blake couldn't help but reflect on the cyclical nature of power and corruption, a theme echoed in the *Tao Te Ching*: "*The softest thing in the universe overcomes the hardest thing in the universe.*" He wondered if his pursuit of justice was the soft water that would eventually wear away the stone of criminality.

In a secluded alcove, Zhou sat waiting, his lean frame coiled with barely contained energy. His sharp and alert eyes scanned the room constantly, a habit born from years of navigating the treacherous waters of Hong Kong's underworld. Though he now moved in legitimate circles, the survival instincts honed during his Triad days remained razor-sharp.

As Blake approached, he felt the weight of the investigation pressing down on him, each step carrying the burden of uncovering truths that could shatter lives and reshape the city's underworld. Zhou greeted him with an enthusiastic smile, though his eyes held a shadow of concern that didn't escape Blake's notice.

"So good to see you, Blake. You look well," Zhou said, his voice a mixture of genuine warmth and underlying tension.

"It's been a while," Blake replied, taking in Zhou's appearance. The man before him was a testament to change, a living embodiment of the Taoist principle that transformation is the only constant in the universe. "It looks like life is treating you well now."

"In no small part due to you," Zhou replied, gratitude evident in his voice.

As they settled into their conversation, the air around them thickened with unspoken dangers and half-formed theories. Blake's mind raced with questions, each one a thread in the complex tapestry of crime and corruption he was trying to unravel.

"I know Raymond Fung. He was in the club several weeks ago, meeting with a man I've never seen before. He looked Hispanic. Raymond didn't notice me, but I was close enough to catch parts of their conversation. They discussed trafficking fentanyl," Zhou said heavily.

After years of police work in Hong Kong, few things shocked Blake anymore. But this revelation was startling. "Zhou, what exactly did you overhear about the fentanyl deal? Any specific quantities or timelines mentioned?" Blake asked, his voice low and intense.

Zhou leaned in closer, his voice barely above a whisper, eyes darting around to ensure their privacy. "They were discussing the specifics of shipment by Raymond's shipping company. The way they talked sounded big, Blake. Really big." The urgency in Zhou's tone sent a chill down Blake's spine.

"What about Raymond Fung? Did he seem nervous or confident? Was there any indication that this was new territory for him?"

"I've been around people trying to make a big score, both legally and illegally, and there's a nervous intensity. It was though he was stalking a prey animal. Or on the verge of a big score," Zhou replied.

Blake absorbed this information, feeling the pieces of the puzzle shifting in his mind. The image of Fung as a desperate gambler clashed with the composed businessman he had interviewed earlier. It was a reminder of the Taoist teaching that appearances are often deceiving, and that true understanding comes from looking beyond the surface.

"One last thing, Zhou," Blake pressed, his voice tight with the weight of unasked questions. "Have you heard any whispers about why the Dragon Heads might be muscling in on this? Any shifts in the Triad power structure I should know about?"

Zhou's expression darkened. "That's the thing, Blake. It's all in flux right now. Simon Chan's Triad is in open warfare with the Min Ho Triad. Old alliances breaking, new ones forming. It's like the whole underworld is holding its breath, waiting for something big to break."

Zhou leaned in closer, his voice dropping to a conspiratorial whisper. "I heard about Chan's assassination. News travels fast. Do you have any suspects yet?"

"You know better than to ask about ongoing investigations. Just let me say, I'll find the assassin." Blake replied, keeping a professional tone while scanning the room for potential eavesdroppers.

"And I'm starting to think Chan's murder is connected. I suspect the Dragon Heads might be competing for a deal with the Cartel," Zhou guessed, his voice barely audible.

"Chow Yung, I appreciate this information. It will undoubtedly expand my investigation. Please let me know if you hear anything else that could help," Blake said appreciatively, though his mind was already racing through the implications.

"Of course, Blake" Zhou agreed, standing up. "I always pay my debts."

As their meeting concluded, Blake felt the weight of unasked questions and unspoken dangers hanging in the air. The Hong Kong Club's refined atmosphere now seemed like a thin veneer, barely concealing the violent currents swirling just beneath the surface of the city's glittering facade.

With each step towards his car, Blake felt the weight of responsibility settling deeper into his bones. He was more than just a detective now; he was a guardian of balance, tasked with navigating the tumultuous waters of change to protect the city he loved. As the neon lights reflected off the rain-slicked streets, Blake steeled himself for the challenges ahead, knowing that amid chaos, there was also opportunity.

Chapter 9

The Fentanyl Bomb

In the murky underbelly of the drug world, a silent killer emerged in the 1980s, forever changing the illegal drug business. Fentanyl, born in a lab as a medical wonder, soon found its way into the hands of those who saw its darker potential. This synthetic opioid, a distant cousin to the ancient opium poppy, would prove to be a wolf in sheep's clothing.

Imagine a substance so potent that a pinch could fell a giant. That's fentanyl - a hundred times stronger than morphine and fifty times more potent than heroin. It's a devil's bargain for drug dealers, offering sky-high profits from tiny amounts. And it comes in all shapes and sizes - patches, pills, sprays, even innocent-looking lollipops. But make no mistake, two milligrams is all it takes to snuff out a life.

The true horror of fentanyl lies in its chameleon-like nature. It slips into other drugs undetected - a dash in some cocaine here, a sprinkle in some heroin there. Sometimes it even masquerades as common prescription pills. This deadly game of Russian roulette leaves users and first responders in a terrifying dance with death.

From heroin to party drugs like MDMA, fentanyl's tendrils reach far and wide. The economics are chilling - a kilo of fentanyl-laced heroin can fetch over one hundred thousand on the street, while producing pure fentanyl costs a mere six thousand. It's a grim equation that spells disaster for communities worldwide.

And at the heart of this global menace? Most fentanyl labs call the mainland home, with Hong Kong's Triads playing a deadly game of middleman. These shadowy figures have been pulling strings since the '80s, weaving a web of distribution that spans continents. In the end, it's a story of greed, power, and lives hanging in the balance - a dark tale written in the language of addiction and despair in North American streets.

The sun beat down mercilessly on the dense forest carpeting the back slopes of *Volcán Nevado de Colima*. Angela Torres wiped a sheen of sweat from her brow, her eyes never leaving the makeshift landing strip and warehouses below. She could make out two guards through her binoculars, their Barrett M82 rifles glinting in the harsh light.

Beside her, Juan Moreno shifted slightly, his DEA training evident in his controlled movements. They were here unofficially, observing and ready to "assist" Jimmy Candelero, a mountain of a man whose reputation in the Mexican Federal Police was as outsized as his hulking six-foot-three, two hundred and twenty pounds of muscle and meanness.

Candelero's voice, low and gravelly, broke the tense silence. "Our government's tried to clean house. Root out the corruption in the police and the military. But for every rat we catch, two more scurry in." His eyes, hard as granite, scanned the horizon. "Can you believe it? In six years, we lost one hundred and fifty thousand soldiers to the Cartels. Killed or recruited."

Angela's brow furrowed. "What's being done about it, Jimmy?"

A humorless chuckle escaped Candelero's lips. "The International Narcotics Control Board says we're making 'good efforts.' But when your own Federal Investigations Agency is rumored to be on Cartel payrolls? It's like trying to bail out the ocean with a teaspoon."

The air hung heavy with more than just heat. The specter of corruption, of the *Pax Mafiosa* that saw politicians trading favors for votes, seemed to loom over them like the volcano at their backs.

As they waited, Candelero regaled them with tales of his time in Peru, of helicopter raids and cocaine busts worth millions. But beneath the bravado, Angela sensed a weariness, a frustration with a system that seemed rigged from the start.

"We should see a plane arrive soon if the intel we received was accurate," whispered Candelero.

Off to Candelero's right, about fifty feet away, was a team of Mexican police accompanying Candelero, all armed with Glock handguns and AR-15 rifles, along with explosive grenades and tear gas. Angela and Moreno were armed with Glock 17 handguns, AR-15 automatic rifles, and Candelero had a Glock and a Remington 12-gauge shotgun.

"Agua," Angela whispered, her throat parched from the oppressive heat. Candelero passed her the canteen with a knowing smirk.

"It's all in the mind, *gringo*," he chuckled, tapping his forehead. Angela fought the urge to roll her eyes as she took a careful sip, savoring the tepid water like a fine wine. She passed the canteen to Moreno, along with a salt pill.

As they waited, Angela's mind drifted to the enormity of what they were up against. The global drug trade was a hydra, and fentanyl was its newest, deadliest head. She turned to Candelero, her voice low and intense.

"Walk me through it again, Jimmy. How are they getting this stuff into the States?"

Candelero's eyes narrowed as he began to explain, his voice a mixture of frustration and resignation. "It's coming in from China, mostly. Either the finished product or precursor chemicals arrive at ports like Manzanillo and Lazaro Cardenas. From there, it's a nightmare. Fentanyl labs are popping up faster than we can shut them down."

"So, what has the Mexican Police uncovered so far, Jimmy?" she asked.

Seventy-five per cent of the fentanyl moves across the Tijuana-San Diego border, mostly under the control of the Tijuana Cartel. There are five Mexican Cartels now vying for control of the fentanyl trade. It appears like the Tijuana Cartel is making a move to become the most powerful."

Angela listened intently, her jaw clenching as she processed the information. The scale of it all was staggering, and for a moment, she felt overwhelmed. But she pushed the feeling aside, focusing on the task at hand.

"And production?" she pressed, needing to understand every aspect of this deadly trade.

"Manzanillo port cranes lift newly arrived containers filled with everything from clothes and powdered milk to car parts. The port handles over nine thousand containers a day. Even with the help of the navy, we struggle to find every tiny amount of precursor chemicals or final fentanyl. It's not a needle in a haystack. It's a hole in the needle in the haystack," Candelero sighed.

"What happens to the precursor chemicals then?" Angela asked.

Candelero took another sip of water. "Then, after delivery at the port, the chemicals are taken to Mexico's various locations in the north, mixed and pressed into pills. The thing about busting fentanyl production sites is that the labs can be set up quickly in houses or any building without anyone noticing. And unlike cocaine or heroin, which required thousands of agricultural laborers, the entire fentanyl industry in Mexico can function with only a few hundred 'cooks.'"

"You don't need a science degree. Teenage boys can be trained to produce it." Morena added.

"And we're catching on to the enormity of the problem in the US late and by accident," Morena said. "Our investigations have shown that eleven pounds of fentanyl in Mexico sells for about fifteen thousand. In America, the same eleven pounds sell for one hundred thousand. It is easier and inexpensive to produce, and it is ten times more powerful than heroin."

"Can you give me a *Readers' Digest* version of how they produce fentanyl from precursor chemicals?" Angela asked.

Candelero explained. "In a legal lab, N-phenethyl-4-piperidone (NPP) is created as a crucial precursor chemical. Next NPP is transformed into fentanyl base which is turned into a citrate salt for medical purposes because it's water-soluble and easier to work with. This crude form of fentanyl is purified to remove impurities. The clean fentanyl citrate is then prepared into the final product form, like patches or injections by adding necessary ingredients to ensure it's effective and stable.

"What about the Cartels' illegal labs? Do they follow the same procedure?" Angela asked.

"Sometimes, but they can vary it, and quality control is not great. Sometimes, it is mixed with other chemicals and drugs like cocaine, Xylazine, caffeine, acetaminophen and methamphetamine. They usually come into the U.S. in pill form or sometimes gel form and can be packed. And fentanyl is much easier to hide than cocaine or heroin. The pills are often wrapped in carbon paper and tape. The tape protects them from sniffing dogs. The paper hides them from X-ray machines. Often, the fentanyl made from the precursor chemicals is pressed into pill form counterfeited to look like Xanax, Percocet or Oxycodone."

Candelero's explanation was interrupted by movement below. Angela's body tensed, her hand instinctively moving to her weapon. Two men emerged from the warehouse, AK-47s slung casually over their shoulders. They jumped into a pickup truck and drove to the landing strip, where they lit signal fires at each end.

Angela's pulse quickened as more figures appeared: a muscular man with a holstered handgun driving a small tractor, and a portly man in a wide-brimmed hat, flanked by two scurrying dogs. The scene unfolding before them was like a carefully choreographed dance of the damned.

The low drone of an approaching plane filled the air, and Angela held her breath as an old C-130 materialized from the cloud cover. It bounced onto the makeshift runway, taxiing towards the waiting vehicles. As the plane's doors opened, Candelero's camera whirred to life, capturing crucial evidence.

The crates were unloaded from the plane and carried into the warehouse. When all the traffickers and pilot below entered the warehouse, Candelero's signal triggered his team in motion to descend on the warehouse.

Candelero's Mexican police team swarmed down on the men below, and positioned themselves just outside the warehouse doors, while Candelero, Angela and Moreno scrambled up into the loft in the building, positioning themselves directly above the traffickers.

Cinderella, Moreno and Angela aimed their weapons at the men below, and Candelero yelled out, *"La Policia! Deje caer sus armas y congelar,"* repeating it in English, "Police! Drop your weapons and freeze!" At the same time, Candelero's team stormed through the doors, weapons ready to fire.

Candelero repeated *"La Policia! Deje caer sus armas y congelar."*

The men below looked up into the loft and at the doors in shock. Several of them immediately raised their hands in submission. But one of the armed guards grabbed his rifle and began shooting at the police who had stormed in. He was met with a firestorm of bullets from the assembled assault team. Dozens of bullets tore the man into pieces, and he fell to the pavement in a heap.

The short, fat man yelled, *"Deja de disparar, me rindo!* Stop shooting, I surrender!"

"Lie on the floor face down and put your hands behind your backs," Candelero called out.

Candelero's men quickly attached handcuffs to the men lying on the pavement. Candelero motioned to have the fat man and the pilot to be sat on two chairs. One of Candelero's men pried open a crate and called out, "M16s, grenades, Glocks."

Candelero pulled out his large field combat knife and pushed it against the fat man's crotch. "What's your name?" Candelero asked, dragging the tip of the knife across the fat man's shorts.

"Gonzales, Juan Gonzales," the fat man replied.

"Well, Juan, you'll tell us everything we want to know, or you'll be a soprano in five seconds."

"Jimmy!" Angela protested.

"We do interrogation differently down here, Angela," Jimmy replied.

A wet stain quickly spread on Gonzales' pants. "Please! I'll tell you everything."

Candelero switched on the camera. Gonzales spilled out the story of the Tijuana Cartel shifting their drug trafficking operations from cocaine to fentanyl and MDA, and how they were in partnership with a Hong Kong Triad.

Angela focused her attention on the pilot. "What's your name, and who do you work for?"

The pilot hesitated. Angela glanced over at Candelero. "You prefer my friend to question you?"

Sweat ran down the pilot's face. "Michael Ransom, I work for AEROCO Airlines."

"Who owns AEROCO?" Angela continued.

"Raul Ramirez."

"What else?" Angela inquired.

"The fentanyl precursors or finished product is shipped from China to Manzanillo in containers disguised as clothing, food, you name it. It's transported by truck to an airport hangar, where I pick it up and fly it here," the pilot replied.

"Why doesn't Ramirez just truck it here directly?" Angela asked.

"More likely to run into Federales, Army and police checkpoints," Ransom said.

"What about the guns and munitions in those crates?" Angela queried, "They are U.S.-made standard military combat equipment."

"I picked them up in Nicaragua and flew them into Manzanillo," Ransom replied.

"Who was your contact in Nicaragua?" Angela pressed him.

"A man named Lopez, if that's his real name," Ransom replied.

"And who does he work for?" Angela continued.

"The CIA," Ransom said definitively.

"What?" "Say that again," Angela said.

"Lopez identified himself as a contractor for the CIA," Ransom replied."

"Alright, you're going to give us the entire story with every detail, right from the time you were first involved, back at police headquarters. And I'm sure you don't want to see this knife again." Candelero said to Ransom and Gonzales.

Candelero motioned to his men, who led the criminals out the door to meet police transport that had been radioed for a pickup.

"We'll leave the follow-up with those two in your capable hands, Jimmy, I need to pursue this CIA and Triad connection further," Angela said, "Please send us a full report, including the photos you took today. I'll be in Hong Kong meeting with Blake Morgan, of the

Hong Kong Police, who oversees investigating and eliminating Triad crime there."

"The evidence we have so far points to some kind of conspiracy involving a Hong Kong Triad, a Mexican Cartel and the CIA," Angela said, walking back to their SUV with Moreno.

"This confirms our informant's information about the CIA," Moreno added.

"Jimmy, it's important we present a united front here in both countries, so we can take down this alliance before it takes hold," Angela said with determination.

"Agreed," Candelero said, " I'll do my part, and let's keep in touch."

On the road back to Manzanillo, Angela's thoughts drifted to Hong Kong. "I hope this Inspector Morgan is as diligent as Jimmy," she thought, "we need two strong fronts."

Chapter 10

The Alliance is Forged

Angela's eyes fluttered open as the Cathay Pacific jet hummed through the sky toward Hong Kong. The gentle nudge of turbulence had roused her from a fitful sleep, a rare respite in the whirlwind of her recent experience in Mexico. As she stretched in her comfortable business class seat, her mind drifted back to the labyrinth of deceit and danger she had been navigating for the past few weeks.

She took a deep breath, centering herself as she recalled Marcus Aurelius's words: *"You have power over your mind—not outside events. Realize this, and you will find strength."* The Stoic philosophy had been her anchor in the tumultuous seas of her career, a constant reminder that while she couldn't control the chaos around her, she could control her reactions to it.

Her recent meeting with Jack Cross gnawed at her, a persistent ache in the back of her mind. His evasive answers and carefully chosen words had only deepened her suspicions. The thought of CIA collaboration with Mexican Cartels sent a chill down her spine, threatening everything she stood for.

"What is within our power, and what is not," she murmured to herself. The potential corruption within her own government was beyond her immediate control, but her response to it, her determination to uncover the truth entirely within her power. Her boss, Roger Jones' promise to confront Cross and leverage White House contacts offered a glimmer of hope, but Angela knew the real work lay ahead. She steeled herself for the challenges to come.

As the captain announced the plane's descent into Kai Tak airport, a flutter of excitement mixed with her apprehension. The infamous approach lived up to its reputation. Angela's breath caught in her throat as the plane banked sharply, skimming over apartment buildings close enough to see laundry flapping on balconies. Her heart raced, partly from the thrill of the landing, partly from the anticipation of what awaited her in this vibrant, dangerous city.

She closed her eyes briefly, focusing on her breathing. *"Fear is the mind-killer,"* she thought, borrowing from one of her favorite science fiction novels. The Stoic teachings on fear resonated with her - fear was a product of the mind, often more damaging than the thing feared itself. She acknowledged her apprehension, then let it go, choosing instead to focus on the task at hand.

Meanwhile, Angela was tasked with a new mission: collaborating with Blake Morgan as he investigated the shadowy nexus of the Hong Kong Triads and their alleged partnerships with the Mexican Cartels. She hoped Morgan was determined to stop the Triads in their criminal activities as she was in battling drug traffickers in Mexico and the U.S..

Stepping off the plane, Angela was enveloped by the humid embrace of Hong Kong. Beyond the airport, the scent of street food, the buzz of conversation, and the kaleidoscope of neon lights welcomed her to a city thriving on the edge of legality. Kai Tak was more than an airport; it was a threshold into a world where danger and opportunity danced hand in hand.

As she scanned the crowd at the gate exit, her eyes locked with those of a man whose gaze seemed to search for her with equal intensity. He approached, a mixture of professionalism and unmistakable attraction in his stride.

"Special Agent Torres," he called, approaching Angela. "I'm Blake Morgan, Royal Hong Kong Police."

Angela took in Blake's appearance, noting that his photo hadn't done him justice – strong jawline, piercing eyes that seemed to look right through her, and an energy that radiated competence and charm. She allowed herself a moment to appreciate his attractiveness, then refocused on the task at hand.

"Inspector. Morgan," she smiled, extending her hand. The moment their fingers touched, a spark of electricity seemed to pass between them. "It's a pleasure to meet you. I didn't expect a personal welcome."

Blake's hand lingered a moment longer than necessary, his eyes never leaving hers. "Please, call me Blake," he said, his voice softening. "And the pleasure is all mine. May I call you Angela?"

Angela smiled broadly, "Yes, I'd prefer that."

As they walked side by side towards the exit, Angela found herself hyper-aware of Blake's presence. The subtle scent of his cologne, the way his shoulder occasionally brushed against hers in the crowded terminal – it all sent little sparks of energy through her body. She chided herself for these distracting thoughts but couldn't entirely push them away.

Blake, for his part, was equally affected. He stole glances at Angela when he thought she wasn't looking, admiring how she carried herself with such confidence and grace. Her beauty was undeniable, but the sharp intelligence in her eyes and the determined set of her jaw genuinely captivated him.

"I'll take you to your hotel so you can freshen up and rest," Blake offered, his voice betraying a hint of eagerness to spend more time with her.

Angela nodded, grateful for the chance to compose herself. "Thank you, Blake. Perhaps we can talk more there. I'm assuming you'll also want to meet at police HQ."

"Sounds perfect," Blake replied, reaching for her bag. "Can I take that for you?"

Their fingers brushed as Angela shook her head, sending another jolt of electricity between them. "It's okay, I've got it," she said, her independence shining through even as she felt a growing desire to lean on this intriguing man.

As they exited the terminal into the pulsing heart of Hong Kong, both Angela and Blake were acutely aware of the delicate dance they were beginning. Professional boundaries blurred with undeniable attraction, all against the backdrop of a dangerous mission in a city of shadows and secrets.

Angela took a moment to absorb the sensory overload of Hong Kong at night. The cacophony of car horns and street vendors, the pungent aroma of fish markets mingling with the sweet scent of egg waffles, the dizzying array of neon signs painting the sky in electric hues - it was an assault on the senses that threatened to overwhelm her. But she centered herself, drawing on her Stoic training to find calm amidst the chaos.

As they navigated the crowded streets, Angela's mind raced, analyzing every detail of her surroundings while simultaneously planning her next moves. She knew that somewhere in this labyrinthine city lay the answers she sought, the connections between the Triads and the Cartels that threatened to unleash a tsunami of destruction across multiple continents.

Yet even as she strategized, Angela couldn't ignore the strong energy of Blake's presence beside her. His steady gait, the quiet confidence in his demeanor, the way his eyes seemed to take in every detail, not to mention his striking good looks, all spoke of a competence that both reassured and intrigued her. She wondered about his own journey, the experiences that had shaped him into the man who now walked beside her.

The weight of their task hung between them, unspoken yet palpable. But as they walked side by side into the neon-lit night, there was also a growing sense of excitement – not just for the mission ahead, but for the possibility of connection in this vast, inscrutable city. Hong Kong awaited them, a new chapter about to unfold, filled with danger, intrigue, and the tantalizing promise of something more.

Chapter 11

Purpose and Passion

Blake and Angela exited the bustling Kai Tak airport, weaving through the crowds towards the storied grandeur of the Peninsula Hotel. The air hummed with the whispered secrets of a city where East meets West, a place where opulence and history intertwine seamlessly. A brief car ride brought them to the historic Peninsula Hotel.

"Opting for the zenith of luxury, I see," Blake mused, glancing at the imposing façade of the Peninsula, a beacon of colonial elegance and an enduring symbol of Hong Kong's storied past.

A chuckle escaped Angela, her laughter a melody in the cacophony of the bustling city. "Trust me, the DEA's budget doesn't stretch to accommodate such extravagance. I've made it clear to my boss that I'm picking up the tab on all my travel expenses."

"I hope your boss appreciates how you're saving the DEA money," Blake quipped, his eyes twinkling with mirth. Angela laughed heartily.

As Blake's car glided to a stop, the Peninsula welcomed them with the silent vigil of its iconic fleet: a phalanx of emerald-hued Rolls-Royce Phantoms, each a testament to the hotel's commitment to unparalleled luxury and service.

Built in 1928, the Peninsula Hotel at Nathan and Salisbury Roads at the tip of Kowloon has long symbolized Hong Kong's opulence. The very walls whispered tales of the bygone era. Founded by the visionary Kadoorie family, it has played host to the dreams and dramas of generations, a silent witness to the ebb and flow of history itself.

Stepping into the lobby, Blake and Angela were enveloped in an ambience that married Edwardian grandeur with modern luxury. The lobby's stained-glass windows, carved woodwork, oriental carpets, and draperies dated from 1928, and the English-style afternoon tea service, in operation since the 1920s, created an atmosphere of timeless elegance. The adjoining hallways connected to the lobby housed one of the oldest fashion arcades in Hong Kong, featuring international luxury brands like Chanel, Gucci, Prada, and Rolex.

Angela checked in at the VIP reception desk while Blake surveyed the lobby with its large staircase leading to the upper floors. His mind wandered back decades to 1945, following the surrender of the Japanese forces in Hong Kong. The British government had arranged for his family to stay at the Peninsula Hotel because his father had been a senior civil servant in the colony's government. In his mind's eye, he imagined his sister's story of chasing his brother up and down the staircase, playing tag. Sadly, both had died a decade ago. He often thought their premature deaths were linked to the terrible health conditions and inadequate diets they endured in the Internment Camp in Stanley where his family were imprisoned by the Japanese in 1941 and remained there until the end of the war.

Angela had completed her check-in. "Blake, I need to freshen up after the long flight."

"Of course," I can pick you up later if you like," Blake replied. "I'd planned to take you to police headquarters and introduce you to my boss."

"Why don't you come up with me and wait? No point in you making two trips," Angela replied.

"Sure, if it's no imposition," Blake responded.

Together, they followed the bellboy toward the elevators and up to Angela's luxurious suite on the 6th floor. Her suite was beautifully decorated with colonial-style furnishings—luxurious and tasteful. The separate bedroom and living room offered a stunning view of Victoria Harbor and the ocean beyond.

After the bellboy deposited Angela's luggage and departed, Angela pointed to the fully stocked bar. "Make yourself a drink if you like. I'm just going to take a quick shower and change my clothes. Feel free to review those files I brought that summarize our current investigations." Angela reached into her briefcase, removed several files, and put them on the table by Blake.

Blake nodded, poured himself a gin and tonic, and reflected momentarily on his impressions of Angela. *"She's what I expected and yet didn't expect. I expected an educated professional, probably with little fieldwork. Why did I automatically think 'little fieldwork' when I heard about a female expert? Would I have made the same assumption about a male colleague? Instead, I got an imposing woman who generates power, confidence and intelligence. I have a feeling working with Angela is going to be an education in more ways than one."*

Twenty minutes later, Angela emerged from the bathroom. "Ah, that feels so much better after a long flight. Do you want to do the same Blake?"

Blake smiled broadly, momentarily letting his eyes rest on Angela's appearance. *"She is a beautiful woman as well,"* he thought. "No, thank you, I'm good for now. Before we head out can you give me the quick rundown on what you've been working on?"

"Certainly, Blake," Angela replied. They sat down together. "The DEA joined the Mexican Police's Drug Enforcement Division on a big bust up country from Manzanillo. I got to see firsthand the production and packaging of fentanyl destined for the U.S. We found from captured perpetrators, including an American pilot transporting a fentanyl precursor chemical, that a Hong Kong Triad was partnering with the Tijuana Cartel to dominate the market."

Blake let out a low whistle, his brow furrowing. "That fits with what we're seeing here."

"Jimmy Canderlero, the Mexican police point man, obtained documentation and testimony from people on a Hong Kong registered ship which transported to Manzanillo."

"Were you able to identify which Hong Kong Triad was involved?"

"No, all we know is that the ship transporting the fentanyl was registered to Fung Shipping."

Blake's expression darkened. "Fung Shipping?" he exclaimed, tension evident in his voice. "That's Raymond Fung's company. His father was just assassinated."

Angela leaned forward. "You'll have to give me more background on this Raymond Fung. Also, could the drugs have been planted?"

"Maybe," Blake said, but his tone was skeptical. "I'm investigating now. By the way, Raymond is married to my best friend Sabrina. Her family, the McDougals, are old money and one of the richest in Hong Kong."

"Hmm. That complicates things." Angela took a deep breath, steeling herself. "There's more, and it's not good." Her voice dropped to almost a whisper. "We have intel that the CIA has been meeting with the Tijuana Cartel headed up by a Raul Ramirez. About fentanyl."

Blake's mouth opened slightly in surprise. "The CIA! Tell me more."

As Angela delved into the CIA's history with drug trafficking, her voice grew passionate, tinged with frustration and disbelief. She painted a vivid picture of Cold War machinations, from Burma to Afghanistan, making the complex history accessible and deeply troubling.

Blake listened intently, his expression growing more troubled with each revelation. When Angela mentioned the Iran-Contra affair, he shook his head, muttering, "It sounds to me that they are operating above the law."

"Exactly," Angela agreed, pouring herself a drink. She sat close to Blake, drawing comfort from his presence. "The CIA's gone way off course. They're into regime change and assassinations - all justified under the banner of fighting communism. And there's almost no oversight."

Blake's eyes were hard now, his voice tight with anger. "How are they funding all this?"

Angela's laugh was bitter. "Off the books. Secret bank accounts around the world. Congress doesn't see half of it." She took a deep breath. "Outside the formal organization of the CIA, it has three kinds of private organizations to provide services for the CIA, many of which leave no documented record. The first are proprietaries that conduct their financial affairs with minimal oversight from CIA headquarters and are free to use the profits however they see fit. The second is an operation that is a front organization for a purported business, which is a sham kept in place to provide cover for other activities. Then there's a third kind of organization, which is truly an independent organization closely aligned with the CIA, where many of its employees are ex-CIA personnel, and they operate independently but in alignment with CIA objectives."

As she finished, a heavy silence fell between them. Blake's eyes met Angela's with a mutual recognition of their uncovered crisis.

"We're in deep here, aren't we?" Blake said softly.

Angela nodded, her voice steady. "Deeper than I knew at first. But now we're in it together."

Their unspoken connection strengthened, a lifeline in the face of the daunting task ahead.

"So, the CIA is essentially a rogue force, working outside the law with impunity? That's... that's terrifying."

Angela nodded, her eyes hard with barely contained fury. "They've gone way beyond intelligence gathering. They've got these shadow organizations - proprietaries, front companies, and aligned independent groups. Makes oversight nearly impossible. And don't even get me started on their black bank accounts."

Blake's expression darkened further. "But doesn't the National Security Council keep them in check? Or Congress?"

Angela's bitter laugh cut through the air. "In theory, yes. In practice?" She shook her head, her voice tinged with cynicism. "The CIA does whatever it wants, Council be damned."

"My God, it's like a cancer in your government."

Angela leaned forward, her voice dropping to a fierce whisper. "And here's something that will shock you. After WWII, many former Nazi Intelligence officers were brought to the U.S. under Operations Sunrise and Safehaven and placed into various intelligence agencies, including the Office of Naval Intelligence (ONI) and the CIA."

Blake's face paled, his eyes wide with disbelief. " How deep does this go?"

"Deeper than we can imagine," Angela replied, her voice heavy with the weight of knowledge. "The CIA has infiltrated many arms of the government, not to speak of corporations and businesses, you name it."

As their conversation continued, touching on the DEA's stance and historical American involvement in Hong Kong, Blake's admiration for Angela grew visibly. His eyes softened, filled with respect and concern. "Aren't you putting yourself at risk by taking this on?" he asked, his voice gentle.

Angela's chin lifted, a fire burning in her eyes. "Maybe. But I took an oath. I can't look away."

Blake nodded, a small smile of admiration playing on his lips. "Where does the DEA stand on all this?"

"The DEA has a different mission, clearly to stop drug trafficking into the US and prosecute money laundering connected to it. The DEA is accountable to the Justice Department and must obey laws; the CIA is not."

"You mentioned meeting with the CIA's Deputy Director of Covert Operations, Jack Cross, to communicate your findings. Has anything come of it?"

"I've known Jack Cross for years. He served in the military with my father. I know him to be a patriot and dedicated to the CIA. At our meeting, though, he denied knowing anything personally about the developments in Mexico or any connection to the Cartels or Triads. He gave me the typical classified information response. He promised to investigate the matter, but I doubt he will."

"So, will you drop the investigation into CIA activity?" Blake asked.

"I guess you don't know me well yet, Blake. I don't give up easily. And this is too important to turn a blind eye," Angela replied.

As they prepared to leave, Blake's hand briefly touched Angela's arm, a gesture of support and growing respect. "I admire you for the work you've done and your commitment Angela. Now let's go meet my boss."

Angela's smile was grateful, her eyes meeting Blake's with a mix of respect and warmth. Their connection had deepened, forged in the crucible of a shared purpose.

With the last echoes of their footsteps fading into the opulent silence of the Peninsula Hotel's lobby, Blake and Angela emerged into the teeming vibrancy of Hong Kong's streets, the city's pulse quickening around them as they made their way to the heart of the police's nerve center. Blake, with the assuredness of one who knows the city's every secret, navigated the dense traffic with an agility that spoke of years on these streets, his car a mere shadow flitting through the neon-soaked evening.

Upon reaching the bastion of law and order that stood imposingly against the city's skyline, they were immediately enveloped in the palpable urgency that filled the air of the police headquarters. The building, a stark contrast to the historical grandeur of the hotel, buzzed with the frenetic energy of a city under the constant watch of its guardians.

In this hive of activity, Blake introduced Angela to his work partner, Dennis Wang, a man whose sharp eyes missed nothing yet whose demeanor spoke of a calm, collectedness. Without lingering, they proceeded to Commissioner Jack Blair's office, a sanctum where the city's safety was quietly orchestrated.

As Blake introduced Angela to Blair, there was a palpable tension. Blair's typically stoic demeanor softened slightly, his eyes betraying a mix of respect and curiosity as he regarded the DEA agent.

"Special Agent Torres," he said, his voice betraying a hint of awe for the reputation that preceded her. Your success in Mexico has not gone unnoticed here."

Angela's response, infused with both humility and a keen awareness of the magnitude of their task, acknowledged the Commissioner's efforts in combating the shadowy tendrils of crime that sought to trap the city. "Your operation," she noted, "is a testament to the resilience of this city against the forces that threaten its harmony."

Blair smiled broadly, something he didn't do often. "I read your report on the Mexican bust, and it's clear now there's a developing alliance between a Triad here and the Mexican Cartel you identified."

As the meeting progressed, the atmosphere grew heavier with each revelation. Blair's face tightened, lines of worry etching deeper around his eyes as he listened to Angela's report on the CIA's potential involvement. Blake noticed the commissioner's hands clench briefly, a tell-tale sign of his growing concern.

"Any further developments, Chief?" Blake inquired.

The tension in the room spiked when David Smith burst in, his face flushed with indignation. Blair's irritation was evident in the sharp look he shot Smith, his patience clearly wearing thin.

"Why wasn't I informed about this meeting?" Smith asked, irritated.

Blair shot him an angry look. "Wasn't necessary; you've got other things to do. But you're here now, so sit down and listen." Gesturing to Angela, he said "this is Special Agent Angela Torres of the DEA Intelligence Division. She'll be working closely on the Triad-Mexican Cartel issues."

Smith politely nodded. "Sorry, boss," Smith replied apologetically.

Blair turned back to address Angela. "We've determined, Agent Torres, that Simon Chan, Dragon Head of a powerful Triad here, was assassinated as part of a war between his Triad and some rival one, which we think was the Min Ho. We've had suspicions about Samual Fung's connection to a Triad, but we don't have any concrete evidence. And then a final disturbing piece as the report from Blake that there has been a meeting here between members of a Triad and the Tijuana Cartel discussing the fentanyl drug trade."

"Well, I can add two pieces to the puzzle, Commissioner," Angela chimed in, "I was on a major bust with Mexican police in Manzanillo, where we seized a large quantity of fentanyl and precursor chemicals, which Fung Shipping Company had shipped. Second, DEA field agents in Mexico have reported that the CIA has been in close communication with the Raul Ramirez' Tijuana Cartel. We can still decide if it's just part of their standard intelligence gathering or something much more dangerous, but I'm determined to find out."

"Thank you, Angela," Blair replied, "the picture is slowly getting clearer."

"David, have you found anything more in your questioning of Fung's staff, his son, Raymond or Sabrina Chan?" Blake asked.

"Nothing new," Smith replied, having regained his composure. "It looks like Samuel Fung had arranged to be alone when he was killed. Looks to me like he didn't want anyone to know who he was meeting with."

"I'd like to follow up with another talk with Raymond Fung," Blake asked.

Smith vigorously shook his head. "That won't be necessary, Blake. My team has the investigation well in hand."

Smith's aggressive response surprised Blake, but before he could object, Blair said, "Do I need to remind you, David, that Blake is empowered to investigate any incident or development related to the Triads. That's his job. So, your team will provide Blake with any assistance he needs and share any information you have with him. And he's free to interview Fung if he needs too."

Smith's face contorted into a scowl, but he said nothing.

"Why is David so obstructionist?" Blake thought, *"there was a resistant undercurrent of something more."*

Blair stood up, a signal that the meeting was over. "Let's get on this. My boss and the Security Bureau are on my butt to get results. And I don't want the Governor to be concerned."

With that, they left Blair's office, with Smith striding out aggressively first.

Blake led Angela over to Dennis Wang's desk.

"Dennis, I will question Raymond Fung again at his home. Angela, if it's alright with you, Dennis can give you a quick tour of the city, and we can meet later for dinner," Blake said.

"Oh, that's so nice of you, Blake and Dennis, but I have some important conference calls I must make. But I'd love to meet up later for dinner Blake," Angela replied graciously.

"Alright, it's settled," Blake said.

When they left the office together, Blake's heart raced as his hand brushed against Angela's. The moment of contact sent a jolt through him. As their fingers touched, he felt a surge of emotions -- desire, connection, and a hint of trepidation about the complexities of their situation.

Angela, too, felt the electricity of the moment. Her breath caught slightly as Blake took her hand, and she was reluctant to let go. Despite their dangers, she felt a sense of security and excitement in Blake's presence.

Chapter 12

Secrets of the Bloodline

Twilight cast long shadows as Blake navigated the maze-like corridors of the Fung estate. Luxury and secrets clung to the walls like ivy. The air was thick with silence, starkly contrasting the usual hum of activity from the servants who ghosted through these halls. This oppressive quietude foreshadowed the revelations that awaited, an uneasy prelude to his meeting with Raymond, the scion of the Fung dynasty and keeper of its darkest mysteries.

Blake's footsteps echoed hollowly on the marble steps leading to the main entrance. The usual bustle of servants was conspicuously absent, replaced by an oppressive silence that seemed to swallow every sound. As he reached for the ornate brass knocker, the door swung open silently, revealing the stoic figure of Tang, Samuel Fung's longtime personal servant and bodyguard.

"Inspector Morgan," Tang greeted him, his face an impassive mask. "We've been expecting you."

"Have the other police officers concluded their interrogation, Tang?" Blake's inquiry cut through the silence, his detective's intuition scanning Tang's carefully neutral visage for any flicker of emotion.

"They have, and I told them everything I know," Tang responded, his voice controlled but betraying his burdens.

Blake's eyes narrowed slightly, detecting a hint of . . . something in Tang's tone. Wariness? Guilt? He pressed further. "Did their questions touch on Samuel's alleged Triad connections?"

A flicker of unease passed across Tang's features, so brief Blake might have missed it if he hadn't been watching closely. "They did inquire about such matters. I assured them I did not know any such associations."

Blake sensed the dance of evasion and revelation, a delicate balance maintained by Tang's unwavering loyalty. Yet, the flicker of unease, the briefest tightening at the corner of Tang's eyes, spoke volumes to Blake's experienced gaze. *"He's not being truthful,"* Blake thought. *"Either he was involved somehow or knew much more than he's admitting."*

"Well, if even a sliver of something in your memory shows that Samuel was meeting with Triad members, I'm sure you'd tell me, wouldn't you?" Blake questioned.

"Of course," Tang replied, trying hard to cover any physical sign of untruthfulness.

"Where can I find Raymond?" Blake asked, filing away the conversation with Tang for future reference.

"He's in the library; the office is still closed off," Tang said.

As Blake moved past him, he caught a whiff of something that might have been fear emanating from the usually unflappable Tang. It was another piece of the puzzle, another shadow to be explored in the labyrinth of the Fung family's secrets.

Following Tang's directions, Blake found Raymond in the library, a room steeped in colonial trappings. Amidst the shadows and the soft glow of lamplight sat Raymond, a figure of solitude against the backdrop of inherited grandeur. The air between them was charged with unspoken words.

The library was a study in colonial opulence, a testament to the Fung family's wealth and influence. Antique furniture, books and priceless artifacts from East and West mingled in carefully curated disharmony. In the center of it all sat Raymond, a solitary figure outlined by the soft glow of a brass lamp.

"Blake, your arrival is unexpected, yet not unwelcome. Will you join me for tea?" Raymond asked, his tone surprisingly upbeat. He gestured towards the ancient Chinese tea set, an invitation to partake in a ritual of hospitality.

With a nod, Blake accepted, momentarily setting aside the formalities to delve into the heart of his visit.

The parlor seemed to contract around them, the opulent furnishings now silent witnesses to the intensifying confrontation. Blake leaned forward, his voice low and measured, each word carefully chosen.

"Inspector Smith's team has been thorough, Raymond, but some questions still linger."

Raymond's frustration crackled through the air like static electricity. "Questions? My father was murdered, Blake. Butchered. This isn't some puzzle to solve – it's a nightmare I'm living."

Blake nodded, sympathy warring with suspicion in his steely gaze. "You're right. And the method—it screams Triad involvement, just like the assassination of Simon Chan." He paused, watching Raymond's face with predatory focus. We need to understand the why, Raymond. Who wanted your father silenced so desperately?"

Raymond's shoulders tensed, a flicker of – was it fear? – passing across his face before being swiftly buried. "As I've told Inspector Smith before, my father had rivals. It's Hong Kong business. But murder?" He shook his head, eyes downcast. "That's a chasm I can't bridge."

Blake pressed on, relentless. "You were deep in the family business. Surely you must have seen, heard something?"

"My father gave me exclusive ownership and control of the shipping business, based both here and on the mainland at Zhoushan. I wasn't involved in any of his other business ventures."

Blake leaned in closer, his voice barely above a whisper. "And in all those years, Raymond, working so closely with your father . . . you never once caught a whiff of Triad connections? Not a whisper?"

The silence stretched between them, heavy with unspoken truths. Raymond's hand trembled slightly as he poured more tea, the porcelain clinking like a warning bell.

"Rumors, Blake. Just rumors," Raymond said, his voice steady but his eyes refusing to meet Blake's searching gaze.

Blake's next words fell like hammer blows. "A fentanyl shipment, Raymond. On one of your vessels. Care to explain?"

" I know nothing of this."

"We'll need to see manifests and question your crew," Blake pushed, sensing weakness.

Raymond nodded, too quickly. "Of course. Whatever you need."

"Upon your father's passing, do you stand to inherit the entirety of your father's estate and business interests?"

"Yes, I am the sole beneficiary. That shouldn't be surprising, I had no siblings. And his companies were all privately owned, not public companies."

Shifting the weight of their conversation, Blake ventured into more personal territory, his tone gentle yet firm. "Perhaps we could shift our focus momentarily to discuss you and Sabrina?"

Raymond exhaled, a semblance of calm returning to his posture. "Alright," he acquiesced, signaling his readiness to tread into the more delicate aspects of his life.

"As her closest friend, Sabrina has shared with me that you initiated divorce proceedings."

"Our personal affairs are none of your concern," Raymond snapped, a hint of jealousy creeping into his voice. "Unless your interest in her is more than friendship?"

Blake ignored the barb, pressing forward. "Wills, Raymond. Samuel's, yours and Sabrina's. We'll need that information."

Raymond's eyes narrowed with anger. "I don't see how any of that is relevant here, and it's private information."

Blake was surprised by Raymond's response. "Anything could be relevant, Raymond. It's my job to ask. If you like, we can get a subpoena."

Raymond's eyes flashed with barely contained anger. "Get a subpoena. This is private."

Blake nodded. "I think that's all for now, Raymond. Inspector Smith may follow up with more questions and provide you with the subpoena. Should you recall anything else that might shed light on your father's death or business affairs that can be helpful, please reach out to me." Blake handed Raymond his business card. My direct number is listed."

Raymond took the card and stared at it but didn't reply. "Should I have Tang show you the way out?" he said sarcastically.

"No, I think I know the way," Blake replied.

As Blake departed the Fung mansion, his mind couldn't help but echo with suspicions about Raymond's candor. "*There's more beneath the surface,*" he mused, his detective's intuition buzzing with unspoken possibilities.

Thoughts of Sabrina intruded, unbidden. Her sadness, her expressed love for him. And now, the complication of his attraction to Angela. Blake pushed the personal turmoil aside. For now, the labyrinth of lies surrounding Samuel Fung's murder demanded his full attention.

Chapter 13

Linked by Duty, Drawn by Desire

Blake knocked on Angela's hotel room door. His eyes widened when she opened the door, and his breath caught. Angela stood before him in a classic black dress, her hair elegantly done, and a gold chain resting on her neck.

She welcomed him with a big smile. "Good news, bad news or no news?"

Blake walked in and sat in an armchair. "I confronted Raymond with our discovery that fentanyl was being shipped to Mexico on one of his ships. He denied any knowledge. We need to question the ship's personnel and review all documentation, but I have suspicions we may not find anything," Blake said, taking a deep sip of the gin and tonic Angela handed him.

"Are you suspicious about Raymond?"

"In spades. But there's no evidence he had anything to do with his father's death. The fentanyl shipping is more promising."

"Well, only if you're up to it, can I suggest we both take a break. Dinner is on me. Gaddi's restaurant in this hotel is supposed to be amazing," Angela suggested, her tone lighter.

"That sounds tempting, but I'm not dressed for it," Blake said, glancing down at his police uniform, rumpled by the Hong Kong humidity.

"That's easy to fix. The Regent Shop in the hotel carries fine clothing and they have quality rentals. Let's get you fitted for something suitable. It's on me."

"I can't accept that Angela, although it's a generous offer. I can go home and change . . . ."

"You told me your home is an hour from here. That's two hours of time we could be spending enjoying dinner and chatting."

Blake laughed, the tension easing from his shoulders. "Alright, I give in. But I'll be paying you back for it."

Angela admired Blake's independence and ethical code. "Alright. And why don't you relax and take a short nap on the bed after they do a fitting. I've got a call to make to Jimmy Candelero in Mexico while you're resting, and I'll make reservations in the restaurant."

"Alright, I give; I'm not used to having someone take care of things for me," Blake said, somewhat embarrassed.

"Ha, don't fancy yourself a kept man, do you?" Angela quipped humorously.

Blake and Angela both laughed heartily.

"I'll head down to the tailor shop now. " He briefly embraced Angela in a friendly hug, feeling a wave of warmth wash over him. Then he quickly departed, reflecting on his attraction to Angela that went beyond a close working relationship.

Angela picked up the phone and called Jimmy Candelero. "Jimmy, good to hear your voice. How are things at your end of the swamp?"

"Not good, I've got some bad news for you, Angela," Jimmy replied with a heavy voice.

"What?"

"The men we apprehended at the fentanyl lab at Manzanillo are dead. Gunned down on their way to the arraignment in court."

"What? Who?"

"Pretty obvious, Ramirez's Cartel. Two of our guards were also seriously injured."

"What about the pilot Ransom?"

"He's been extradited to return to the U.S. for charges."

"Which DEA agent handled it?"

"No one in DEA. It was a CIA agent with someone from the State Department."

"What were their names?"

"I don't know. Our prosecutor, judge and government officials here won't release that information to me. I have a suspicion they are on the take."

"But you've still got the audio recordings and photos you took as evidence, right?"

"They've disappeared from the evidence locker."

"Shit! I can't believe it. So, we've got nothing now!"

"It looks that way, Angela. I'm boiling mad but there's nothing I can do now. It makes all the work we did account for nothing. I can see why so many of my colleagues, prosecutors, police and military quit or are on the take."

"And then the Cartels can continue to operate with impunity."

"Yes."

"What are you going to do now, Jimmy?"

"Take a few days off and decide if I want to keep doing this job."

"If you leave, it will be a huge loss for drug enforcement in Mexico, Jimmy."

"I don't think anyone cares now."

"I understand, Jimmy, but Blake and I are going to fight on and do what we can."

"Good on ya. Let me know if there's anything more I can do to help you."

"I will. *Cuídate, amigo mío* (take care my friend)."

Angela hung up the phone and a wave of anger and despair washed over her. "*This is too important a case to give up,*" she said to herself. "*It means the death of thousands of people in the U.S. caught in this fentanyl juggernaut. I hate to say it, but the war on drugs is becoming a revolving door. You take out a Cartel Kingpin, and someone else takes over, and business continues as usual. You add to that American agencies, banks and politicians aiding the drug traffickers and enforcement is becoming almost impossible. In my darkest moments, I think this will never change. The drug problem is not a Mexican or Columbian or Hong Kong problem, it's a global problem.*"

Angela walked into the bathroom and splashed some cold water on her face. It wasn't like her to give up when the going got tough, and she wouldn't back down now. Besides, the thought of being able to work closely with Blake made her even more motivated.

An hour later, Blake reappeared at the door in a tailored dark blue suit, white shirt, and red silk tie. "I can't believe how fast they did this."

Angela sucked in her breath for a moment. "Oh my, do you look handsome? What a beautiful suit and great fit."

"I'm glad I'm just renting it for the evening. I saw the purchase price tag," Blake said, "but I have something for you." Blake brandished a red rose from behind his and handed it to Angela.

Angela took the rose and kissed Blake on the cheek. "Thank you Blake, how thoughtful."

After smelling the rose, she put it in a small vase with water.

She grabbed her green silk shawl, handed it to Blake and turned. He gently placed it on her shoulders, his hands lingering on her back, bringing a wave of warmth over his body. Blake was smart enough to know that he was feeling an intense attraction to Angela. *"Got to keep this professional,"* he reminded himself.

They walked into Gaddi's dining room minutes later. Blake admired the opulent surroundings—the glittering chandeliers, ornate mirrors, and the soft glow of candlelight reflecting off the crystal glasses. The *Maître D* showed them to a quiet corner table.

"You said you'd tell me about your family history. Do you mind?" Angela asked, her eyes sparkling with genuine interest.

"I'd be glad too," Blake responded enthusiastically. "I was born in Hong Kong. My father, Trevor, was a Welshman in the Hong Kong civil service. My mother, Alicia, was Mexican."

"Now, there's an interesting combination. How did they meet?"

"I don't want to bore you with a long story."

Angela reached over and touched his hand with hers. "I'm not bored. Please?"

"My father ran away from my abusive grandfather in Wales when he was fifteen because my grandfather insisted my father keep working in the coal mine. He stayed with his aunt until he was sixteen and then joined the British Army. His parents willingly signed an agreement to allow him entry even though he was underage. For the next two years he remained on a British Army camp."

Angela leaned forward toward Blake in rapt attention.

"Then, at the age of eighteen, he was shipped to Palestine and spent seven years in action there and in Egypt in what amounted to police action. He served there for the next nine years."

"This is fascinating," Angela said, her eyes sparkling.

"He got disillusioned because of the constant conflict and violence and retired from the army, got some training and took a civil service job in Hong Kong."

"I would have loved to have met your father. He sounds like a resilient and independent man—like you."

Blake smiled. "He was the finest man I have ever known . . . but I never got to grow up with him."

"I'm so sorry. What happened?"

"I'll explain later. First, here's my mother's story. My mother's family was originally from Sonora, Mexico, where many Spanish people settled. Mexicans from there look a lot more Spanish. Her mother and father were very poor and lived in a small farming community. My mother was a warm, loving woman but very frail. She seemed to give away her life force to others. Everyone who knew her loved her."

"How did she end up in Hong Kong?"

"She was the youngest of three sisters. Her oldest sister married an American Chinese businessman when he was travelling on business in Mexico. My mother, her sisters and her mother relocated to San Francisco, where the Chinese businessman lived. One day, he decided to travel to Hong Kong on business. Little did my mother and maybe even his wife know the man was involved with the Triads. Shortly after arriving in Hong Kong, he was murdered, and my mother, her sisters and grandmother were stranded. The younger women had to find jobs and worked in one of the dance halls in Hong Kong. One night my father appeared at the dance hall and was immediately attracted to my mother after having a dozen dances with her. He then asked for permission of my grandmother to date her formally, and several months later, they were married. Little did he know she was only sixteen or seventeen at the time."

"What an incredible story, Blake. Like right out of a romance-adventure novel!"

"Yes, many people are amazed about both their stories and our family."

"Seems like they had love at first sight. Do you believe in that?"

Blake looked intently into her eyes. "It's one of those things you can't prove other than by asking the people it happens to."

Angela looked thoughtfully and with affection at him for a few moments. "How did you lose your parents?"

"My parents, sister and brother I were prisoners of the Japanese in WW II. We were interred in Stanley Camp for almost four years. I was born the last month of the war, and my mother and I almost died at my birth."

"Oh my God, Blake. You and your mother survived?" Blake nodded agreement. "What happened to the rest of your family?"

"We all survived the camp experience, although the deplorable conditions in the camp had a damaging impact on my father's health. After being liberated from the camp by the British we were sent as refugees to Australia to live in a refugee camp for the next two years. Then my father chose to return to Hong Kong to his job, and we moved back."

Tears formed in Angela's eye. "I'm so sorry. That must have been horrible for your family and for you as a child."

"Yes, it was. And we know now from research on civilian detainees in Internment camps that the traumatic experience not only creates post-traumatic stress syndrome (PST), but the experiences have a permanent impact on survivors, including changes in one's DNA."

Angela leaned back, holding herself with her arms. "I don't know how you survived all that," Angela said.

"Survival against great odds gives you a great inner strength, but in a way, it can also make you more detached from people."

"I really want to hear more, Blake. Can you talk about how your mother and father died?"

A lump formed in Blake's throat, and he looked away. "Not now, maybe another time. I promise."

"Of course, Blake, no pressure . . ." She reached over grabbed his hand. "Will you excuse me for a moment, I have to take a washroom break."

Blake stood up and watched Angela walk to the restaurant washroom. He was surprised that he'd opened up so much to her. *"It's as though I've known her all my life, and she created a safe place to talk about the pain from the past. This is one incredible woman!"*

Chapter 14

Den of the Dragons

Angela returned to the table, making eye contact with Blake the whole way. "Blake, I want to thank you for sharing those intimate and painful remembrances from your past. It's an amazing story, and it's obvious to me you are a man of incredible resilience and courage. It's an honor to be your professional partner and get to know you personally," she said after sitting down. "I want you to know that you have a safe space in my life to talk about any of those things you mentioned."

Blake swallowed deeply, emotion rising in him. He hadn't expected to make such a strong emotional connection with Angela so quickly, and it appeared that she too was willing to embrace that. "I appreciate your empathy, compassion and kindness, Angela."

Several moments of silent appreciation for each other passed.

"Blake, I hope you don't mind if we switch to talking about work. I have a very general knowledge of the Triads in Hong Kong," Angela inquired. Can you educate me?"

The question took his focus from the emotional center of his brain to the cognitive center, where painful memories didn't grip him. "Sure, stop me if I start to bore you," Blake replied.

Angela nodded. "You needn't worry about that."

Blake took a deep breath, settling into his role as an expert on Hong Kong's and China's organized crime. His eyes gleamed with the intensity of someone about to share hard-won knowledge.

"Triads and other secret societies in China have a fascinating history," he began. "They've evolved from mutual aid groups and personal networks into full-fledged criminal organizations. But here's the kicker - they started out as patriotic entities."

Angela leaned forward, intrigued. "Patriotic? How so?"

Blake nodded, pleased by her interest. "Initially, they were associated with supporting the restoration of the Ming Dynasty and opposing the Manchu Qing Dynasty. This patriotic facade has been a key factor in their longevity. Throughout history, various regimes - the Nationalists, Japanese, Communists, even the British have collaborated with the Triads when it suited their purposes."

He paused to take a sip of his drink, then continued. "The term 'Triad' itself has an interesting origin. Europeans coined it during the Qing Dynasty to describe these secret societies. It refers to the emblem used by groups like the Heaven and Earth Association, Three United Association, and others. Modern Cantonese speakers typically call them *'Hak Sh'e'* or Black Societies."

Angela's eyes widened. "So, they've been around for centuries?"

"Absolutely," Blake confirmed. "Some believe these organizations played roles in revolutionary movements like the White Lotus, Taiping, and Boxer Rebellions. But their involvement with the Chinese Nationalist movement, the Kuomintang or KMT from the early 1900s onwards, is particularly noteworthy."

"They opposed the Communists, right?" Angela interjected.

Blake smiled approvingly. "Correct. The relationship between the Kuomintang, the political party that ruled China from 1927-1949 and Triads, especially the Green Gang, a Chinese secret society and criminal organization in Shanghai, was crucial. The Green Gang became a source of muscle for the KMT. In fact, Chiang Kai-shek, a key figure in the KMT and one of the founders of Taiwan, was believed to have joined the Green Gang in 1919 while working in Shanghai."

Angela shook her head in amazement. "So even then, politicians were either part of or used Triads for their purposes."

"Exactly," Blake said. "After the Communist takeover in 1949, Mao Zedong ordered a suppression of secret societies in mainland China. Most relocated to Hong Kong, Taiwan, Southeast Asia, and even the United States. Over time, they turned to illegal drugs as a major source of income. I find it fascinating that people change history to suit their beliefs. Both Chiang Kai-shek, who was the head of the KMT and Dr. Sun Yat Sen, also a leader in the KMT were revered in Western nations even though they were involved in Triads, criminal organizations," Blake said ironically.

Angela steered the conversation to another area "What happened during World War II?"

Blake's eyes lit up at the question. "The Japanese invasion of Hong Kong on December 8, 1941, revealed the fractious nature of Triads to the British. The battle was short, but it severely impacted the local Chinese population. The Triads split into three camps: one supporting the Nationalists, another assisting the Japanese, and a third waiting to see the outcome."

"Where did the Triad loyalties lie?" Angela pressed.

"It was complicated," Blake explained. "The British Hong Kong Police had tried to crack down on Triads before the invasion, fearing they might become fifth columnists. After the British defeat, the Japanese utilized some Triad societies to maintain control, allowing them to continue their operations in return."

"Did the Japanese occupiers collaborate with the Triads?"

Blake shook his head. "Not all, but some. For instance, the Luen Lok Tong Triad grew to several thousand members during the occupation, continuing their protection rackets, extortion, and prostitution rings. The Japanese even employed their leader as a detective in Wanchai police."

"It sounds like a nightmare, Blake."

"It is estimated that there are fifty Triad gangs in Hong Kong. The Triads have been active in Hong Kong almost since its inception. They were engaged in the local opium trade and helped and were assisted by the corrupt British police force. Before my time, corruption was so entrenched in Hong Kong that half the police force was dismissed for accepting bribes."

"So, it sounds like political and police corruption are not unique to the U.S."

Blake nodded. "The British cracked down on the Triads in Hong Kong in an aggressive anti-corruption campaign that began in the 1970s, sharply curtailing the influence of the Triads on the police and the civil service. After the crackdown in Hong Kong, many of the Triads moved the bases of their operations across the border into southern Chinese provinces such as Guangdong, Fujian, Guanxi and Yunnan, and into Macau. The Triads have done well in the developing free-wheeling cowboy capitalism in China, but it is hard to gauge how well because they operate quietly behind the scenes. They are involved in bribery, extortion, prostitution, smuggling, and involved in shady real estate and stock market deals."

"Are the structures of Chinese Triads the same as those in Hong Kong?"

"The Hong Kong Triad is distinct from mainland Chinese cousins. Two distinguishing features are the extent to which the organization can control local markets and, unfortunately, in some cases, police protection can be obtained. In stark contrast to the sprawling empires of international crime, the Triads of Hong Kong danced to a different tune, a symphony of independence and autonomy, with each faction crafting its destiny, unbound by the iron chains of centralized command as often depicted in the Italian Mafia."

"And I understand drug trafficking is not the only criminal enterprise Triads are involved in."

"That's right. Triads engage in a variety of crimes, from fraud, extortion and money laundering to trafficking and prostitution, and are involved in smuggling and counterfeiting goods such as music, video, software, clothes, watches and money."

"And I thought I was busy chasing drug traffickers."

"It keeps me busy, to say the least."

"Can you tell me something of their organization and structure here in Hong Kong?"

Blake leaned forward, his eyes gleaming with a mix of intensity and long-harbored frustration as he delved into the world of Hong Kong Triads. His voice carried the weight of years spent combating these elusive organizations. " They operate on a complex web of reciprocity and favors, a network woven from trust and mutual aid."

Angela found herself drawn in by Blake's passion. She leaned closer, her curiosity piqued, and her professional interest ignited. "And their drug focus has been primarily heroin, right?" she prompted, eager to confirm her understanding.

"Exactly. Their power stems from their proximity to the Golden Triangle." His brow furrowed as he added, "But their move into fentanyl, that is unexpected and deeply concerning."

As Blake detailed the Triads' involvement in legitimate businesses—from entertainment to property trading —Angela's eyes widened, her expression a mix of shock and dawning comprehension. "My God," she breathed, feeling overwhelmed by the scope of Triad influence. " never realized it went this deep. When most Americans think of drug trafficking, they think of Central American, Mexican and Mafia organizations."

Blake's tone grew somber, tinged with a hint of shame. "It's a source of embarrassment for those who've worked hard to eradicate the Triads. In the '60s and '70s, police corruption was rampant. We've made progress, but" he hesitated, his eyes darting around as if checking for eavesdroppers. "I suspect some officers are still on the take."

Angela, visibly shaken by these revelations, suggested another drink, the weight of this new knowledge settling heavily on her shoulders.

Undeterred, Blake continued, his words painting a vivid picture of Triad culture. He described their structure, elaborate initiation rituals, and complex code names with a mix of fascination and revulsion. "The mystique surrounding the Triads is arguably more intriguing than the Italian Mafia," he admitted.

As Blake concluded his explanation of the Triad hierarchy, from the Dragon Head down to the foot soldiers, Angela let out a long, heavy sigh. Her mind was reeling, struggling to process the intricate world Blake had unveiled. "And I thought I'd heard everything," she muttered, her voice a mix of awe, disbelief, and a touch of fear.

The atmosphere in the room grew thick with tension, weighted by the information shared. Blake's determination to fight the Triads was palpable, his jaw set and eyes burning with resolve. Meanwhile, Angela grappled with the shocking realities of Hong Kong's underworld, her previous understanding of organized crime shattered and reformed.

"This is a lot to take in," Angela admitted, running a hand through her hair. Her analytical mind was already racing, connecting dots and seeing implications for her own work. "How do you even begin tackling something deeply ingrained in society?"

Blake's expression softened slightly, recognizing the overwhelming nature of what he'd shared. "It's not easy," he confessed, a hint of weariness creeping into his voice. "*But understanding their world is the first step. Knowledge is power, especially when dealing with shadows,*" he thought.

"Do you want to know about Triad structure?" Blake asked, his eyes glinting with suppressed excitement and grim determination. His fingers drummed lightly on the table, betraying his eagerness to share his hard-won knowledge.

Angela poured herself another drink and sat closer to Blake. "Yes, please." Her professional curiosity was piqued, but there was also a hint of apprehension in her eyes, as if she sensed the weight of what she was about to learn.

Blake leaned in, his voice low and intense. "Triads are tribal-like organizations, following a strict Confucian code where elders are deeply respected. They use an intricate system of secret signs, exotic code names, and hidden tattoos." His tone held a complex mix of fascination and disgust. "Symbolism is crucial in their world - even a simple glance or how a cigarette is offered can convey volumes of information."

He paused, gauging Angela's reaction before continuing. "New members undergo elaborate initiation rituals lasting up to six days. Though these ceremonies are highly symbolic, they're becoming less common now." Blake's voice dropped even lower, taking on an almost reverent quality. "Many Triads have mandatory oaths. I can quote one from memory: 'I shall not disclose the secrets of the Hung Family, not even to my parents, brothers or wife. I shall never disclose the secrets for money. I shall die by a swarm of swords if I do so.'"

Blake continued, his voice hardening. "They operate on a system of favors and mutual support, unlike the rigidly structured Italian mafia. They value living outside societal norms, bound by strong oaths of loyalty and secrecy." His jaw clenched slightly. "Their code sanctions violence for revenge, upholding agreements and establishing dominance. Betrayal is considered the gravest offence."

"And their organization?" Angela pressed, leaning forward, her food forgotten.

Blake's response was rapid-fire, his words charged with a strange mix of admiration and contempt. "At the top is the Dragon Head, or Mountain Master - *Shan Chu*. Below him is the Deputy Lodge Master, *Fu Shan Chu*, essentially a Chief Operating Officer." He went on to detail the roles of the Incense Master, Guardian, Red Pole, and White Paper Fan, explaining their responsibilities and significance within the organization.

His eyes gleamed with a hint of dark humor as he added, "They even use complex numerical codes from the *I Ching* to indicate positions, 489 for the leader, 438 for the deputy, and so on. It's like a twisted corporate structure, but with far deadlier implications."

As Blake finished, Angela slumped back in her chair, visibly overwhelmed. The opulent dining room, with its golden chandeliers and fine china, seemed to fade into insignificance around her. "Good heavens, Blake," she sighed, her voice barely above a whisper. She reached for her wine glass with a slightly trembling hand. "I need time to digest all this," she said, gesturing weakly at their untouched meal. "Let's not let this sumptuous dinner go to waste."

Blake nodded, his expression softening as he recognized Angela's emotional turmoil. He leaned back, giving her space to process. "Take your time," he said gently. " We've been battling these organizations for years, and sometimes it feels like we're just scratching the surface."

As they turned to their meal, both were lost in thought. Angela's mind raced, trying to connect this new information with her DEA work, while Blake's eyes held a steely determination. The weight of their shared knowledge hung between them, a silent acknowledgement of the challenges ahead in their fight against the Triads.

The night unfolded like a delicate tapestry, woven with threads of fine cuisine, rich wine, and intimate conversation. For an hour and a half, Blake and Angela found themselves ensconced in a world of their own making, the restaurant's ambient noise fading to a distant hum as they delved into stories of their families, shared personal experiences, and explored the landscape of their beliefs and values.

As the last course was cleared away, Blake raised his glass, the crystal catching the soft light and transforming the golden liquid within into a beacon of warmth. "To the serendipity of our meeting," he declared, his voice carrying a note of genuine gratitude that seemed to resonate between them. His eyes, usually sharp with the keen edge of a detective, now softened with an emotion that surprised even him.

Angela felt a rush of warmth flood her cheeks, a rosy flush that wasn't entirely due to the wine. "To us, then," she agreed, her voice a melodious echo of Blake's sentiment. As their glasses clinked, a spark of connection flashed between them, bright and ephemeral.

However, the moment of levity was fleeting. As the last drops of wine were poured, Angela felt the weight of their situation settling back upon her shoulders. She glanced around the now-quieting restaurant, suddenly feeling exposed. "Perhaps we should continue this evening in a more comfortable setting?" she suggested, her voice low and tinged with a hint of nervous anticipation. "My suite offers a more private ambiance."

Blake's response was immediate, his voice smooth as velvet and rich with unspoken promise. "An excellent proposition," he agreed, rising from his chair with a grace that belied the late hour and the wine they'd consumed.

The transition to Angela's suite was seamless, the plush surroundings enveloping them in a cocoon of privacy. Angela shed her shawl with a fluid motion, the act also seems to shed some of her professional armor. She appeared almost ethereal in the soft, golden glow of the suite's lighting, a side of her Blake had yet to witness.

"Gin and tonic for you?" she offered, moving towards the well-stocked bar with an easy familiarity.

Blake nodded, easing out of his jacket and sinking into the embrace of the plush couch. "Sounds perfect," he murmured, his voice carrying the weight of the evening's revelations. As Angela poured their drinks, he found his eyes drawn to her, noticing the graceful curve of her neck, the way the light played off her hair.

Angela opted for wine, the deep ruby liquid a stark contrast to the lingering tension between them. As she settled beside Blake, close but not touching, the air seemed to crackle with unspoken words and possibilities.

"Our next step should be a discussion with David Smith," Blake suggested, his tone betraying the urgency that still thrummed beneath their relaxed exterior. "His findings could be crucial."

"Agreed," Angela replied, her mind already racing ahead, plotting their next moves like a complex chess game.

As the night deepened, however, the toll of the day began to show on Blake. His usual sharp focus gave way to a bone-deep weariness. "I think it's time for me to head back," he announced, though his unsteady attempt to rise betrayed his exhaustion.

Angela reacted immediately, her professional concern mixing with a more personal worry. "Stay here, on the couch," she insisted, her tone brooking no argument. "You're in no shape to drive."

Gratefully, Blake acquiesced, sinking back into the sofa that now promised the rest his body craved. Angela busied herself fetching a comforter and pillow, her care a soothing balm to the harshness of their shared world. As she leaned into place the pillow, their faces drew close. For a moment, time seemed to stand still. Then, with a tenderness that surprised them both, Angela softly kissed Blake's cheek.

It was a moment of shared vulnerability, a silent acknowledgment of the bond forming between them. As sleep claimed Blake, deep and unyielding, Angela retreated to the bedroom, her mind whirling with emotions and half-formed thoughts.

The peace of the night was shattered in the early morning by the sound of Angela's sharp, distressed voice. "Don't do it. Drop it. Don't do it," she called out, her words echoing from the bedroom.

Blake was awake in an instant, his protective instincts overriding his grogginess. He rushed to Angela's side, his heart pounding. "Angela, are you okay?" he asked, gently holding her shoulders. At that moment, as Angela's eyes flew open, filled with residual fear and confusion, Blake realized how deeply he had come to care for his partner in this unspoken dance they were engaged in.

Angela awakened, visibly upset. "It's a reoccurring nightmare I have had. Once on assignment when I first worked as a field agent, we were involved in a huge cocaine bust in Miami on the docks. A firefight ensued, and I killed one of the "perps." All the training and psychotherapy in the world doesn't prepare you for the psychological impact of killing another human being, and it stays with you, maybe permanently. At least it has for me."

Angela pulled the sheets up to her neck, as though it would protect her.

Blake took her hand in his. "I know what you're going through. I've been there. I want to say it eventually fades away, but I can't. But you can't change the past. But you can be compassionate with yourself. It doesn't mean you are weak."

Suddenly, Angela pulled him towards her and kissed him passionately. "Blake!"

He returned her kiss with equal fervor.

"I'm here and I'm not going anywhere."

Blake gently pulled the sheets from her. The morning light streamed through the window, casting a golden glow on Angela's naked body. His hand traced the lines of her silhouette, his touch tender and reverent. Their lips met in a slow, deep kiss.

After a slow-moving time of passionate love, they rest gently, wrapped in each other's arms.

"Blake, I hadn't meant for this to happen," Angela whispered, her voice soft and vulnerable.

"Neither did I. But it feels right," Blake replied, his eyes searching hers.

Angela nodded, a small smile playing on her lips. "We'll figure it out. Together." Angela whispered.

They leaned back together on the pillows and held each other for a long time, each minute seeming like an eternity.

Angela took a deep breath. "Without meaning to spoil the incredible importance of the last hour, Blake, I mentioned that Senator Bryce Connor, Chairman of the Senate Intelligence Committee contacted me. His committee is investigating CIA wrongdoing. He has asked you and I to meet with him and perhaps testify before his Committee regarding our investigations. Are you okay with that?"

"Of course, the more allies we have the better."

"I thought you'd say that. I've booked a flight back to Washington for us, if you're agreeable."

Blake laughed. "Now, who's in charge?" Angela joined in his laughter.

She kissed Blake and stood up, displaying her magnificent body without any shyness. "Could you order room service for me? Coffee, fruit and one poached egg for me."

"That sounds good. I'll join you."

Angela scampered into the bathroom and Blake called room service for breakfast. Soon after she emerged from the bathroom, wearing a jade green pantsuit. During breakfast, they chatted warmly, talking about their personal lives in a manner suited to a happy married couple, realizing the time was quickly approaching that would immerse them in what could be the fight of their lives.

Chapter 15

Unmasking the Truth

The DEA car sliced through Washington D.C.'s bustling streets, its tinted windows a barrier between the oblivious world outside and the tense atmosphere within. Angela's voice cut through the engine's hum, her words sharp and clipped as she briefed Blake on Senator Connor's battles.

"Connor's committee is caught in a political maelstrom," she explained, her as she gripped a leather portfolio. "They're knee-deep in the Iran-Contra affair, going toe-to-toe with the President and CIA despite mountains of damning evidence."

Blake's eyes narrowed, his gaze fixed on the passing monuments that seemed to mock the very ideals they represented. "Give me the highlights," he prompted, his tone betraying a mix of curiosity and growing unease.

Angela took a deep breath, steeling herself. "Reagan's top officials orchestrated an illegal arms deal with Iran, violating an embargo to funnel funds to the Contras in Nicaragua." Her voice dropped as if the car itself might be bugged. "They claimed it was to free American hostages, but Lieutenant Colonel Oliver North, a member of the National Security Council diverted the funds to the Contras."

Blake nodded. "Any pushback?"

"The Tower Commission, created by President Reagan, implicated a dozen officials but conveniently spared Reagan and Bush," Angela replied, her tone bitter. "We're talking heavyweights - Defense Secretary Weinberger, National Security Adviser MacFarlane, North himself." She paused, her eyes meeting Blake's. "And it gets worse. Senator John Kerry's Foreign Relations Committee has been uncovering a web connecting drug Cartels, the Contras, and even the State Department."

Angela continued, explaining the CIA's alleged involvement in drug trafficking to support the Contras—a saga shadowed by persistent allegations despite official denials.

"So much for accountability," Blake said.

Angela continued, delving into the murky waters of CIA involvement in drug trafficking to support the Contras—a saga of denial and dismissal by official reports, yet shadowed by persistent allegations of the CIA's complicity.

As their car pulled up to the imposing government building, both felt the weight of what lay ahead. The marble steps seemed to stretch endlessly upward, a physical manifestation of the uphill battle they faced.

They quickly found their way to Senator Connor's office and waited for him.

Senator Bryce Connor's entrance was like a sudden gust of wind, instantly commanding attention. Connor was a man of medium height in his mid-sixties with chiseled, handsome features, sparkling Irish green eyes, and thick black hair freckled with grey. His Hollywood good looks and charismatic personality helped propel him into a successful political career. He'd made a name for himself by aggressively expanding the scope of his committee's investigative powers, sometimes to the embarrassment and displeasure of the White House.

"Special Agent Torres," he greeted, his voice a perfect blend of charm and authority.

"Good to see you again, as well, Senator Connor; I'd like to introduce a colleague of mine, Blake Morgan, who is Chief Inspector of the Royal Hong Kong police force's Triad Crime Division. We've been working together on a startling new development in the drug trafficking problem."

Connor and Blake exchanged firm handshakes and direct eye contact, sizing each other up.

"You've piqued my interest," Connor said, leaning back in his leather chair. "What's this new development that couldn't wait?"

Angela leaned forward, her voice low and urgent. "Two months ago, we got reports of CIA field agents meeting with Mexican Cartel members." Her eyes flashed with barely contained frustration. "When I confronted Covert Operations Deputy Director Cross, he stonewalled me completely."

"Why am I not surprised about Cross' response?" Connor said sarcastically. "How does that report connect to Hong Kong Triads?" Connor queried.

"Well, with my counterparts in Mexico, we conducted a raid on a fentanyl lab in Manzanillo. We found out the Tijuana Cartel is connected to Triads providing precursor chemicals. The freelance pilot there indicated that the CIA was involved," Angela said.

"Around the same period, I had reports that a member of a Mexican Cartel, probably from the Tijuana Cartel, headed by Raul Ramirez, had been meeting with a Triad member in Hong Kong, and the subject of the CIA was part of their conversation," Blake chimed in.

"So, it appears the drug world may be reinventing itself. Fentanyl is far more powerful than cocaine or heroin and easy to manufacture and distribute. The prospect of a global conglomerate behind this with the potential of killing and harming millions is very real," Angela said.

The temperature in the room seemed to drop several degrees. Connor's face darkened, the lines around his eyes deepening. "What you say is disturbing, but sadly, not surprising." He stood, moving to gaze out the window at the city below. "This pattern goes back further than you might think."

"Angela has told me that your Intelligence Committee has been holding hearings as part of its oversight of the CIA, Senator," Blake said. "If you don't mind me asking, what has spurred your interest in the CIA?"

"My concern about the CIA goes a long way back. When I worked for the Office of Naval Intelligence (ONI), which preceded the CIA, during World War II, I discovered that Meyer Lansky and Lucky Luciano were asked by the ONI to assist in fighting Communist-leaning unions on New York's docks. After the war, Luciano returned to New York, rebuilding his criminal empire. Lansky settled in Cuba to run mob activities there and support Cuban dictator Juan Batista. When Castro came to power, Lansky returned to Miami to run the mob rackets."

"Are you saying, Senator, that the U.S. government worked with known criminals?" Blake asked.

"I'm saying that the ONI had a cooperative relationship with Luciano and Lansky, both criminals, to fight Communists," Connor replied.

Senator Connor leaned forward in his chair, his eyes burning with an intensity that belied his years. The weight of the knowledge he was about to share seemed to press down on his shoulders. "Even though the Tower Commission is doing its work, I couldn't let it go. I dug deeper, much deeper," he began, his voice low and gravelly. "I interviewed General Maurice Montagne, former head of SDECE - the French equivalent of our CIA. What he told me was chilling."

Connor paused, allowing the tension in the room to build. "Montagne revealed that the SDECE had funded most of its covert operations through the opium trade in Indochina, working hand in glove with Corsican gangsters in Marseilles and Naples, to destroy the Communist Party's influence on the dock workers union there. But here's the kicker - when France left Indochina, the CIA inherited this sordid network and continued the same practices."

"So, the CIA was actively involved in drug trafficking by their connection to these criminal organizations?" Blake asked.

Connor nodded grimly, his expression a mixture of resignation and disgust. "Oh, it gets worse. In '68-'69, CIA assets set up a cluster of heroin labs in the Golden Triangle in Southeast Asia. Hmong tribes were loading opium onto CIA planes, supplying our own troops in Vietnam." He reached for a file on his desk, his hands trembling slightly. "A 1972 CIA Inspector General report admitted they turned a blind eye to drug trafficking because these heroin drug lords were useful in the fight against Maoist communists."

Angela, who had been listening intently, her body coiled like a spring, suddenly interjected. Her tone was sharp, cutting through the heavy atmosphere. "Assets, actual CIA personnel - let's not kid ourselves. It's a conceived dividing line to divert responsibility away from the CIA."

Connor's eyes met Angela's, a flicker of appreciation for her directness passing between them. "By 1971, according to a Pentagon report I've seen, nearly thirty percent of American troops in Vietnam were addicted to heroin. The CIA had working relationships with known drug traffickers like the KMT and the Hmong tribes. Air America, a CIA proprietary, was involved with South Vietnamese armed forces in transporting large amounts of heroin."

"And the Administration . . . they knew about this?" Blake asked.

Connor's face hardened. "In 1971, the DEA sent a team of agents to Laos. Upon arrival, they were stonewalled, prevented from conducting their investigations by the U.S. Embassy, the CIA, and the Laotian government." His fist clenched involuntarily. "Our own army's Criminal Investigation Division uncovered damning evidence that South Vietnamese armed forces officers were drug traffickers.

These reports went through channels to the U.S. Embassy in Saigon, which took no action."

The weight of these revelations hung heavy in the air, almost suffocating. Blake and Angela exchanged glances, their faces a complex mix of shock, disgust, and grim determination. The truth they sought was darker and more dangerous than they'd ever imagined, stretching back decades and implicating the highest levels of government. The enormity of what they were up against began to sink in, along with the realization that their investigation could put them in the crosshairs of some very powerful, very dangerous people.

Angela's eyes flashed with determination as she leaned forward, her voice cutting through the hushed atmosphere of Senator Connor's office. "Senator, let's cut to the chase. What has happened to the CIA?"

Connor's weathered face seemed to age another decade as he met Angela's gaze. The weight of his years in intelligence work hung heavy in the air. He glanced at Blake, then back to Angela, his voice low and gravelly. "The CIA, an institution I once believed in, is rotting from within. A trinity of cancers plagues it: objectives that shift like sand, methods that would make Machiavelli blush, incompetence and botched missions, and an absence of accountability that's nothing short of terrifying."

Blake felt a chill run down his spine, his policeman's instincts screaming that this was bigger than anything he'd ever encountered. He leaned in, hanging on every word.

Connor's eyes took on a faraway look, his words pouring out like a confession. "Born from the ashes of the OSS in '47, the CIA was meant to be our eyes and ears in a dangerous world. But somewhere along the line, it morphed into something else entirely -- a shadow government, operating beyond the reach of law or morality." He opened his hands widely. "A former Director once bragged to me over drinks, 'We lied, we cheated, we stole . . . hell, we even taught courses on it.' He said it with pride!"

Angela felt her blood boil, a mix of outrage and vindication surging through her. Her voice was steel when she spoke. "I've heard whispers, read fragments about toppled governments, shattered nations. But to hear it confirmed . . . ."

"The chaos they've sown is beyond measure," Connor growled, years of pent-up frustration etched in every word. "From Iran to Guatemala, Chile to Cuba – the list goes on. And yet, the CIA remains untouchable, cloaked in layers of secrecy and bureaucracy."

Blake asked, "But why? What drives them to such extremes?"

Connor glanced out the window. "Ah, the million-dollar question. Good intentions paved this road to hell, my friends. President Truman wanted to stop the spread of Communism and protect America. But fear is a potent drug, and absolute power, well, you know how that saying goes." He shook his head. "Even now, with the Cold War long over, they find new 'threats' to justify the unjustifiable."

The Senator took a shuddering breath, seeming to deflate slightly. "And it's only grown worse over the years. What was once a single agency has metastasized – SAC/SOG, SAC/PAG, a whole alphabet soup of Black Ops units, many of them contractors, not employees, all operating in the shadows, beyond the reach of oversight or consequence."

Angela leaned forward, her posture radiating determination. Her voice was steely, tinged with a mix of hope and trepidation. "You mentioned that Blake and I can help, Senator. What's the plan?"

Connor nodded, outlining a plan to leverage the Senate Intelligence Committee to scrutinize CIA communications with criminal organizations, requiring Angela's and Blake's testimonies.

With agreements made and hands shaken, Connor excused himself, leaving Angela and Blake alone. They understood the complexity of uncovering the CIA's involvement in drug trafficking, made daunting by the agency's perceived invincibility and misguided missions.

As they departed Connor's office, the weight of their conversation lingered, a mix of optimism and sobering reality. Angela's determination was unwavering, a trait Blake admired deeply. Their journey was far from over, with new developments in Hong Kong beckoning them back into the fray.

"Do you have confidence in Senator Connor?" Blake asked.

Angela's gaze was unflinching, her jaw set with resolve. "I do. He's one of the good ones. But he's isolated with only a few allies and a reticence by his party to enforce accountability. He is swimming against a powerful current." Her expression softened slightly, a hint of warmth breaking through. "I want you with me when we talk to Jack Cross next. We're in this together now."

Blake nodded, then hesitated, running a hand through his hair. "I heard from Dennis while we were in there. He's got new intel on the Hong Kong angle, but he didn't want to discuss it on the phone – he wants to meet in person."

A ghost of a smile played at Angela's lips, a moment of lightness in the heavy atmosphere. "Looks like we're heading back to Hong Kong, partner. And I've cleared it with Commissioner Blair and my boss, that I'm picking up the tab for you on first class travel. They were quite happy to save the money from their budget this time. I've got more airline points than I know what to do with."

Blake couldn't help but grin, grateful for the momentary release of tension. "Well, how can I refuse when you put it that way?"

As they walked away from Connor's office, the weight of their task loomed before them like a mountain. The CIA's tendrils ran deep, and they were about to tug on them hard. Yet in that moment, a spark of hope flickered between Angela and Blake – a shared determination to shine a light into the agency's darkest corners, no matter the cost.

The corridors of power echoed with their footsteps as they left, two figures united—and now a third, Connor -- against a shadowy goliath.

"The DEA car headed to Angela's home. And what a home it was.

The taxi wound its way through Massachusetts Avenue Heights, D.C.'s most opulent neighborhood. Blake's eyes widened as they passed sprawling estates -- Colonial mansions, Tudor revivals, and Mediterranean villas nestled among manicured gardens and towering trees. The air seemed different here, rarefied and thick with old money.

As they pulled up to a grand colonial home on Brandywine St., Angela's eyes danced with excitement. "This is me, Blake."

Blake let out a low whistle, a mix of awe and sudden self-consciousness washing over him. "I knew you came from money, but this is... wow."

Angela squeezed his hand, sensing his unease. "It's been in my family for two generations."

The moment they stepped through the imposing oak and brass door, Blake felt like he'd entered another world. The entryway was a testament to American history, with gleaming hardwood floors and walls adorned with portraits spanning a century. The air carried the weight of countless stories, a subtle scent of lemon polish and old books.

Sally Thompson, the housekeeper, greeted them with the warmth of a longtime family friend. Her easy acceptance of Blake's presence and Angela's instructions to place his things in her bedroom spoke volumes about the trust and openness in this household.

As Angela led Blake on a tour, her fingers intertwined with his, he felt the walls between them crumbling. Angela's voice softened with memory in her father's study, surrounded by floor-to-ceiling bookshelves and antique furniture. "This room . . . it's where I truly knew my father."

Blake's gaze fell on the framed military medals, the purple heart, a bronze star. "He was a war hero?"

Angela's eyes glistened. "He was my hero. A man of unshakeable principles, who taught me the value of truth and courage." Her voice caught as she touched her father's photo. "

Blake picked up a photo of a woman from the desk." And this is your mother? She is very beautiful."

"Yes, tragically, she died when I was eleven years old. She was so gentle, kind and delicate, as though she would break if you touched her too hard. It crushed my father, who loved her so much. he channeled that pain into raising me and building his legacy. He never remarried and threw himself into building a business empire and spoiling me. He died when I was still in university. I'm the only one left in the Torres family now."

Blake felt a surge of connection. "We're both shaped by loss, aren't we?"

Angela's answering squeeze of his hand spoke louder than words.

Angela grabbed Blake's hand. Let's go out onto the veranda. It's so peaceful there."

The large wood and tile veranda overlooked a glass-enclosed swimming pool, manicured gardens, and, beyond, the lights of Washington below. Blake felt a serene silence here.

Angela retrieved two drinks from the bar on the terrace and handed one to Blake.

Blake took his drink and held it up *"perfer, obdūrā,* (endure, persist.)"

Angela clinked his glass with her own, *"Defiende lo que es correcto. Incluso si eso significa estar solo* (Stand for what is right. Even if it means standing alone)."

They finished their drinks and grazed on the refreshments. The light of day faded into night, and the lights in the pool and gardens switched on.

"How about a swim, Blake?"

Taken by surprise, "I don't have swimming trunks. I could go in my underwear."

"We don't need swimming suits. It's entirely private, and Sally is otherwise occupied. Shy, are you?"

"Okay, okay. Let's do it."

Angela left momentarily and returned with towels and two robes. Then she quickly removed her clothes, revealing her beautiful, fit body. Blake, his lean muscular body marked with the scars of his work, promptly followed her, and they dove into the water.

Under the moon's tender gaze, the garden around the secluded pool whispered with the rustle of leaves, crafting a sanctuary away from the world's prying eyes. The air, warm and fragrant with the scent of blooming night flowers, wrapped around them like a soft cloak as they stood by the water's edge, their fingers intertwined, a silent promise hanging between them.

Blake looked into her eyes, finding the reflection of the starlit sky within them, and saw the universe mirrored back at him—a vast, beautiful mystery that he longed to explore with her by his side. With a gentle squeeze of her hand, they stepped forward, the world around them fading into a hush of anticipation.

Together, they swam in the pool, the cool water enveloping them. The water danced around them, caressing their skin, as they moved closer to one another. Below the surface, the silence of the underwater world was profound, a serene backdrop to the intensity of their connection.

As they surfaced, laughing softly, droplets of water cascading down their faces, they found themselves in an ethereal world of their own making. The moonlight cast a silvery glow on the water, turning it into a canvas of light and shadow that danced around them. They shared a look, a moment suspended in time, where all that existed was the bond that drew them together, as inevitable as the tide.

In the tranquility of the night, they came together, a gentle collision of souls that felt like coming home. Their kiss was a whisper of promises yet to be spoken, a tender exploration of deep affection and the quiet strength of a love that had found its equal.

They explored each other's bodies with passion and tenderness in the soft caress of the water. Blake kissed Angela deeply, and she returned the kiss with great love.

Afterwards, in her bedroom, Angela lay back in Blake's arms. "I love you, Blake. I can't imagine going through life without you."

Blake caressed the smooth skin of her shoulder. "That's something that you won't have to worry about. I'm in love with you Angela."

They spent the rest of the night in each other's embrace, pledging their bodies, minds, and souls before they crashed into restful periods of sleep until the morning. Together, they had found a sanctuary, a source of strength to face whatever storms were brewing on the horizon.

Chapter 16

The CIA in the Crosshairs

The air in the waiting area outside the Senate's Sensitive Compartmented Information Facility (SCIF) crackled with tension. Angela and Blake perched on the edge of their seats, their bodies rigid with anticipation. The sterile, cold room seemed to pulse with the weight of past secrets, its thick walls muffling the world outside but amplifying the thundering of their hearts.

Blake's hand found Angela's shoulder, his touch a lifeline in the sea of uncertainty. "Ready for this?" he murmured, his voice barely above a whisper.

Angela's eyes, bright with determination, met his. A small smile played at the corners of her mouth, a stark contrast to the moment's gravity. "Ready? Not quite. But armed? Absolutely," she replied, her voice steady despite the tremor in her hands. "We've got the truth on our side, Blake. That's our armor. Our sword." She paused, drawing a deep breath. "We lay it all out there. After that?" She shrugged, a gesture of both resignation and resolve. "It's in Senator Connor's hands."

Blake nodded, his face a canvas of conflicting emotions -- resolve, fear, anticipation. "They have no idea what's coming," he said, his voice low and tinged with a mix of dread and excitement. "The Triad's activities . . . it's going to hit them like a freight train."

Leaning in, Angela's voice dropped to a conspiratorial whisper. "Your testimony is the linchpin, Blake. And don't forget about Connor's mystery witness. Whoever it is, he's got something big on the CIA's covert operations."

A dark chuckle escaped Blake's lips, the sound incongruous in the tense atmosphere. "I can't wait to find out who and what it is."

Their hushed exchange was cut short as the door swung open with a soft hiss. An assistant, her face a mask of professional detachment, stepped into the room. "The committee is ready for you," she announced, her crisp tone slicing through the tension. "Please, take your seats facing them. The Chairman will provide further instructions."

Inside the SCIF, the air felt heavier, charged with the gravity of what was about to unfold. Chairman Bryce Connor sat at the center of the long, curved table, his presence commanding attention even in silence. The committee members flanked him on either side, their faces etched with varying degrees of anticipation and wariness.

When Connor spoke, his voice filled the room with authority. "Let the record show that the Committee is now in session for a confidential hearing on allegations of misconduct within the Central Intelligence Agency." The words hung in the air, each syllable weighted with significance.

Leaning forward, Connor's eyes swept across the room, his gaze intense. "Committee members, we gather today under the darkest of clouds," he began, his tone grave. "Reports have reached us, allegations that the Central Intelligence Agency has engaged with a certain Mexican drug Cartel, the purpose of which has been called into question by DEA authorities. If proven true, such actions undermine the fabric of our national security and betray the trust of the American people and our international partners."

The silence that followed was deafening, broken only by the rustle of papers and the almost imperceptible shifting of bodies in seats. Connor continued, his voice steady but laced with an underlying tension. "Our task is clear but far from simple. We must sift through the evidence, separate fact from fiction, and chart a course forward - not just for the Senate or the President, but for the very soul of our nation."

Many Committee members nodded their agreement, with a few shaking their heads in silent disagreement.

"Before we hear testimony from our witnesses, I'd like to make a few introductory comments, and committee members are welcome to comment after that with a maximum time limit of two minutes each," Connor declared.

Connor shifted in his seat and surveyed the Committee members. "Let us be clear: Our aim is not to undermine the CIA or its critical role in national security. However, oversight is a cornerstone of democracy. Should any part of our government stray from the principles upon which this nation was founded, it is our duty to correct its course. Our agenda focuses on grave accusations against the Central Intelligence Agency. If such allegations hold any water, the implications for our national security and moral standing are profound and deeply troubling. In addition to thoroughly examining these accusations, we'll hear from an intelligence expert who can provide some context to CIA activities, and finally hear from a CIA official."

Committee members nodded their agreement.

"The Chair recognizes the Senator from Arizona," Connor said.

Freshman Senator John McHenry switched on his microphone.

"Chairman Connor, I served this country for twenty-two years in the military, and during that time, I was trained to believe and still believe that people in the service of this country are bound to serve with honesty, honor and ethics. That also applies to our intelligence services, such as the CIA. If their conduct is such that contravenes that code, then they should be held accountable. No one person or agency is above the law. They must know when the values that define our nation are intentionally disregarded by our security policies, even those policies that are conducted in secret. They must be able to make informed judgments about whether those policies and the personnel who supported them were justified in compromising our values, whether they served a greater good, or whether, as I believe, they stained our national honor, did much harm and little practical good."

"Thank you Senator McHenry. The Chair recognizes Senator William Gladstone from Texas."

"Thank you, Chairman Connor. Senator McHenry's statement is a fine platitude, but the ultimate test for our government and its agencies, such as the CIA, is any threat to American national security. In protecting against those threats and keeping us safe, there may be times that our agencies, such as the CIA, must bend the rules a little and exercise discretionary judgment. Having said that, if there is absolute proof that the CIA violated their official mandate or the law, it must be held accountable. And I stress absolute proof."

"The Chair recognizes Senator Alice Wilson from Massachusetts," Connor said.

"Thank you, Chairman Connor. I won't repeat what Senator McHenry said so succinctly. However, I do want to stress that our duty today is to the Constitution and the American people, not to any agency. I've long warned about the dangers of unchecked power within our intelligence agencies. This investigation must be thorough, unbiased, and, above all, conducted to protect American citizens, and we must not be fearful of shining light on the truth wherever it leads us. The eyes of the nation are on us."

Connor's gaze settled on the dossier before him, the gavel held loosely in his other hand. "Let us begin. The future of our intelligence operations, international relations, and principles may depend on our deliberations."

With a curt nod to the clerk, Connor set the wheels in motion. The door opened, and Angela and Blake entered, their footsteps echoing in the hushed chamber. Angela's chin was held high, her eyes bright with determination. Blake, by contrast, seemed to carry the weight of the world on his broad shoulders, his face a mask of grim resolve.

"Special Agent Angela Torres," Connor announced, his tone a complex mix of respect, wariness, and barely concealed anticipation. "Please stand and be sworn in."

Angela rose, smoothing her tailored suit with her hands. She raised her right hand, and as she swore to tell the truth, her voice rang out strong and clear.

"In what capacity do you work and can provide evidence that pertains to our investigation?" Connor asked.

"I am a Special Agent for the Intelligence Division of the DEA, which helps initiate new investigations of major drug organizations, strengthens ongoing investigations and subsequent prosecutions, develops information that leads to seizures and arrests, and provides policymakers with drug trend information upon which policy and laws can be made," Angela replied. "Since I joined the Division, the DEA has become much more aware of the growing tentacles and power of drug trafficking throughout the world. And of particular interest to us is Mexico and Southeast Asia."

Connor leaned forward, his piercing gaze fixed on Angela. The wrinkles around his eyes deepened, evidence of long nights and heavy burdens. "Agent Torres," he began, his voice low and intense, "can you state briefly the nature of your investigations relevant to today's hearing?"

Angela's response came in measured tones, her words crisp and professional as she outlined the DEA's role and her division's responsibilities. But as she approached the crux of her testimony, a change came over her. Her voice took on an edge of urgency, her eyes flashing with a mix of righteous anger and trepidation.

"Over the past two years," she said, each word deliberate and weighted, "we have uncovered evidence of someone within the CIA actively meeting with the Tijuana Cartel."

"And what evidence do you have to support your statement?" Connor pressed.

Angela's confidence seemed to grow as she presented her case. She clicked through damning photos and documents and audio tapes, her movements precise, her explanations clear and concise. With each piece of evidence, her eyes gleamed brighter, a mix of triumph at finally bringing this information to light and apprehension about its implications.

"And has the CIA person been identified?" Connor asked?

"Yes, we have been able to ID him from the photographs. In addition, our Agent surreptitiously followed the CIA individual to his lodgings and gained further corroborating evidence."

"And who is this CIA individual?"

"Under the advice of my superiors and the Department of Justice (DOJ), I've been directed not to reveal this individual's identity until the DOJ and the FBI conduct further investigations."

"I see. Well, we will contact the DOJ about this. Is there any more evidence you can present that incriminates the CIA?"

"Yes, Chairman Connor. I took part in a combined drug enforcement bust of the Tijuana Cartel involving fentanyl with the Mexican police in Manzanillo, Mexico a few months ago. In addition to apprehending drug traffickers in a large drug bust, the pilot who was involved in transporting the drug fentanyl to the warehouse flew for an airline called AEROCO, which, upon investigation, is an airline owned by the Tijuana Cartel. The pilot, a man named Michael Ransom, told us his job was to fly the guns and munitions found in the confiscated crates with the drugs from Nicaragua to Manzanillo. He identified his contact man in Nicaragua as a man named Juan Lopez, who is a CIA asset."

"What has happened to this man, Ransom, and the others you apprehended in Manzanillo?"

"Initially arrested and charged with various drug trafficking offences under Mexican law. But the bad news I received just recently is that the Mexicans who were apprehended and charged were killed on their way to arraignment in court. My guess is by someone who didn't want them to testify. And I received a report from my Mexican counterpart that the pilot Ransom had been extradited here to the U.S."

"Oh, some good news," Connor interjected. "By the DEA?"

"No, I was told it was someone from the State Department who was accompanied by someone from the CIA. When I attempted to contact the State Department and the CIA to gain the identities of these individuals, they had no such knowledge or record of it. Subsequently, Michael Ransom cannot be found."

"So, an important part of your evidence has now disappeared," Senator Gladstone interrupted, obviously anxious to cast doubt on Angela's testimony.

"Not all of it Senator." Angela replied. "During my investigations, I was put into contact with Senior Inspector Blake Morgan of the Royal Hong Kong Police, who is charge of combatting Triad criminal organizations in Hong Kong. The DEA and Hong Kong Police are now collaborating in their investigations as they intersect in alarming ways. But before you swear in Inspector Morgan, I want to set off some alarm bells regarding drug trafficking. Committee members and the government in general, if not the public, have a general awareness of drug trafficking for cocaine and heroin, but they pale in comparison with what is occurring now."

"And what might that be, Agent Torres?" Connor asked.

"Illegal trafficking of fentanyl. We've uncovered evidence that there is a growing global drug trafficking conspiracy in which Asian criminal organizations are collaborating with Mexican drug Cartels for trafficking fentanyl into the U.S. The danger this presents is that fentanyl is fifty times more potent than heroin and one hundred times more potent than morphine. Increasingly, cocaine overdose deaths have been found to contain fentanyl. Fentanyl is a killer drug that can be laced with other drugs, and many more people will die."

A heavy silence hung in the room for a long minute.

Throughout the exchange, Blake sat in taut silence. His eyes darted between Angela and Connor, watching the interplay with a mix of pride in Angela's performance and a little anxiety about the reception her report was receiving

"Disturbing indeed, Agent Torres," he finally managed, his voice barely above a whisper. The words seemed to catch in his throat, as if reluctant to acknowledge the gravity of what he'd just heard. Connor's eyes, usually sharp and calculating, now held a haunted look. "This goes beyond mere criminal activity. It strikes at the very heart of our institutions, the very foundations of our democracy."

Connor's words struck a chord with the majority of the Senators on the Committee. "Now, we'll hear from Mr. Blake Morgan, Inspector and Head of the Triad Investigation Unit for the Royal Hong Kong Police. Inspector Morgan, please stand and take the oath."

Blake rose slowly, each movement deliberate and measured. As he raised his hand to swear, his eyes met Connor's. In that moment, a silent communication passed between them — a shared understanding of the gravity of the situation and the potential consequences of what was about to be revealed.

"Inspector Morgan," Connor began, his voice low and intense, "how do your investigations into Triad crime relate to our inquiry into CIA activity?" The question hung in the air, laden with unspoken implications. Every ear in the room strained to catch Blake's response.

Blake took a deep breath, his chest rising and falling as he gathered his thoughts. He squared his shoulders, as if physically bracing himself for the weight of his words. When he spoke, his voice carried a hint of passion, a fervor born of years dedicated to his work.

"The Triads, Mr. Chairman," he began, his words measured but intense, "are not merely local thugs or common criminals. They are a global force, with roots stretching back centuries, intertwined with the very fabric of Chinese history and politics." His hands moved as he spoke, painting invisible pictures in the air, bringing his words to life.

As Blake delved into the rich and complex history of the Triads, the room hung on his every word. He spoke of secret societies evolving from revolutionary movements, of oaths sworn in blood, and empires built on the backs of the oppressed. His narrative wove a tapestry of intrigue, violence, and power that spanned continents and centuries.

Connor's eyebrows shot up, a mix of surprise and grudging admiration crossing his face. "Politicians using criminals for their own ends?" he muttered, a touch of cynicism coloring his voice. "Some things, it seems, never change." His fingers drummed a soft, contemplative rhythm on the polished wood of the table.

Blake nodded grimly, a flicker of shared understanding passing between him and the Chairman. "Indeed, sir. The lines between politics and crime have always been blurry." His voice took on a harder edge, tinged with frustration born of years fighting an uphill battle.

As Blake delved deeper into the Triads' wartime activities, Connor's expression darkened progressively. The horror of what he was hearing etched itself clearly on his face, deepening the lines around his eyes and mouth. His complexion paled visibly, the blood draining from his face as the full implications of Blake's words sank in.

"Are these Triad organizations large in size and number?" Connor asked.

"In Hong Kong alone, we estimate there are one hundred thousand Triad members. Their influence is pervasive. Insidious." Blake paused, his eyes taking on a distant look, as if seeing beyond the room to the streets he'd patrolled. "They've woven themselves into the very fabric of our society. They're in our markets, our schools, sometimes even our police force."

Connor's knuckles whitened as he gripped the edge of the table, leaning in further. "And now they're involved with fentanyl?" he asked, his voice tight with barely contained alarm. "As if heroin wasn't destructive enough."

Blake's eyes flashed with a complex mix of emotions – frustration, determination, and a hint of something deeper, more personal. Perhaps a memory of lives lost, communities destroyed. "Yes, sir. It's a new challenge for us, and a deadly one. We've made significant progress against corruption within our ranks, but." He paused, shame coloring his words, his gaze dropping momentarily to the table. "I must admit, there may still be officers on their payroll. The temptation of easy money is . . . powerful."

"Can you bring us up to date with recent developments and the connection to Special Agent Torres' work?"

"Yes, through informers and documents, we have determined three things. First, there is an internal war among Triads in Hong Kong going on; we think about drug trafficking, including the assassinations of powerful Triad leaders. Second, we have evidence to show that a Triad is involved in a cooperative venture with the Mexican Tijuana Cartel for the production and distribution of fentanyl to the U.S. The Triad provides the precursor chemicals, and the Cartel carries out production and distribution. And third, evidence indicates that the CIA has been involved in discussions with Triad leaders. The detailed evidence is contained in my written report that I have provided for the Committee."

Connor sat back in his chair, the leather creaking softly. His face was a mask of concern and resolve, but his eyes betrayed the turmoil within – a man clearly grappling with the enormity of the situation before them. He took a deep breath, his chest rising and falling slowly as he collected his thoughts.

"Inspector Morgan," Connor said, his voice low but carrying clearly in the silent chamber. "I think I speak for the entire committee when I say your testimony has been deeply troubling." He paused, carefully choosing his next words, each weighted with significance. "The picture you and Agent Torres have painted for us today is one of a world far more complex and dangerous than many of us imagined. A world where the lines between law enforcement, intelligence agencies, and criminal organizations have become dangerously blurred."

Connor straightened in his seat, a new resolve hardening his features. His voice took on a steely quality, ringing with determination. "This committee will not rest until we've uncovered the full extent of these operations and their implications for our national security. The road ahead may be long and dangerous, but the truth must prevail. For the sake of our nation, and for the countless lives affected by these criminal enterprises, we must press on."

"Thank you for your testimony, Inspector Morgan," Connor said, stretching out his arms. "The hearing is now open for Committee members to ask questions of Inspector Morgan or Special Agent Torres," Connor announced.

"The Chair recognizes Senator McHenry," Connor said.

"Thank you, Mr. Chairman. Special Agent Torres, you've worked in the DEA for some time now. How concerned are you about the drug trafficking picture you presented so ably?"

"If I were to describe it in terms of a fire, I believe this should be a five-bell fire alarm. Illegal drugs are continuing to pour into our country despite our best efforts to stop it, and the appearance of large amounts of fentanyl coming across our borders is frankly frightening," Angela replied.

"And do you believe that the information you have to date regarding possible involvement in some way of the CIA with these criminal organizations is a serious threat to our national security?" McHenry continued.

"I believe this Committee and the administration in general needs to determine what is the nature of activities by the CIA with these criminal groups," Angela replied.

"The Chair recognizes Senator Gladstone," Connor said.

"Thank you, Mr. Chairman. Special Agent Torres and Inspector Morgan, did you personally witness CIA personnel being actively involved with criminal groups in Mexico or Hong Kong?" Gladstone asked.

"No, I did not, Senator," Angela replied, "But we have eyewitness testimony from reliable field agents and informers."

"I did not, Senator," Blake replied.

"Then I would conclude that the information is second-hand and insufficient for us to cast aspersions on the agency protecting our national security," Gladstone replied curtly.

"The Chair recognizes Senator Wilson, of Massachusetts" Connor said.

"Thank you, Mr. Chair. First, I'd like to emphasize that our witnesses here today have no axes to grind. They are fulfilling their duties to their agencies and governments by reporting what they see as a serious problem, so we can take necessary steps to act upon those problems. It matters not which agency or branch of government may be involved. No one is above the law and Constitution. And I believe we owe a debt of thanks to our witnesses today to help us do our job."

"Thank you, Senator Wilson. I endorse your comments. If our witnesses have no further questions, I'd like to take a twenty-minute break before we hear our next witness. I want to thank Special Agent

Torres and Inspector Morgan for their testimony, and we will be entering your written reports into the record," Connor stated and banged his gavel.

Blake and Angela stood up and were led from the hearing room. Outside the Senate offices, they stopped to discuss what happened.

"Well, what do you think?" Blake asked Angela.

"I think there are a few Senators that share Connor's perspective and are really concerned about the CIA's clandestine activities." Still, there are others who see the agency as a necessary evil," Angela replied. "What do you think?"

"I agree with you. And we've seen it in Hong Kong. It's the ends that justify the means argument. My impression of America now is that it is obsessed with fighting Communism or Socialism or even the threat of it, that any means, legal or illegal or immoral, is justified to protect the country," Blake said.

"Exactly. If some reports are accurate the CIA's mission has gone far beyond fighting Communism. It now sees as legitimate playing a key role in regime change and support for groups plotting political assassinations in countries around the world."

"I know you well enough, Angela, to know that you believe in personal responsibility and accountability. For you, this means speaking out and acting when you encounter injustice, doing what you can personally to correct it, and holding those bad actors accountable. It's a belief I share with you."

Angela put her arms around Blake. "Which is another reason I love you." She kissed him passionately. "Alright, let's return to my house, have dinner, and plan our next moves. I'll check in with Senator Connor tomorrow for his thoughts."

Arm in arm, they walked together to hail a taxi. Blake looked up at the sky and noticed a dark cloud moving in.

Chapter 17

The Chronicles of Deceit

The SCIF's atmosphere grew even more charged as Chairman Connor called for the next witness. The committee members shifted in their seats, a collective tension palpable in the air. A stocky, bald man in his early 60s made his way to the witness table, his footsteps echoing in the hushed room. James Reynolds, his face etched with the lines of a man who had seen too much, took his place and raised his hand to take the oath.

"Can you tell the Committee who you are and what you do?" Connor asked, after Reynolds had taken the oath.

"My name is James Reynolds. I have been a special investigator for the FBI and the Department of Justice (DOJ) for the past twenty-eight years," he replied.

Connor leaned forward, his eyes boring into Reynolds. "Mr. Reynolds, please summarize your findings on alleged CIA misconduct for this committee." The chairman's voice was taut with anticipation, a mixture of dread and determination evident in his tone.

"I have served on staff for the Senate Foreign Relations Committee's Subcommittee on Terrorism and International Operations and the Senate's Church Committee, which has investigated the CIA's clandestine activities."

"You've provided a lengthy written report of your work, Mr. Reynolds, which has been entered into this Committee's record. For this hearing, can you give us a summary of some of the more relevant findings?"

Reynolds nodded gravely, his weathered hands clasping together on the table before him. "Mr. Chair, members of the committee," he began, his voice low but clear in the silent room. My investigation reveals a disturbing pattern of CIA covert operations that have systematically undermined democracies worldwide." His words hung heavy in the air, each syllable weighted with the gravity of his discoveries.

"The first area to summarize is the CIA's covert operations, including assassinations and political coups that deposed democratically elected governments across multiple continents. The populations of at least twenty-five countries were denied the right to choose their leaders by the CIA," Reynolds said.

"And what were those countries?"

"Mr. Chair, I'll provide the summary in bulletin point form, which you'll see." Reynolds pointed to the screen on the wall. "Detailed descriptions are in my report."

For the next twenty-five minutes, Reynolds described in detail how the CIA was actively involved in coups of governments around the world, from the 1970s to the modern era in Angola, Bolivia, Cambodia, Chile, Iraq, El Salvador, Laos, Nicaragua, Panama, Greece, Iran and many more.

The Committee members leaned forward almost as one, their faces a tableau of shock, dismay, and growing anger. Some furiously scribbled notes, while others sat frozen, as if physically struck by Reynolds' words.

"One area that needs special mention Mr. Chairman is the Nugan-Hand bank affair and alleged "unofficial" coup of the Australian government." Reynolds continued.

"Proceed," Connor replied.

He leaned forward, his voice dropping slightly as if sharing a terrible secret. "The bank, established by Frank Nugan and Michael Hand, a former CIA operative, defrauded depositors of at least fifty million dollars. But that's just the tip of the iceberg."

Reynolds' eyes swept the room, making sure he had everyone's full attention. "There are strong suspicions of the bank's involvement in drug dealing, arms trafficking, and covert intelligence operations. The staff included high-ranking former U.S. military and CIA personnel."

He paused, allowing the implications to sink in. "But here's where it gets truly alarming. There are allegations that the bank, with CIA involvement, played a role in the dismissal of Australian Prime Minister Gough Whitlam in 1975."

"The evidence suggests," Reynolds continued, "that $2.4 million was transferred from the Nugan-Hand Bank to the Liberal Party of Australia. And the Governor General, Sir John Kerr, who was pivotal in Whitlam's dismissal, was allegedly referred to by the CIA as 'our man.'"

"And do you have proof of these allegations?" Connor asked.

"I do. You'll find documentary evidence in my report, which I will submit to the Committee."

"What, in your opinion, would be the motivation for CIA actions in this case?" Connor asked.

"Pine Gap," Reynolds responded. "The Whitlam government was contemplating closing the Pine Gap surveillance system a joint effort between Australian intelligence services and the CIA."

As Reynolds concluded, a heavy, oppressive silence fell over the room. The enormity of the revelations seemed to press down on everyone present, an almost physical weight of responsibility and horror. Connor took a deep breath, visibly shaken, his usual composure cracked by the weight of what he'd heard.

"Mr. Reynolds," he said finally, his voice hoarse with emotion, "your testimony paints a picture of an agency operating far beyond its mandate, with devastating consequences for global democracy and stability." He paused, struggling to find the right words. "We have much to consider."

The committee members exchanged grim looks, the weight of responsibility clear on their faces. This was more than just a hearing; it was a reckoning with a dark chapter of American history, a confrontation with truths that had long been buried.

As Reynolds's testimony's implications settled over the room, there was a palpable sense of change in the air. It was clear to everyone present that everything would be different after this day. The truths revealed here would ripple out, challenging long-held beliefs about America's role in the world and the true nature of its intelligence operations.

"There's more," Reynolds continued. "During the 1960s and 1970s, the CIA enlisted the Hmong tribe of Laos to combat communist forces, encouraging opium cultivation. The CIA transported the opium, leading to widespread heroin addiction among U.S. soldiers in Vietnam. These controversial relationships remained largely unnoticed until exposed by a Christian Science Monitor correspondent. The report revealed the CIA's involvement in opium trafficking, with shipments receiving special CIA clearance. By that time, about thirty thousand U.S. servicemen in Vietnam had developed heroin addictions."

Reynolds continued, "Separate inquiries into the CIA's conduct have uncovered numerous controversial activities, including Operation MKULTRA, COINTELPRO, and Family Jewels, involving mind control experiments, surveillance, infiltration, and assassination plots. These activities, conducted under programs like Project Artichoke and Project Chatter, involved hundreds of unknowing participants subjected to various drugs, including LSD."

Reynolds cleared his throat. "Here are some other examples. In 1975, Mexican police, with U.S. support, arrested drug lord Alberto Sicilia Falcon, a CIA protégé, who facilitated arms trafficking for the agency while managing a drug empire. His lieutenant, Jose Egozi, a CIA-trained intelligence officer, secured agency backing for a coup attempt in Portugal."

"And in 1985, DEA agent Enrique 'Kiki' Camerena was kidnapped and murdered in Mexico. Investigators accused the CIA of stonewalling to protect assets, including top trafficker Miguel Angel Felix Gallardo, linked to the Contras. Felix Gallardo's partner, Juan Ramon Matta Ballesteros, received U.S. funds to transport 'humanitarian supplies' to the Contras, despite involvement in drug trafficking."

Connor cleared his throat. "You mention in your report that the CIA has operated outside of Presidential and Congressional oversight with respect to financing its operations. Could you elaborate?"

"Certainly Senator. "Secret funds have been the heart of the CIA's secret operations. The CIA has had since 1948 an unfailing source of untraceable cash, according to a top-secret paper sent to the State Department and the White House."

"Could you elaborate Mr. Reynolds?"

"As all of you are undoubtedly aware, the Marshall Plan and the Truman Doctrine were created to help rebuild and strengthen the democratic governments of Western European countries after WWII. The Marshall Plan was financed to the tune of approximately fourteen billion dollars. Five percent of those funds, or about six hundred and eighty million, was made available to the CIA through the plan's overseas offices. The CIA had sole discretion of how to use those funds with no Congressional oversight. Dean Acheson, Secretary of State in the Truman Administration said in his memoirs, 'I had the gravest forebodings about this organization [the CIA] and warned the President that as set up neither he, the National Security Council, nor anyone else would be in a position to know what it was doing or to control it.'" Reynolds paused.

"Continue Mr. Reynolds," Connor said encouragingly.

"The National Security Act of 1947, which created the CIA, said nothing about secret operations overseas. It instructed the CIA to correlate, evaluate and disseminate intelligence information, and perform other functions and duties related to intelligence affecting national security. It did not specifically sanction in covert activities. Just during the Truman administration alone, the CIA engaged in hundreds of covert actions."

"I'd like to hear more about the financial issue, Mr. Reynolds," Connor asked.

"The CIA used financial incentives to persuade politicians in foreign countries to take action favorable to the US. The Agency delivered millions into the bank accounts of Italian Americans, who then entered the money into newly formed political fronts created by the CIA, with the bonus that the donations were tax deductible. It has been a long-standing practice of the CIA to purchase elections and politicians with bags of cash. Secret funds were the heart of secret operations," Reynolds said.

"Why was the CIA granted such wide latitude?" Connor asked.

"With The CIA Act of 1949, Congress gave the Agency the widest conceivable powers, which gave it the ability to do almost anything it wanted, as long as Congress provided the money in an annual package. Those in the know understood approval of the secret budget by a small armed services subcommittee to constitute a legal authorization for all secret operations. The CIA ended up with free rein: unvouchered funds, untraceable money buried under falsified items in the Pentagon's budget," Reynolds continued.

"And to top things off, the 1949 Act allowed the CIA to let one hundred foreigners a year into the US in the name of national security and guaranteeing them permanent residence without regard to their inadmissibility under the immigration or any other laws. And they admitted people like Ukranian Mikola Lebed who the CIA felt had helped them in insurgency efforts against the Soviets, but CIA records show that he led a Ukrainian faction which was labelled a terrorist organization, and the Germans in WWII had recruited his men into two German Army battalions."

Reynolds referred to some papers before him. "By the 1960's the CIA was a worldwide force with fifteen thousand people, half a billion dollars in secret funds to spend each year and more than fifty overseas stations."

"Mr. Reynolds, can you explain why the CIA has been viewed so positively by the American public in general, and the news media specifically?" Connor asked.

"Simple," Reynolds replied, "Beginning with the first civilian Director of Central Intelligence (DCI) Allen Dulles, the CIA waged a relentless propaganda campaign, cultivating America's most influential publishers and broadcasters, courting newspaper columnists and public relations machine that came to include more than fifty news organizations, TV and film movie studios and a dozen publishing houses."

Reynolds continued. "In most recent years, the CIA, like the Pentagon, started subcontracting its missions and work to private contractors. It proved to be extremely profitable for big business. In effect, the Agency had two workforces -and the private one which paid better. As a result, large numbers of CIA employees quit the Agency and went to work for these private companies. And while technically, the private subcontractors were subject to the same rules and regulations as regular Agency personnel, it was rarely enforced."

"These reports are deeply disturbing, Mr. Reynolds. Looking at all the evidence you've provided, can you explain why the CIA would be involved in illegal and corrupt practices?" Connor asked.

"Founded in 1947, the CIA inherited the dual roles of intelligence gathering and subversion from the OSS. The agency's mandate included providing intelligence and engaging in subversive activities against perceived adversaries. These activities have significantly impacted global stability and challenged U.S. rule of law principles. Over the years, the CIA has functioned like a secret army, operating globally with minimal accountability. Other than Senator Frank

Church's investigation, the Agency has only been subjected to substantial public scrutiny once—in 1975."

Reynolds cleared his throat. "I'd like to add that, looking at the CIA's history, the CIA has evolved from an intelligence gathering organization to one that predominantly focuses on covert operations and has no hesitation in hiring known criminals and foreign agents of questionable moral character."

Connor replied, "The picture you paint for the CIA is very dark, Mr. Reynolds, and one that this committee, Congress, and the administration need to address. I'll hear questions and comments from committee members now."

Senator McHenry asked, "Thank you, Mr. Chair, and thank you, Mr. Reynolds, for your eye-opening testimony. Are there any other investigations or reports that point to CIA wrongdoing?"

Reynolds nodded. "In 1974, investigative reporter Seymour Hersh published an account of illegal CIA operations against the Vietnam antiwar movement. The CIA conducted intelligence surveillance on at least ten thousand U.S. citizens. Additionally, the agency engaged in break-ins, wiretapping, and mail inspection of American citizens."

McHenry asked, "Any other reports, Mr. Reynolds?"

"Yes, the Tower Commission found CIA-Contra networks involved in drug trafficking in Costa Rica. Key operatives included John Hull, a major base for Contra activities, and George Morales, a Miami-based drug trafficker. The U.S. government blocked Costa Rican attempts to extradite Hull. Cuban Americans employed by the CIA were implicated in drug trafficking, using Contra aircraft and a shrimp company for cocaine transport. Guatemala, with close ties to the CIA, also served as a conduit for cocaine trafficking."

Reynolds added, "Ramon Milian Rodriguez, the Medellin Cartel's accountant, testified about channeling millions to the Contras through Felix Rodriguez, a CIA operative. The Contras provided infrastructure for CIA-linked drug networks. Historically, U.S. intelligence agencies engaged with criminal elements, including the Italian Mafia and Chinese criminal syndicates, to gather intelligence and combat communism. These relationships facilitated heroin trafficking into the U.S. and other regions."

Senator Gladstone asked aggressively, "Mr. Reynolds, much of the evidence you provide is circumstantial or hearsay. Are there official documents showing the CIA's wrongdoing?"

Reynolds replied, "Yes, Senator. My report and the Church and Tower Committees provide documented evidence. And you should know that the CIA has also destroyed or 'misplaced' critical files."

Gladstone scowled. "Isn't it true that the CIA has kept America safe from its enemies?"

Reynolds replied, "Yes, that is true, in some instances. However, I would argue, it has also made our country less safe and engaged in morally indefensible activities. The CIA has been successful in intelligence gathering, but its shift to predominantly covert activities has led to some illegal and unethical activities, certainly ones that are inconsistent with our projected image of a democracy."

Senator Williams thanked Reynolds for his testimony and asked, "Do you believe the ends justify the means in the CIA's actions?"

"Unequivocally, I do not," Reynolds replied. "The rule of law and ethical frameworks must guide government actions. The CIA should operate within legal confines and be subject to rigorous oversight."

Connor concluded, "Thank you, Mr. Reynolds, for your invaluable testimony. We will review your written report and supporting documents and decide whether to hold a public meeting or submit a report to the Senate. And unless there are objections, I adjourn this hearing." He banged the gavel, the ominous sound echoing in the chamber.

Chapter 18

The Director's Defiance

The austere SCIF of the Senate Intelligence Committee crackled with an almost palpable tension as Senator Connor reconvened the hearing the next day. The wood paneled walls seemed to close in, amplifying the gravity of the moment. Jack Cross, the last witness scheduled that day, sat alone at a stark table facing the committee. His isolation was striking, a physical manifestation of the weight he carried as the guardian of the CIA's deepest secrets.

Cross, a man forged from steel and shadows, exuded a military bearing that seemed to challenge the very air around him. His steely gaze swept the room, meeting each Senator's eyes without flinching. As he was sworn in, his right hand raised with a practiced steadiness, his face remained an impenetrable mask. Yet, those who knew him best might have noticed the slight tightening around his eyes, the only outward sign of the tempest surely raging within.

"Deputy Director Cross, what is the CIA's mission?" Connor asked bluntly.

"Senator, the CIA's mission is to protect American interests and keep this country safe from its enemies. We are one of the country's best agencies to provide national security," Cross replied quickly.

"Deputy Director Cross, you have been asked to testify in camera to the Senate Intelligence Committee because serious accusations of CIA wrongdoings in your division have been made. The Committee would like to hear your response to these accusations. After I describe them and your response, Committee members will ask you questions."

The questioning intensified as Connor laid out the accusations. With each damning word, the room seemed to shrink, the air growing thicker and more oppressive. Cross remained outwardly calm, a statue of composure, but a keen observer might have noticed the slight tightening of his jaw, the almost imperceptible narrowing of his eyes. These micro-expressions were telling – but the only cracks in his otherwise impenetrable facade.

"Deputy Director Cross, we have heard testimony from three credible witnesses, one from the DEA and a Hong Kong policeman, who are jointly investigating a fentanyl drug trafficking conspiracy involving a Mexican drug Cartel and a Hong Kong Triad, as well as a special investigator formerly with the DOJ and FBI," Connor stated.

"How is that relevant to the CIA? It sounds like an issue for drug enforcement agencies," Cross replied flatly.

"We've heard testimony that describes CIA operatives meeting with Mexican Cartel members in Mexico City discussing the drug trade," Connor replied. "And we've heard testimony that a Triad member was meeting with a CIA operative in Hong Kong, discussing fentanyl. I ask you, Mr. Cross, is any of this true?"

Cross appeared unfazed by the line of questioning, his confidence unshaken. "It's possible, Mr. Chairman, but I'd have to determine the accuracy of these accusations by talking to eyewitnesses and examining documents. Sometimes the Agency may work with unsavory characters to accomplish our mission."

"I'll turn over the questioning to Committee members at this time," Connor said, "but I reserve the right to ask further questions later. The Chair recognizes Senator McHenry from Arizona."

"Thank you, Mr. Chair. Deputy Director Cross, I believe Chairman Connor's question to you was very simple, and I'd like it answered simply. " Did any CIA operatives meet with members of a Mexican drug Cartel in Mexico? Yes, or no?"

Cross's response was a masterclass in evasion, a verbal dance that would have made the most skilled diplomat proud. "I am not aware personally, but it's possible," he parried, his words forming an invisible shield around him. "If it did occur, it may have been part of a classified operation related to our national security." His eyes never wavered, challenging anyone to push further.

"And did CIA operatives meet with members of a Hong Kong Triad in Hong Kong to discuss fentanyl drug trafficking?" Deputy Director Cross?

"I am unaware of such a meeting, but it is possible. I'd have to check in with our Southeast Asia branch. Senator, we make hard choices to keep this country safe. But we don't traffic drugs. We help the DEA disrupt Cartels and dismantle networks. We play a secret, dangerous game, but it is for a greater purpose."

"Excuse me, Deputy Director Cross, how could you not know if such operations were occurring? Are you not aware of all the activities in your division?" McHenry replied.

Cross stared McHenry down. "Of course, I am, Senator McHenry, but I'm not obliged to share information with you if it's classified."

"And may I remind you, Deputy Director Cross, that it is the responsibility of the Senate and House Intelligence Committees to exercise oversight of the CIA and other intelligence agencies," McHenry stared back.

Cross sat there and said nothing.

"The Chair recognizes Senator Gladstone from Texas," Connor said.

Senator Gladstone's effusive praise provided a momentary respite, a brief lessening of the suffocating tension. "Men like you have kept our country safe, and for that we owe you a debt of gratitude," Gladstone effused, his voice warm with appreciation. But this interlude only served to heighten the stark divide between those seeking answers and those determined to protect the nation's secrets at all costs.

Cross nodded. "Thank you Senator, it's been my honor."

"For security reasons, it is my understanding that the CIA's involvement in covert activities is shared with a minimum number of people from the President down. Is that correct?" Gladstone asked.

"That's correct." Cross replied.

"Then, Mr. Chairman, I see no reason to continue investigating this issue unless the President authorizes the Committee to obtain all the relevant information," Gladstone lectured.

"I'm not going to rush into any action of any kind, Senator, until the Committee is satisfied that we've thoroughly examined the accusations against the CIA. Now, let us continue with the hearing. I recognize Senator Williams from Massachusetts."

"Thank you, Chairman Connor," Senator Williams replied. Deputy Director Cross, can you describe the CIA's mandate for covert operations?"

"Covert operations can be defined as any activity to influence political, economic or military conditions abroad, where it intended that the role of the U.S. Government will not be apparent or acknowledged publicly," Cross replied.

"And what might be those activities, Deputy Director Cross?"

"Propaganda, psychological and economic warfare, preventive direct action, including sabotage, demolition and evacuation measures, subversion against hostile states, including assistance to the underground resistance movements, guerrillas and refugee groups and support of indigenous anti-Communist elements in countries that potentially be a national security risk. The CIA oversees and facilitates collecting, evaluating, and disseminating foreign intelligence collected by clandestine sources. Our Special Activities Center conducts direct action-like raids, ambushes, assassinations, and guerrilla training. But we operate in the grey areas. We make hard choices to keep this country safe. We do what's necessary. We walk the tightrope between morality and survival.'"

"And so, if the report of CIA liaison with a Mexican drug Cartel is accurate, the covert action could fall within one of the areas you just described?" Senator Williams asked.

"I repeat, Senator Williams, I cannot confirm or deny that such a meeting took place, as it may at this time be classified."

"If such a meeting did take place, Deputy Director Cross, what could possibly be the purpose of meeting with a criminal organization such as the drug Cartel?" Williams persisted.

"If such a meeting did take place, there could be several reasons ranging from gathering intelligence on Cartel activities to gathering information regarding the growth and strength of Socialist and Communist groups in Mexico, which certainly could pose a threat to national security—but I'm just speculating," Cross replied.

As the hearing progressed, Cross's responses became a litany of carefully crafted non-answers, each one a brick in the wall he was building between the committee and the truth they sought. "We make hard choices to keep this country safe," he intoned, his voice a mixture of unwavering conviction and veiled warning. "We play a secret, dangerous game, but it is for a greater purpose." The subtext was clear – "You cannot handle the truth, and I will not give it to you anyway."

"Deputy Director Cross, do you have any final comments for the Committee," Connor said.

"Only this, Mr. Chairman. Since 1948, the National Security Council directed the Central Intelligence Agency to carry out covert operations in support of U.S. foreign policy. To do so means the Agency engages in various forms of intelligence and espionage operations that are not widely known, even by various branches of the government, to keep our country safe from potential and actual external threats. The greatest threats come from existing and potentially new Communist organizations and countries. The CIA will continue to be aggressively vigilant in carrying out this mandate, and I make no apologies or excuses for what those activities may be, despite the Committee's concerns. Unless I receive a directive from my chain of command to share specific information, I will continue to decline." Cross said confidently.

The climax came as Connor, his patience clearly frayed to its last thread, leaned forward, his hands gripping the edge of the table. "Do you think you and your division are above the law, Deputy Director?" The question cracked like a whip in the tense atmosphere.

Cross's reply was chilling in its certainty, delivered with the calm assurance of a man who had faced far worse than a room full of politicians. "We do what's necessary, we protect this country, even when it means getting our hands dirty." The room fell silent, the weight of his words hanging in the air like a threat, or perhaps a promise.

"You've been heard, Deputy Director Cross. And you should know that this Committee has its mandate to exercise oversight of the CIA, a responsibility it takes seriously and will pursue with all vigor, despite your apparent lack of cooperation. Be on notice that we may issue a subpoena for documents the Agency has in connection with the reports of CIA activity related to the Mexican Cartel and Hong Kong Triad drug organizations. I thank you for your testimony. We reserve the right to recall you for further questioning," Connor summarized unemotionally but emphatically.

The room held its breath. Cross met Connor's resolute gaze fearlessly, and for a brief moment, the two warriors were locked in a silent combat. The ticking of an old clock on the wall echoed like a countdown—a reminder that time was slipping away, and that secrets were unravelling. The Senate Intelligence Committee had become their battleground.

Cross nodded but said nothing, quickly leaving the room.

As Cross left the room, his departure as composed as his entrance, the committee erupted into debate. Voices rose and fell, emotions bubbling to the surface as the implications of what they had heard sank in.

At this moment, within these wood-paneled walls, the very soul of American democracy was being questioned, challenged, and redefined. Even if they couldn't fully articulate it, the Senators knew that their decisions here would echo far beyond this room, shaping the nation's future and its place in the world. The weight of this responsibility was palpable, a physical presence that pressed down on each of them as they grappled with the thorny questions of power, secrecy, and the true meaning of national security.

"I'll call the matter to a vote," Connor said, "all those in favor of taking the hearings public."

Connor and a majority of Senators, predominantly Democrats, voted in agreement. Notably, Senator Gladstone voted no.

"The motion is passed. I will advise witnesses to be prepared to appear again and testify in an open hearing. I'll discuss with the administration and the National Security Council our proceedings and get their support. In addition, the Committee will issue a subpoena to Deputy Director Cross for documentation if he does not comply voluntarily. Before I entertain a motion to adjourn, I'd like the Committee to have its own discussion regarding the evidence presented thus far by the witnesses. This is on the record, but I'll forgo the usual time limits and the Chair's procedure."

The Senators nodded in agreement.

"Let me begin by stating what I think is the core issue here. Do the ends justify the means? Is the CIA entitled to use whatever means possible to achieve its goals and outcomes," Connor began, "or are there legal, ethical and moral boundaries that cannot and should not be crossed?"

"My colleagues, the ends justify the means regarding our national security. During the Cold War, the CIA understood that Communism posed an existential threat to our way of life. They had to act decisively, sometimes ruthlessly, to protect democracy. Covert operations against the Soviet bloc, like backing anti-communist movements in Latin America or conducting surveillance of suspected subversives at home, were necessary. We can't afford to play by conventional rules," Senator Gladstone stated emphatically.

"I understand the need for national security. However, compromising our values and legal frameworks is not the way to achieve that. When covert operations overstep ethical and moral boundaries, they tarnish our nation's credibility, erode public trust, and can lead to blowback that undermines long-term goals," Senator McHenry said.

"We need to be pragmatic when it comes to covert operations. Sometimes, these men employ strategies the public may not fully approve of. How can we prevent threats without proactive intelligence gathering and action before they materialize? Often, these covert operations are the only way to effectively disrupt criminal activity, terrorist plots or political organizations that are a threat to our country. The ends—protecting our country—justify the means whatever they are," Gladstone rejoined.

"I'm not against proactive measures, but those operations must be accountable. They should respect international law, human rights, and the sovereignty of other countries. If we justify every questionable tactic under 'national security,' we risk normalizing overreach that leads to a slippery slope, " Senator Williams said.

Gladstone responded, "But we already have checks and balances. That's what this committee, other committees, and the Inspector General are for."

"Even so, history has shown us these mechanisms can fail, as our witness, Mr. Reynolds so graphically illustrated for us. For example, the CIA's MK-Ultra, an illegal human experiments program to develop brainwashing and psychological torture procedures and identify drugs to weaken people and force confessions or the CIA's Operation CHAOS, a domestic espionage project targeting American citizens operating from 1967 to 1974, established by President Johnson and expanded under President Nixon, whose mission was to uncover possible foreign influence on domestic race, anti-war, and other protest movements. And more recently the abuses uncovered in the Iran-Contra affair, " Senator McHenry added.

Gladstone nodded. "I don't deny that excesses may have occurred. But hindsight is always 20/20. The threat of global Communism was real and immediate. Our adversaries would have gained the upper hand without a willingness to bend the rule to counter it. Even today, in the fight against communism, our intelligence community must act swiftly and decisively to keep America safe."

"Swift action is possible within legal and ethical frameworks. While we need to oppose Communism wherever it appears, our opposition should not have come at the expense of other democratically elected governments or our own civil liberties. Just because an outcome was achieved doesn't mean the methods were justified," Williams replied.

Gladstone replied in a lecturing tone, "Senator, history has shown us that achieving security sometimes requires moral ambiguity and decisive measures, however distasteful they may appear."

"Let me jump in here, my colleagues," Connor said. The perception that America is willing to disregard democratic norms when convenient is a perception that emboldens adversaries to do the same and alienates our allies. Security should never come at the cost of the very principles we claim to defend. America has stood for some sacred principles that have been a beacon and a light for peoples for over two hundred years—democracy, the rule of law, and dedication to the principle that the ends cannot justify the means. Without our protection and observance of those principles, we cease to be that guiding light, that shining city on the hill."

Senators McHenry and Williams tapped the table in agreement while Senator Gladstone shook his head in disagreement.

"I thank you for expressing your views openly and honestly. We must have an open discussion about this important topic. With that, I will entertain a motion to adjourn our hearing," Connor said, "I remind Committee members not to discuss our deliberations or the content of the witnesses' testimony with anyone until the Committee holds its public meeting."

Connor banged his gavel, and the committee members slowly filed out of the room. Connor remained. *I don't want this committee's work to end up a report shelved in Congressional Archives, like so many other investigations,"* he thought. *"But it's clear Cross's confidence comes from a position of power. I'll have to get the support of the National Security Council, and talk to Cross' boss. And I'll continue to rely on the support of Special Agent Torres and Inspector Morgan, who have proven to be staunch allies."*

And with those thoughts still filling his mind, Connor left, angry but determined.

Chapter 19

The Money Trail

As Blake and Angela sank into their sumptuous first-class pods on Cathay Pacific, heading back to Hong Kong, the air crackled with a palpable mix of excitement and tension. Blake's eyes darted around, taking in the opulent surroundings.

As if on cue, a flight attendant materialized beside them, proffering crystal glasses filled with perfectly mixed gin and tonics, the ice clinking musically against the sides. Angela accepted hers with a gracious nod, her eyes never leaving Blake's face as she continued, "Just wait until you experience the privacy, the mood lighting that'll make you forget you're hurtling through the stratosphere, and with our lie-flat beds you'll get a good sleep on this long flight."

Blake couldn't help but relax as he stretched out, feeling the tension melt from his body. "You might be onto something here," he admitted, a slow smile spreading across his face.

As they settled in, savoring the first sips of their drinks and perusing a menu that read more like a Michelin-starred restaurant than airplane fare, Blake's mind turned to the task at hand. His voice lowered, eyes glinting with determination. "We should compare notes on what we know about the drug money laundering operation."

Angela's demeanor shifted instantly, her posture straightening as she leaned in, her voice dropping to match Blake's intensity. "Did you know," she began, her words laced with a mix of fascination and disgust, "that the term 'money laundering' originated with the Mafia using laundromats? A brutally efficient way to wash their blood-stained cash clean."

Blake's eyebrows shot up, a sardonic chuckle escaping his lips. "That's ironic. And now, casinos have become the new laundromats -

spinning dirty money clean in a whirlwind of chips and slot machines."

Angela nodded grimly, her fingers tracing the condensation on her glass. "Meyer Lansky," she continued, her voice heavy with the weight of history, "he was the pioneer who first exploited Swiss bank accounts for laundering. It's only recently that Western governments have started to tighten the noose on these practices."

"Refresh my memory on the stages this dirty money goes through. I want to make sure we're on the same page," Blake said.

Angela's eyes gleamed with a fierce intelligence as she began to speak, her words painting a vivid picture of a shadowy underworld. "Picture it, Blake," she breathed, her voice barely audible over the hum of the engines. "A three-act play of deception and greed, played out on a global stage."

She paused, allowing the tension to build before continuing. "Act One: Placement. This is where our nefarious drug lords make their opening gambit, slipping their blood-soaked bills into the veins of legitimate finance. They're clever, these bastards, using every trick in the book to disguise the origins of their ill-gotten gains. It's all about stealth at this stage, ensuring their mountains of cash don't set off a cascade of red flags."

Blake nodded, his jaw clenching as he absorbed the information. "I'm with you so far," he murmured.

Angela's eyes blazed as she launched into the next phase. "Act Two: Layering. This, Blake, is where things get truly Byzantine. It's a dizzying dance of deception, a financial shell game played out across continents. The goal? To slice and dice the money, scattering it to the four winds through a labyrinth of transactions so convoluted that even the most tenacious bloodhounds lose the scent."

She leaned in closer. "They wire it offshore, bouncing it through a maze of shell companies and ghost accounts. Now you see it, now you don't - a magician's sleight of hand played out with billions of dollars."

"And the final act?" he prompted.

Angela's smile was razor-sharp as she delivered the *coup de grâce*. "Act Three: Integration. The grand finale, where our villains take their final bow. The once-dirty money appears on the other side, scrubbed clean and gleaming, ready to mingle with legitimate funds. This is where they cash in their chips, Blake. Luxurious homes, gleaming yachts, priceless art - all perfectly legal purchases that blend seamlessly into their carefully crafted facade of respectability."

She sat back, her eyes never leaving Blake's face. "And all the while, the authorities are left grasping at shadows, always one step behind."

Angela's voice was steely when she spoke, cutting through Blake's momentary silence. "And let's not forget our banks are in on this sick game. HSBC, Wachovia, Deutsche Bank - all caught red-handed laundering billions. And those so-called 'hefty' fines? Nothing but a slap on the wrist, a joke that barely dents their profit margins."

Blake nodded grimly, a sardonic smile twisting his lips. "As Bob Dylan might say if he were writing today: 'Deal a little dope, rot in jail. Launder billions? Get a politician's thanks.' Another issue I see on the horizon, Angela, is that we are not keeping up with detection and financial tracking technology required to thwart these sophisticated schemes."

"I agree, Blake. We don't think of those banking barons as the financial services wing of a Mexican Cartel. The stark truth is that the Cartels' best friends are those people in pinstripes who, after a rap on the knuckles, return to their golf in Connecticut and drinking parties. The notion of any dichotomy between the global criminal economy and the legal one is a fantasy. Worse, it is a lie. They are seamless, mutually interdependent –the same," Angela replied.

"And very few see this, or they turn a blind eye," said Blake.

"Right, in the U.S., very few U.S. money big money laundering cases have been prosecuted. Law enforcement, national security, and military agencies have lobbied vociferously and successfully for anti-narcotics enforcement appropriations to offset reduced, post-cold war budgets. Add to these roadblocks interference by the CIA in our efforts, and we have a losing cause, Blake. It's hard not to be pessimistic."

"Indeed. Oh, and I should add one more wrinkle at my end. While Hong Kong and Chinese Triads have access to traditional banks, those banks keep records. Increasingly, the Triads are forging alliances with mainland China's Triads and underground banks. I feel like I'm fighting a battle on all fronts."

"Tell me more Blake."

Blake's eyes gleamed as he delved deeper into the ancient roots of their modern nemesis. The soft ambient lighting of their business class pod seemed to dim, as if the weight of his words was physically darkening their surroundings.

"Angela," he breathed, his voice tinged with awe and a touch of fear, "this goes back centuries. What we're facing is not just some new criminal innovation. Chinese underground banking is a beast born from the Silk Road, perfected over millennia of trade and secrecy."

He leaned in closer, his words rushing out in a torrent of barely contained excitement and dread. Blake painted a vivid picture of ancient traders and brokers, of vast sums changing hands without a single coin moving across borders. His hands moved animatedly as he spoke, tracing invisible maps and connections in the air between them.

"Imagine it, Angela. Merchants from distant lands, speaking a dozen different languages, exchanging fortunes with nothing more than a whispered word and a scrap of paper. They call it *'hawala'* in the Islamic world," Blake explained, his eyes wide with the implications. "It's not just an old system – it's the grandfather of all modern banking, reborn as a digital monster in our age of global crime."

The world outside their little bubble of light and luxury ceased to exist as she hung on his every word. Blake's voice dropped to a conspiratorial whisper, forcing her to lean even closer as he outlined the intricate, deadly dance between Cartels and Chinese money brokers.

"Go on," Angela said hanging on to Blake's every word.

"Step one," he murmured, "the Cartel reaches out, fishing for the cheapest rates among the brokers. It's like they're shopping for groceries, Angela, except they're moving millions in blood money."

He continued, each step more outrageous than the last. Code words passed in shadows, secret meetings in broad daylight, and money vanished and reappeared across continents as if by magic. Blake's voice grew hoarse with the effort of containing his emotions – disgust at the criminals' audacity, grudging respect for the system's efficiency, and a burning determination to bring it all crashing down.

"Blake," she whispered, her voice shaking with a mixture of awe and terror. "We're... we're outgunned and outmaneuvered at every turn. How can we possibly hope to fight this?"

Blake nodded grimly, reaching out to clasp Angela's hand. The warmth of his touch seemed to ground her, pulling her back from the edge of despair. "We need backup," he said, his voice low but filled with iron determination. "Big guns. Connor, Congress – hell, we'll need to build a private army to take this on."

Little did Blake know his words would foreshadow the future.

Angela's eyes suddenly hardened with fierce determination. She squeezed Blake's hand tightly, drawing strength from his unwavering resolve. "I'm on it," she said, her voice steadying. "We'll build our army, piece by piece if we have to. These bastards might have centuries of tradition on their side, but we've got justice and the law. And between us we have a giant potful of money to finance it."

They outlined their Hong Kong strategy rapid-fire, the urgency palpable in every clipped word and sharp nod. As they finished, the weight of their task settled over them like a heavy cloak.

"We're in this together," he murmured, his voice rough with emotion. "No matter how deep this rabbit hole goes, no matter how many ancient secrets or modern criminals we have to face. You and me, partner."

"Just try and get rid of me," Angela replied.

"Here's my immediate plan for Hong Kong. First, on a personal note, I've committed to attending Samuel Fung's funeral and meeting with Raymond and Sabrina. Also, I'd like us both to meet with David Smith and Commissioner Blair to get updated on the investigations and give them a report on our Senate testimony," Blake said.

"Sounds good," Angela replied. "Now let's enjoy our meal and a glass of wine and try to get a little sleep before we get to Hong Kong."

Chapter 20

Grave Doubts

Blake stood at the edge of Chiu Yuen Cemetery, his eyes tracing the contours of Mount Davis as it loomed above. The air was thick with incense and the weight of unspoken words. He couldn't help but reflect on a passage from the *Tao Te Ching*: *"Life and death are one thread, the same line viewed from different sides."* As he watched the mourners gather around Samuel Fung's grave, Blake wondered which side of that thread they were truly standing on.

The cemetery, nestled at the foot of the mountain, was a stark reminder of the divide between rich and poor in Hong Kong. Each plot here, Blake knew, cost upwards of thirty thousand dollars - some fetching up to four times that amount. It was a graveyard for the elite, a final resting place that commanded as much prestige in death as its occupants had in life.

Traditional Chinese funerals are elaborate and symbolic affairs. For example, a long-standing belief in Chinese culture is that the dead should rest on mountains facing the sea for positive feng shui. A magnificent view lay below Samuel Fung's grave.

Chinese funerals in Hong Kong blend Buddhist, Confucian, and Taoist rituals. In Taoist tradition, if a person dies violently or tragically, they may become vengeful spirits lingering around the place of their death. The dead who performed misdeeds in life face punishment in the underworld.

As Blake's gaze swept over the assembled mourners, it settled on Raymond Fung. The new head of the Fung empire stood rigid beside his father's ornate coffin, his face a mask of grief carved from stone. But beneath that mask, Blake could see the tempest raging. Raymond's eyes burned with a fury that seemed to simmer just beneath the surface, threatening to boil over at any moment.

Across from Raymond, on the other side of the coffin, stood Sabrina. Draped in traditional white mourning clothes, she presented a stark contrast to the somber black suits surrounding her. Despite the palpable sorrow that hung in the air, there was something about Sabrina that drew Blake's eye and held it. A quiet strength radiated from her, a resilience that refused to be diminished by grief or circumstance. Behind her eyes, Blake could see a fire burning - an indomitable spirit that whispered of hope even in this darkest of moments.

The Taoist priest, clad in his ceremonial robe and skull cap, stood at the head of Samuel Fung's coffin, chanting incantations while two monks shook discordant bells. To the right of the coffin, Blake, Raymond, several distant male relatives, and business associates, all dressed in dark suits, stood solemnly. Sabrina and the other women, dressed in white, stood to the left of the casket. White and yellow chrysanthemums adorned the coffin, with incense and candles burning around it. The priest's assistants burned paper money to ensure Fung's safe journey to the next world.

Honoring tradition, family members placed personal items and food for the journey in the coffin. Raymond laid a jade ring his father gave him on his thirteenth birthday, while Sabrina chose an ivory comb Samuel had given her.

The ceremony unfolded in a blur of ancient rituals and modern grief. Paper money was burned, its ashes carried away on the breeze to ensure Samuel Fung's safe passage to the next world. The coffin was lowered into the ground, and everyone turned away as custom dictated. The sharp crack of firecrackers suddenly split the air, their explosive bursts meant to ward off evil spirits. Blake felt the tension in his chest echo each detonation, his nerves as taut as bowstrings.

As the crowd began to disperse, the air was heavy with unspoken emotions, leaving Raymond alone with Blake and Sabrina. Raymond's voice suddenly cut through the somber atmosphere. "Why haven't the police come up with any suspects?" he demanded, his words sharp with frustration and shame. "Father's death must be avenged, or I will lose face!"

Blake tried to soothe him, "Raymond, the investigation is in Inspector Smith's hands. He's doing everything he can to find those responsible and bring them to justice. You must be patient."

"That's not good enough, Blake!" Raymond snapped, his composure finally cracking. "And there are other ways to find out."

The raw pain in Raymond's voice was palpable, but there was something else there too - a dangerous edge. Before he could respond, Raymond had already turned away, striding towards his waiting limousine with Tang in tow.

As Raymond's car pulled away, Blake turned to Sabrina, his heart heavy. "I'm sorry, Sabrina. It was rude of Raymond to leave without you."

Sabrina shook her head, a sad smile playing at the corners of her lips. "That's alright, Blake. We had arranged for me to leave separately. I've started to move into my family home."

Her eyes met his, and Blake was struck by the maelstrom of emotions swirling in their depths - grief, fear, longing, and something else he couldn't quite name. As he walked her to her car, he felt compelled to offer some comfort. "Is there anything I can do to help you get through all this, Sabrina?"

Her response came in a rush, barely above a whisper. "Take me away from all this," she pleaded. "Australia, Canada - anywhere but here. Just Away!"

Blake's heart raced, caught between empathy for her pain and the cautious voice of reason in his head. He loved her, yes, but not in the all-consuming way she seemed to need right now. "I . . . we . . ." he stammered, searching for the right words. "It's best not to make rash decisions," he finally managed, his voice gentle but firm. "Take your time to decide what you really want."

As he helped her into her waiting car, Sabrina's arms suddenly wrapped around him in a fierce embrace. She clung to him for a moment, as if he were a lifeline in a stormy sea. "I can wish, can't I?" she murmured against his chest, her words muffled but heavy with emotion.

Then she was gone, the car pulling away and leaving Blake alone with his tumultuous thoughts. He stood there for a long moment, watching the vehicle disappear down the winding cemetery road. His emotions were a tempest, friendship, and duty warring with the ghosts of what might have been.

As the sun began to set over Mount Davis, casting long shadows across the graves, Blake couldn't shake the feeling that this was only the beginning. The death of Samuel Fung had set something in motion, something dark and dangerous that threatened to engulf them all.

Chapter 21

Blood Oath

The stucco mansions of Victoria Peak appeared and disappeared among sculptured trees and fortified walls. At the end of the narrow road, a large, red-tiled pagoda towered above grey granite walls.

Tang, the Fung family's ancient, grizzled servant and driver, stopped the black Rolls Royce thirty yards from two massive metal gates.

Raymond Fung sat in the back seat, twisting his father's twenty-four-carat gold ring on his middle finger. His delicate fingers smoothed his Hong Kong Jockey Club tie under his white linen suit. The jacket collar stuck up above his shirt, ruffling the nape of his neatly trimmed salt-and-pepper hair. He shifted in his seat, glancing at his reflection in the rearview mirror.

Tang drove past exquisite gardens of bauhinias, roses, ponds, and painted bird statues. Victoria Harbor stretched across the horizon like a glossy photograph from an expensive travel magazine, surreal against the dark hills of Kowloon, the Nine Dragons.

Tang steered the car up to the garage and parking area, past a dozen Mercedes-Benzes. Limousine drivers knelt in a circle, playing Pai Kau and handling handfuls of paper money. A hulking bald man in a too-small suit nodded to Tang, who nodded back.

A hulking bald man in a suit one size too small and sitting on his haunches nodded to Tang. He nodded back.

"Sei gau jais (Triad foot soldiers)," Raymond thought to himself.

Tang parked the car and waited there; Raymond walked up a dozen stone steps and along a wooden bridge that curved over a large pond. A thirty-foot stone dragon undulated in the water, its gaping jaws and bulging eyes warning all who approached. Soon, they stood before two weathered wooden doors. The door opened and a muscular young man in a leather jacket and blue jeans stepped forward. He bowed slightly and stepped aside for Raymond, who strode confidently into the house.

Dust-covered, century-old vases and silk wall tapestries adorned the dark hallway. Two expressionless men in black robes stood by the door at the end. They opened the double doors to a large room thick with burning incense.

An old man in his seventies, scarred and with piercing eyes, dressed in a long white robe, approached. Tattoos adorned the backs of his hands, a signature of Triad members.

Robert Lee, the Dragon Head of the Min Ho Triad, exchanged bows with Raymond, who bowed lower out of respect. Lee had risen from the streets, proving his worth in street battles and expanding Min Ho's protection racket. Now, his body and mind showed signs of age.

Raymond, as the White Paper Fan or leader in charge of the Triad's business and finance arrangements, was given secondary respect by Triad members, who bowed appropriately.

Lee and Raymond joined a half-dozen high-ranking Min Ho members at a large black cherry table, all in black robes. A tiny middle-aged man with one hand waved his stump while talking wildly to another man, who just nodded. A younger man with slick-backed hair and a tranquil expression sat quietly, oblivious to the commotion.

Lee stood at the head of the table. "*lái dìnggòu!* (come to order!)." He smashed a large copper gong by his chair.

Lee brandished a parchment document. "First, I want to thank our White Paper Fan, Raymond Fung, for negotiating a strategy that will propel us to the top of the Triads here and in China—the partnership with the Tijuana Cartel to produce and distribute fentanyl." He paused, breathing deeply. "Our elimination of Dragon Head Simon Chan was essential to crush his decaying Triad. We mourn Samuel Fung's assassination by Chan's men, but Raymond has ably replaced his father as our White Paper Fan. Raymond, would you like to add anything?"

"Inspector Blake Morgan is proving to be an obstacle to our plans, and he must be eliminated," Raymond replied. "You and I should talk privately after about this." Lee nodded.

"Our unified commitment is crucial," Lee continued. "We will all be making blood oaths for our commitments." He unfurled a parchment document. "I will read it, and you will all sign, then take the blood oath."

Lee read the oath, emphasizing loyalty to the brotherhood, the destruction of opposing Triads, and the partnership with the Tijuana Cartel. The penalty for betrayal was death for the Triad member and his family.

He passed on the document for the signature of all the men at the table, with Raymond and Lee signing last. Lee left the room, returning quickly, carrying a black canvas bag. The bag shook and wiggled, accompanied by the sharp squawking of an animal. He pulled a box of matches and a bottle of brandy from the bag. When the signatures were complete, he held the yellow parchment over the bowl and set fire. Flames licked at his fingers, and a bluish-yellow smoke curled in the air. The Min Ho leaders, seated at the table watched, stone-faced and silent.

"This is the breath of the God of Vengeance, *Kwan Kung*. May he strike down anyone who is not true to our cause," Lee announced. The red-faced old warrior held the burning paper between his yellowed thumb and forefinger until the paper's ashes floated into the bowl. He uncorked the bottle of brandy, poured some into the bowl, then unsheathed the ivory-handled knife in his sash and held it over the foul mixture. "Blood will purify the truth," he said.

He pulled a black-feathered chicken from the bag, slammed it on the table, and drew the knife across its neck. The chicken screeched and thrashed, its blood splattering onto the bowl and table. Lee held it firm until it was still, then dropped the carcass into the bag. He mixed the ashes, brandy, and blood, then sipped from the bowl. "Whoever breaks the oath will die by the ten thousand cuts."

He passed the bowl to the other men at the table. The one-armed man held the bowl with his stump and good hand, spilling some liquid down his chin as he drank. He wiped it with his sleeve and passed on the bowl.

When it came to the last man, Lee paused momentarily, looking at the bowl and said, "and may their families be broken as this bowl is broken." He threw the bowl on the floor and crushed it with his foot.

The men dispersed, and only Raymond stayed behind to talk to Lee. "I have a request. "

The old man nodded.

"I want you to complete the job of eliminating Inspector Blake Morgan." Raymond said unemotionally.

"I don't think that's a good idea right now. Since the first failed attempt, he will be on guard, and we wouldn't want him to come knocking on our door," Lee replied.

"Morgan could expose and destroy our whole operation—he must be eliminated!" Raymond yelled.

Robert Lee rose up from his normal hunched posture, and he shook his fist at Raymond. "I'll remind you who is in charge of Min Ho. I'll decide who is our enemy, and who is to be eliminated and when and how. Understood?"

Raymond stormed out of the room, resisting the impulse to end the old man's life on the spot. He walked out to the garden to calm down. He now knew it was time to take over as Dragon Head of the

Min Ho. He had many supporters, and it was necessary to be able to deal with Blake and get the partnership with Ramirez safe.

Chapter 22

Criminal Conclave

Kowloon during the 1980s was a place where time seemed warped, a blend of the past with the future beneath the glow of neon signs. Here, amidst the dense urban jungle, the air thrummed with an unending symphony of life's hustle, the streets a living, breathing entity that never slept.

The labyrinthine streets of Kowloon, a network of serpentine alleyways and vibrant main arteries, each twist and turn unveiling a new layer of its multifaceted soul. The air was a rich tapestry of scents - the divine fragrance of temple incense interwoven with the mouth-watering allure of street food: the succulent *dim sum*, the savory fish balls, and the zest of stir-fried noodles. Markets sprawled like living organisms, spilling over with abundant goods - from the vivid allure of textiles and the seductive whisper of futuristic electronics to the silent stories encased within ancient antiques.

The night in Kowloon unfurled like a scene from a dream, with neon signs cutting through the darkness, beckoning with the promise of escape and revelry. Nightclubs and bars throbbed with the heartbeat of Cantonese pop, a kaleidoscope of sound and color. Yet, beneath this façade of effervescence, the undercurrents of a harsher reality pulsed, with enigmatic figures conducting their nocturnal ballet, their dealings as ephemeral as the smoke trailing from their cigarettes.

The narrow streets of Kowloon writhed with life, a pulsing organism of humanity pressed between towering, crumbling tenements. In a narrow alley slick with the day's rain and other, less savory fluids, the Jade Serpent dive bar nestled like a dirty secret.

Inside the Jade Serpent, Raymond Fung reclined in a corner booth, a dragon mural snarling above him. His tailored suit, immaculate despite the bar's grime, exuded an aura of lethal elegance. His eyes, cold and black as obsidian, scanned the room with predatory focus. When they settled on Inspector David Smith, a cruel smile played at the corners of his mouth.

Smith sat across from him, rigid and ill at ease. His collar, normally crisp, was wilted with sweat. His eyes darted nervously, never settling, like prey sensing a circling predator. When he spoke, his voice quivered slightly, betraying his fear.

"No leads on your father's murder," Smith stammered, his British accent faltering.

Raymond's smile widened, revealing teeth too sharp, too white in the dim light. "David," he whispered, voice dripping with malice, "I never expected the police to solve anything. We know it was Simon Chan's Triad. The score is even." He leaned forward, eyes gleaming with cruel amusement. "You just keep up appearances. Especially for Blake."

Smith flinched at Morgan's name, a bead of sweat trickling down his temple. "The anti-corruption commission," he began, voice barely above a whisper, "they're watching closely. And Morgan . . . ."

"Let me worry about Morgan," Raymond cut him off, voice suddenly hard as steel. His hand shot out, gripping Smith's wrist with bruising force. "Your only concern should be me. Or have you forgotten our arrangement?"

Smith's face drained of color. He tried to pull his hand away, but Raymond's grip was unyielding. "I haven't forgotten," he managed, eyes wide with fear.

Raymond's laugh was a low, menacing sound that seemed to chill the air around them. "Good. Because if Morgan or Blair were to learn of your . . . indiscretions." He released Smith's wrist, reaching instead for his glass of baijiu. "Let's just say, accidents happen in Kowloon. Terrible, tragic accidents to wives and children."

"Are you threatening my family?" Smith snapped defiantly, a shaft of courage finding some light.

"Don't be naïve," Raymond replied sarcastically. "Of course I am!"

Smith's hand trembled as he raised it to loosen his tie, gasping as if the air had suddenly become too thick to breathe. "What do you want from me?" he asked, defeat and terror mingling in his voice.

Raymond's eyes glittered with malicious glee. "Information. Misdirection. You'll be my eyes and ears in the force. And you'll bury any leads on my operations so deep they'll never see daylight." He paused, savoring Smith's visible distress. "Oh, and my father's case? It never existed."

"You know that the heat has been on since the police anti-corruption commission was established. And Morgan is watching me carefully. I must consider the risks."

"Consider this risk: what if Morgan or your boss Jack Blair found out you've been on the take for years?" Raymond said menacingly.

Smith looked away, the reality of the pit he had dug for himself consuming him. "I'll do what you ask," he said abruptly.

Raymond watched with sadistic satisfaction as Smith stumbled to his feet, swaying slightly. "Remember, David," he called as the inspector turned to leave, "I own you now and you're paid well for your services. Don't disappoint me." Smith lurched out of the bar without a backward glance, leaving Raymond to savor his victory. Around them, the Jade Serpent continued its nightly business, indifferent to the moral destruction that had just unfolded.

The Jade Serpent writhed with life, a microcosm of Kowloon's underworld. Smoke hung thick in the air, defying Hong Kong's smoking ban with the same casual disregard its patrons showed for most laws. The acrid scent mingled with the sweet-sour notes of spilled baijiu and the earthy musk of unwashed bodies.

Raymond moved to isolated corner booth, his tailored suit a jarring contrast to the bar's dingy interior. The peeling wallpaper behind him depicted a faded dragon, its scales seeming to undulate in the flickering neon light. He drummed his fingers on the sticky table, eyes fixed on the door, waiting.

When Raul Ramirez entered, the entire room seemed to hold its breath. He cut through the haze like a shark through murky waters, his presence commanding even in this den of iniquity. As he slid into the booth opposite Raymond, the fake leather creaking ominously.

"You could've chosen a more upscale setting for this meeting," Ramirez remarked, his voice a low growl barely audible over the tinny Cantopop leaking from a battered jukebox.

Raymond's lips curled into a predatory smile. "Upscale doesn't buy silence, my friend. Here, everyone's too busy guarding their own secrets to care about ours."

A heavily tattooed waitress approached, her eyes carefully averted. Raymond ordered without looking at her, "Baijiu for me, tequila for my associate." She nodded and melted back into the crowd and returned with the drinks quickly.

"To a future of lucrative ventures," Raymond toasted, his glass held aloft, catching the light in a dance of shadows.

Glasses chimed in agreement, a fleeting moment of camaraderie amidst the tension.

"Now," Raymond leaned forward, his voice dropping even lower, "tell me about Manzanillo."

Ramirez's face darkened. "We were betrayed. The Mexican Police and DEA were waiting. They seized everything – the product, our men, even the AEROCO pilot, Ransom."

Raymond's knuckles whitened around his glass. "And the fallout?"

"Minimal, thanks to our friends in high places," Ramirez's smirk was cold. "Jack Cross intervened. Our men are free, the witnesses silenced, Ransom was taken to the U.S. by the CIA."

"And the price for the CIA's intervention?"

Ramirez's eyes gleamed with a mixture of amusement and disdain. "What we've been doing already. The Infiltration, assassination, sabotage of Mexico's Socialist and Communist parties. And the CIA's cut from our profits. They want to keep them in check, maintain their grip on Mexico's politics and ensure whoever is in power is friendly to the U.S."

Raymond nodded, satisfaction evident in his posture. "Good. Now, let's discuss the future. I propose we totally shift our strategy."

"Up until now, we've been sending you both precursor chemicals to make fentanyl as well as the finished product. The latter is much easier for customs and police to identify and destroy. The main precursor chemicals that are used to make fentanyl legally are NPP and 4-ANPP. There are now multiple forms of fentanyl that can be produced in labs."

"So, what are you proposing?"

"I'm proposing that we only send you the easily packaged precursor chemicals, and you set up your lab to produce the finished fentanyl product. We would train your lab technicians to do the manufacturing process, but it's quite simple. A high school kid could do it with training. And if you wish, they can be mixed with heroin or cocaine. If you manufacture them in pill form from our precursors, you could produce five hundred thousand pills from a kilo of fentanyl. And you can cut the fentanyl and add any other drug like cocaine, methamphetamine, cocaine or heroin as you please."

"Hmm. If it results in less interception by the authorities, I agree, let's do it," Ramirez responded enthusiastically.

"Alright, I'll start all the preparations at my end, including sending over to you a couple of people to show you how to set up a lab and use the precursor chemicals for fentanyl production. Once that's done, I can proceed with the next shipment."

"Right."

Raymond raised his glass. "Here's to our successful partnership and growing empire."

Ramirez raised his glass, *"quien no arriesga, no gana* (who doesn't risk, doesn't win)."

As they drained their glasses and rose to leave, the dragon on the wall seemed to leer at them, a silent witness to their dark covenant. The Jade Serpent swallowed their secrets, adding them to the countless others buried in its smoky depths.

Chapter 23

Deadly Disclosure

The Hong Kong skyline shimmered beyond the floor-to-ceiling windows of Sabrina Fung's 30th-floor office, a dazzling tapestry of light and shadow that belied the storm brewing within. The fading sunlight painted the city in hues of gold and amber, glinting off the glass-and-steel monoliths that stood as testaments to the city's economic might. Sabrina moved with the grace of a panther, her crimson Louboutin shoes clicking a staccato rhythm on the Italian Carrara marble floor. Her perfectly tailored peach-colored Chanel suit, worn as if on a Milan runway, masked the steel trap of her mind—a mind honed by generations of business acumen and colonial power.

As she gazed out at the city she'd known all her life, Sabrina's thoughts drifted to her family's legacy. The Fung name carried weight, but not like the mighty Jardines, or her family, the McDougals, the taipans of Hong Kong. For three generations, they had woven themselves into the very fabric of the city's economy—shipping lanes that stretched across oceans, real estate that touched the sky, financial deals that could make or break empires, insurance that protected the dreams of millions, and retail empires that clothed the elite.

Sabrina had been raised in this world of privilege and power, her childhood a blur of exclusive social circles, private tutors, and summers spent in the family's villa in the South of France. But amidst the opulence, there was a scar—the brutal years in the Japanese prisoner-of-war camp in Stanley during WWII. Those years had stripped away the veneer of invincibility, showing her the fragility of life and the strength hidden within her. That crucible had forged her into something harder, something unbreakable and yet at the same time, painfully vulnerable.

Her success and family wealth a brilliant beacon in the stock trading world, was a constant thorn in the side of her husband, Raymond. His insistence on her surrender to the conventional role of a businessman's wife had been a battle line drawn between them, a silent war of wills and wants.

Her voice, measured and confident, filled the room as she spoke to a client on the phone. "I'd counsel holding that stock a tad longer, Mr. Nakamura," she said, her tone brooking no argument. "The horizon shows an upturn, especially with the upcoming release of that research study from the University of Hong Kong. Then, we pivot aggressively into a buying spree, focusing on the emerging tech sector in Shenzhen." Her words danced on the edge of prophecy, painting futures not yet realized with the surety of an artist's brush.

As she hung up the phone, her gaze fell upon a Baccarat crystal photo frame on her desk—a triptych of smiles and solemnity featuring herself, Blake, and Raymond. Her fingers traced the edge of the frame, a moment of vulnerability in her otherwise impenetrable facade. Blake's warm smile contrasted sharply with Raymond's serious, calculated gaze. The photo had been taken at the Hong Kong Jockey Club, a bastion of old money and new power.

A sudden crash—a casualty of her multitasking—sent the glass picture frame tumbling from her desk to shatter upon the floor. A sigh escaped her, frustration momentarily piercing her composed exterior. "Damn . . . no not you," she said to the caller, "you know what to do. We'll speak again tomorrow," she concluded, ending the call.

Stooping to gather the remnants of the frame, her gaze captured the moment within herself, Blake, and Raymond, a triptych of smiles and solemnity.

A sudden knock shattered her reverie. Raymond entered without waiting for a response, his presence filling the room with an oppressive weight. Sabrina straightened, her chin lifting in defiance, even as a chill ran down her spine.

A sharp knock shattered her reverie. Raymond entered without waiting for a response, his presence filling the room with an oppressive weight. Sabrina straightened, her chin lifting in defiance, even as a chill ran down her spine. She inhaled deeply, catching a whiff of his cologne—an expensive blend that somehow managed to smell cheap on him.

Raymond's eyes, cold and calculating, swept over her. His suit, though bearing the label of a top London tailor, lacked the effortless elegance of old money. It was a constant reminder of the gulf between them—Sabrina's generations of refined wealth versus Raymond's nouveau riche criminality. His cufflinks, flashy diamonds that caught the light, seemed to wink at her mockingly.

"Do you have a moment?" Raymond's voice was smooth, practiced—the voice of a man accustomed to getting his way through charm or force. There was an edge to it, a hidden blade waiting to strike.

"Of course, come in," Sabrina replied, her voice a blend of invitation and wariness. She gestured to the Eames chair across from her desk, a piece she'd inherited from her grandfather.

As Raymond spoke of their impending divorce and his decision to amend his will, Sabrina felt a mixture of relief and trepidation. She had long suspected that Raymond's wealth was built on a foundation of shadows and secrets, a stark contrast to her family's legitimate empire. Whispers in exclusive clubs, nervous glances from his associates, mysterious late-night phone calls—all pieces of a puzzle she was only now beginning to solve.

"Your legacy is yours to direct, Raymond," she said, her fingers clenching around the edge of her rosewood desk, imported from Brazil. "My journey was never anchored by the weight of gold or the trappings of your success." She thought of her own holdings— diversified, clean, built on generations of shrewd but ethical business practices.

Something flickered in Raymond's eyes—surprise, perhaps, at her easy acquiescence. Or was it a threat? The air between them crackled with unspoken tensions and half-buried secrets. Sabrina felt as if she were standing on the edge of a precipice, the winds of change threatening to push her over.

"I've moved back into my family's home on the Peak. You'll find I've left nothing behind."

As Raymond turned to leave, his hand on the doorknob, Sabrina steeled herself for what came next. Her heart raced, blood pounding in her ears. She reached into her desk drawer, feeling the cool touch of the manila envelope. This was it—the moment of truth.

"One more thing, Raymond," she called out, her voice quavering slightly. She produced some documents from her desk drawer, watching Raymond's face carefully as she explained her discovery. "I found these papers mixed with mine last week. They show my name, and my company listed as an exporter for something bound for Mexico. A list of chemicals, but what they are used for is heavily redacted on the documents. There is a portion of a word that was not completely redacted—'tanyl.' What is that, and can you explain these documents?"

The change was subtle, but to Sabrina, who had spent years studying this man, it was as clear as day. Raymond's shoulders tensed, his eyes darting to the side—classic signs of deception that sent a chill down her spine. She saw his hand twitch, as if reaching for something that wasn't there.

"I don't know what this is about," he lied smoothly, taking the papers. His fingers left slight indentations on the crisp white sheets. "I'll have to question my accountant. It must be a mistake." The words hung in the air between them, a flimsy shield against the truth they both knew.

Sabrina felt uneasy about his response, her instincts screaming danger. "I want an answer as soon as possible. I find it surprising that you don't know what's happening in your company." She leaned forward, her eyes boring into his, searching for a flicker of truth.

Raymond's eyes flashed dangerously, like storm clouds gathering on the horizon. "I said I'll look into it!" The threat in his voice was unmistakable now, a growl beneath the polished exterior.

As Raymond left, documents in hand, promising answers he'd never deliver, Sabrina felt a wave of terror wash over her. Her hands shook as she reached for the phone, her fingers flying over the keypad. The cool receiver against her ear did little to calm her racing heart.

"Blake? It's Sabrina," she said, her voice trembling. She glanced at the door, half-expecting Raymond to burst back in. "We need to talk. It's about Raymond. I ... I'm scared, Blake. I think I've stumbled onto something that threatens me."

Blake's voice came through, warm and reassuring—a beacon of safety in the gathering storm. "Slow down, Sabrina. What's going on?" His concern was palpable, even through the phone line.

"I'd rather not explain over the phone," Sabrina replied, glancing nervously at the door. Her eyes darted to the vintage Cartier clock on her desk—9:45 PM. The office around her was silent, most employees long gone. "Can you meet me at my parents' house? I've moved out of Raymond's place."

"Of course," Blake answered, his tone a mixture of worry and determination. "I'll be there as soon as I can."

As she hung up, Sabrina didn't notice the door, slightly ajar. She didn't see Raymond, lingering just outside, his face twisted with a mixture of rage and calculation as he listened to her conversation. His hand was in his pocket, fingering something cold and metallic.

In the fading light of day, Sabrina stood at her office window, the glittering city below a stark contrast to the darkness closing in around her. The neon signs of Wan Chai blinked in the distance, a riot of color against the encroaching night. She was raised in the corridors of power, trained in the art of business warfare. But for the first time in years, she felt truly afraid. The documents in her possession were a double-edged sword—a damning indictment of Raymond's underworld dealings, but also a potential death sentence for her.

As night fell over Hong Kong, Sabrina gathered her things, her mind racing. She slipped a copy of the damning documents into her Hermès Birkin bag. She had always been suspicious of Raymond's business practices—the way he'd dodge questions about certain investments, the mysterious meetings with men whose names never appeared in any official records. But this . . . this was beyond anything she had imagined.

With a deep breath, she stepped out of her office, the click of the lock sounding like a gunshot in the empty hallway. The elevator ride down her office building in Central was interminable, each floor a countdown to an uncertain future. As she crossed the marble-floored lobby, her heels echoing in the cavernous space, Sabrina felt exposed, vulnerable.

Outside, the humid night air hit her like a wall. She hailed her driver and directed him to drive her to her parents' home, now hers. As the car wound its way up the twisting roads, the lights of the city receding below, Sabrina clung to one thought like a lifeline—Blake. In a world of shadows and lies, Blake was her anchor, her one chance at navigating the treacherous waters ahead.

As she waited for Blake, Sabrina paced the terrace, her fingers trailing along the spines of leather-bound books. Outside, the mist rolled in from the harbor, shrouding the Peak in an ethereal glow. In the distance, a lone ship's horn sounded, mournful and haunting.

Sabrina's mind raced with possibilities and fears. What exactly had she uncovered? How deep did Raymond's criminal connections go? And most terrifyingly—what would he do to keep his secrets buried?

Back at police HQ, Blake walked over to his work colleague, Dennis Wang's desk. "Dennis, I'm going to meet Sabrina Fung at her parents' home. She wants to talk to me about something involving Raymond she wouldn't discuss over the phone."

Dennis looked up. "Sounds mysterious, Blake, you want company?"

"No, no, I'll deal with this myself."

On the way to Sabrina's home, Blake stopped by the Peninsula Hotel. Angela was on the phone when Blake walked into her suite.

"Thank you, Senator Connor; I've made a note in my calendar for the Senate Intelligence Committee Hearing. You are certainly moving fast on this. Blake Morgan and I will both be prepared and look forward to giving testimony. Goodbye." She replaced the phone in the cradle, walked over, and embraced and kissed Blake. "Sweetheart, this is a surprise. I wasn't expecting you until later. As you've heard, Senator Connor made good on his promise and has scheduled a Senate Intelligence Committee open public hearing."

"That is good news. I received a call from Sabrina. She wants to see me immediately about some information about Raymond. She wouldn't talk over the phone, so I'm going to her parents' home on The Peak which is where she lives now."

"Her message sounds mysterious."

"I know. Every day, I feel that Raymond's stories may not be true, and there's something else there, but I don't know what. Maybe she's found a missing piece. Anyway, I shouldn't be long, and we'll still have dinner tonight here."

"Alright, Blake, return safe and sound to me."

Blake embraced and kissed her once more passionately. "I promise."

Blake put on his jacket and was about to walk out the door when Angela said, "Haven't you forgotten something?" holding up his service revolver he had left on the coffee table.

"I doubt if I'll need it to talk to her, but I should get in the habit," Blake replied. He took the SIG HAUER P229 handgun and holster, put it on and left the suite.

Chapter 24

Exposure and Death

The night air hung heavy over Victoria Peak, a suffocating blanket of humidity that seemed to trap the very essence of foreboding. Blake's heart thundered in his chest as he ascended the winding granite steps to Sabrina's parents' home, each footfall echoing like a funeral drumbeat in the oppressive silence. The magnificent teak and brass door loomed before him, a gilded sentinel guarding secrets he couldn't begin to fathom, its ornate carvings throwing eerie shadows in the dim light.

Sabrina answered the door, and Blake could see immediately the look of stress and anxiety in her face. Her eyes, usually sparkling with intelligence, now held a shadow of fear.

"Oh, Blake," Sabrina whispered, "I'm so glad you came quickly." She embraced him, but the warmth he once felt was replaced by an icy dread that seemed to seep into his very bones.

Blake's senses were on high alert as they moved through the vast house. The furniture, still shrouded in white dust clothes, loomed like ghosts of happier times, silent witnesses to the unfolding drama. The air was thick with the musty scent of disuse, mingled with the faint trace of Sabrina's familiar perfume – a jarring juxtaposition of past and present.

On the veranda, the glittering lights of Hong Kong spread out before them, a dizzying tapestry of life and commerce that seemed mockingly oblivious to the darkness closing in around them. The city's constant hum was a stark contrast to the deathly quiet that enveloped them. Blake's mind reeled as Sabrina revealed her concerns about Raymond, her words punctuated by the nervous clink of ice in their gin and tonics.

"I have a serious concern about Raymond, which has nothing to do with our divorce," she said, her voice thick with emotion.

"What is it?"

"While boxing up my business papers, I came across documents identifying me as connected with Raymond's shipping company."

"What was the concern?"

"First, I am not involved whatsoever with Raymond's or Samuel Fung's businesses. Second, the documents were heavily redacted so that I couldn't discern the exact nature of my involvement. However, the reference to my business and me indicates that I exported some product from one of his ships bound for Mexico. I showed the documents to Raymond, and he said he knew nothing about them, and he'd have to check with his accountant. And he took the documents."

Blake's alarm bells went off. "Has he gotten back to you with an explanation?"

"No, but I took the precaution of making a copy before I gave them the originals. They're right here."

Sabrina got up, retrieved the documents from behind the bar, walked back to Blake, and handed them to him.

In a horrifying instant, the night exploded into chaos. The sharp crack of gunfire shattered the silence, a sound that would echo in Blake's nightmares for years to come. Sabrina crumpled to the floor, her coral dress blooming crimson, a macabre flower unfurling in the moonlight.

Pain seared through Blake's arm as he dove for cover, his heart pounding so furiously he thought it might burst from his chest. The acrid smell of gunpowder filled the air, mixing with the coppery tang of blood. He returned fire, his vision blurred by rage and adrenalin. A cry of pain from the darkness brought little satisfaction -- all that mattered was Sabrina bleeding out before him, her life ebbing away with each passing second.

From behind the veranda's railing, Blake peered into the dark to the garden below to determine the shooter's location. Again, he saw the muzzle fire from a gun in the bushes, the bullets hitting the wall behind him. He returned a burst of fire in that direction. He heard a loud yell, indicating he had hit someone. Then there was silence. His immediate concern was Sabrina, whose life was ebbing from her body.

Blake cradled Sabrina in his arms, his hands slick with her blood as he desperately tried to stem the flow in her chest. The weight of regret and lost opportunities crushed down on him as he gazed into her fading eyes. Each labored breath she took was a dagger to his heart, a cruel reminder of the fragility of life and love.

"Blake," Sabrina gasped, her fingers weakly grasping at his shirt, leaving crimson streaks like accusatory brushstrokes. "I didn't think ... it would end like this. I wanted . . . needed . . . to be happy . . . with you." Her voice was barely a whisper, each word a battle against the encroaching darkness.

"Stay with me, Sabrina," Blake pleaded, his voice raw with emotion, cracking under the strain of unspeakable grief. "Fight it, please! I'll get help!" The words felt hollow, a futile command against the inevitable.

Sabrina's eyes locked onto his, a lifetime of love and longing reflected in their depths. A terrible clarity replaced the fear that had clouded them earlier, a final moment of truth hovering between them. "I always loved you, Blake. Always. Did you . . . did you ever love me?"

Blake's heart shattered into a million pieces, each shard a memory of what could have been. Years of denial and missed chances crashed down around him, a tidal wave of regret threatening to drown him. He bent down, kissing her gently, tasting the salt of his own tears mingling with the metallic tang of blood. "Yes," he choked out, his heart and head in conflict. "I did."

A smile of transcendent peace graced Sabrina's lips as she exhaled one final time, her body going still in Blake's arms. The vibrant, passionate woman who had been his best friend, his almost-lover, his greatest "what if," was gone. The silence that followed was deafening, a void that seemed to swallow all light and hope.

Blake held her, his body wracked with silent sobs that shook him to his very core. The glittering city below continued its indifferent dance of light and shadow, oblivious to the tragedy unfolding above. In that moment, surrounded by danger and loss, Blake made a silent vow. For Sabrina, for the love they'd never fully realized, he would find her killer.

The implications of Sabrina's death extended beyond the personal; they signified a battle cry against the corruption festering at the heart of Hong Kong. For Blake, every step forward was now laden with the dual purpose of honoring Sabrina's memory and dismantling the corruption that sought to silence her. Amidst the luxury of her estate, a scene of profound loss, Blake's resolve hardened into something unbreakable.

Amidst his grief, a deep and violent anger rose in him, a tsunami of rage that threatened to obliterate everything in its path. It spoke to the primal need for revenge and retribution, a dark whisper urging him to cause as much pain to Sabrina's killers as he could humanly inflict. This newfound fury both terrified and energized him, a dangerous ally in his quest for justice.

The pain in his arm jolted him into action. He crawled across the veranda into the house and ran down the stairs that led to the garden below toward the direction he thought the shooter might lie wounded. There, tangled in the bushes, was a young Chinese man with a sniper's rifle. Blake's shot had hit his mark in the shooter's neck, which was bleeding profusely.

Blake grabbed the shooter, ripped off a piece of his sleeve and pressed it on the wound. "I will get you medical help. Now tell me who hired you!"

The shooter didn't answer but grasped at Blake's arm.

"Who were you hired to kill? Tell me, and I'll get help for you."

Blake could not stop the flow of blood from the assassin's neck, and within a minute, he was dead.

In the eerie stillness that followed the tempest of violence, Blake, clad in clothes that bore the grim tapestry of the day's horrors — his own blood, Sabrina's, and the assassin's—rose with a heaviness that seemed to anchor his very soul to the earth. With deliberate steps that echoed the tumult in his heart, he navigated the chaos-strewn path back to the house, a silent testament to the catastrophe that had unfolded.

Blake's hand trembled as he reached for the phone, not from fear, but from the receding tide of adrenaline that had kept him alive moments before. He dialed David Smith's number at police headquarters, each beep echoing in the suddenly too-quiet room.

When David answered, Blake's voice came out as a hoarse whisper, thick with emotion he struggled to suppress. "David," he began, clearing his throat to steady himself. "I need you to mobilize a team to Sabrina Fung's parents' residence on Victoria Peak. Sabrina's been ... murdered." The word caught in his throat, a bitter pill he was forced to swallow. "I managed to neutralize the assailant. I'll wait until you get here."

"I'll be there ASAP," David replied, his tone clipped and professional. "Do you need medical attention?"

Blake glanced at his arm, the pain only now registering through the fog of shock. "Nothing serious. Just send a paramedic." He paused, a sudden thought striking him. "Oh, and bring Dennis with you."

As the line went dead, Blake stood motionless momentarily, the weight of what had just happened crashing down upon him. His eyes drifted to Sabrina's still form, and a wave of nausea threatened to overtake him. With mechanical movements, he retrieved a furniture sheet, his fingers brushing against the soft fabric that had protected the furnishings from dust – furnishings that would never again feel Sabrina's touch.

Approaching her body, Blake felt as though he were moving through water, each step an immense effort. As he draped the fabric over Sabrina, his composure finally cracked. He grasped her hand, still warm but growing colder by the second, and held it with a gentleness that belied the storm of emotions raging within him.

The arrival of David Smith, Dennis Wang, and the forensic team and medic shattered the bubble of grief that had enveloped Blake. He stood, wiping his face and squaring his shoulders, the mask of the professional detective sliding back into place even as his heart continued to bleed.

Dennis approached first, his face etched with concern. Forgetting his policeman decorum, he embraced Blake. "I'm so sorry, Blake. I know you have been life-long friends and how important she was to you," he said softly, "Do you ...."

David's voice cut through the air, sharp and businesslike. "Alright Blake, tell me what happened here."

Blake's eyes snapped to David, a flash of anger igniting in his chest at the other man's callous tone. He bit back a scathing retort, reminding himself that the job came first – it's what Sabrina would have wanted. Still, he couldn't help the cold edge that crept into his voice as he recounted the events of the evening.

As the medic treated and bandaged Blake's arm, Blake spoke, and found himself hyper-aware of every detail – the metallic tang of blood in the air, the slight tremor in his own hands, the way David's eyes seemed to glaze over with disinterest at certain points. When David suggested there "must have been another reason" for the murder, Blake felt his tenuous control on his temper slip.

"Why are you so anxious to look elsewhere for a motive?" he snapped, the words escaping before he could stop them.

David's response was equally terse. "Isn't it our job to consider all possibilities?"

Blake chose not to reply, instead focusing on steadying his breathing. He couldn't afford to let emotion cloud his judgment, not when the stakes were this high. As he continued his account, he found himself unconsciously positioning his body between David and where Sabrina lay as if to shield her from the man's indifference even in death.

"Sabrina called me at the office asking me to meet her in person here because she had information that was a serious concern for her. When I arrived, she briefly filled me in on the status of her divorce from Raymond Fung, then showed me a document with her name listed as an originator of an export on one of Raymond's ships to Mexico."

"Why would that be a concern for her?" David asked.

"Because she was not involved in Raymond's or his father's businesses. Also, the document was heavily redacted, so the product was not identified, Blake replied.

"Did she ask Raymond to explain?" Dennis asked.

"Yes, and he denied any knowledge, but took the document, promising to check into it," Blake replied.

When the subject of the document arose, Blake felt a surge of protectiveness. This piece of paper, possibly the key to understanding why Sabrina died, was not something he was willing to relinquish just yet. As David reached for it, Blake pulled back, his voice steady but brooking no argument. "I'll make a copy for you when I get back to the office. I'll hang onto this right now."

The flush of anger that colored David's neck did not escape Blake's notice, nor did the man's increasingly aggressive stance. Something was off, a dissonant note in an already chaotic symphony. Blake filed the observation away, adding it to the growing list of inconsistencies that would need to be addressed.

"And it will be entered as evidence in this case—by me," Blake said curtly.

"We can recover the text that's been redacted with this new tool that's been developed and shared among police agencies throughout the world," Dennis said optimistically.

"Great, Dennis. Let's get on it when I get back to the office," Blake said heavily. If there are no more questions, David, I'll head back to the city. I've got to stop in and tell Angela what happened. Then I'll brief Commissioner Blair."

David said nothing and turned his attention to his forensic team, which was still collecting information from the scene.

As the interview wound down, Blake felt the adrenaline finally leaving his system, replaced by a bone-deep weariness. The grief he had pushed aside threatened to overwhelm him once more, but he held it at bay. There would be time for mourning later. For now, he had a job to do – a job that had just become the most important of his life.

"I'll walk out with you, Blake," Dennis said. Blake nodded.

"Something's not right about David," Blake said, once outside. "He's acting weird and very aggressive towards me."

"I've noticed that too, Blake," Dennis replied, and he seems jittery all the time, with a quick fuse. I don't know what his problem is."

"Until we find out, I want to share information with him only on a need-to-know basis when it comes to Sabrina's and Samuel Fung's deaths and our work on the Triad-Cartel-CIA conspiracy."

"Agreed." Dennis nodded. "One final thought. Have you considered you were the assassin's target, not Sabrina, and our shooter wasn't a great shot?"

Blake looked at Dennis for a long time, thinking. "A good question, one that we'll have to get the answers to."

"And Blake, maybe you should consider taking a little time off to deal with your grief and loss. Jack Blair would understand," Dennis said empathetically.

"Thank you, Dennis, for your compassion," Blake said softly, "there will be time for that."

Blake waited for the paramedic to finish patching up his arm, then got in his car and headed back to the Peninsula Hotel and Angela.

He swallowed his grief. Sabrina's death had unearthed a kaleidoscope of tumultuous feelings he wasn't yet ready to process.

Leaving the scene, Blake cast one last glance at the sheet-covered form of Sabrina. *"I'll find out who did this,"* he promised silently. *"No matter what it takes."*

But before he reported to Blair, he wanted to see Angela. Her love and support were what he needed right now.

Chapter 25

Corruption Within

The soft glow of lamplight bathed Angela's suite at the Peninsula Hotel in a warm, deceptive calm. She sat on the plush sofa, her brow furrowed in concentration as she pored over a stack of documents. The muffled sounds of the city beyond the windows seemed distant, unreal, as if the world outside had ceased to exist beyond the confines of this room.

Angela glanced at her watch, a flicker of concern crossing her face. Blake should have been back by now. He'd mentioned meeting Sabrina, but that was hours ago. She reached for her phone, debating whether to call him, when the sudden click of the door latch shattered the quiet, causing her to look up sharply.

Blake stood in the doorway, a silhouette of anguish and despair. Blood smeared the front of his shirt and sleeve where an assassin's bullet had grazed him, a stark crimson against the crisp white fabric. His shoulders, usually squared with determination, now sagged under the weight of an invisible burden. His head hung low, as if the very act of holding it up required more strength than he possessed. The sight of him, so utterly broken, sent a jolt of fear through Angela's heart.

"Oh God, Blake!" The words tumbled from her lips as she leapt to her feet, documents scattering forgotten to the floor. In three quick strides, she crossed the room and enveloped him in an embrace, her arms a fortress against the world that had so cruelly battered him.

Blake's body trembled against hers, a man on the verge of collapse. His arms hung limply at his sides for a moment before slowly, almost reluctantly, wrapping around her. When he spoke, his voice was a ghost of its usual self, raw and ragged. "Angela . . . Sabrina's . . . dead," choking on the words.

"Shh, I've got you," Angela murmured, her hand gently cradling the back of his head. "Come, sit down. You're hurt."

Blake sank into the sofa, his body seeming to deflate further. "It's not serious," he muttered, but the pallor of his face and the slight tremor in his hands betrayed the toll the injury – and something far worse – had taken on him. "Sabrina ... she's gone, Angela."

Angela's breath caught in her throat, her hand finding Blake's and squeezing tightly. "What happened?" she asked softly, her thumb tracing soothing circles on the back of his hand.

Blake's eyes, usually sharp and alert, now seemed unfocused, gazing at something beyond the hotel room walls. "She called me, asked to meet at her family home. She sounded terrified, Angela." His voice cracked, a fissure in his usual composure. "When I got there, she showed me documents. Raymond had falsified her name, her company's name, on shipping manifests for Mexico. She'd confronted him, and he just ... brushed it off."

Angela's hands shook slightly as she poured him a glass of brandy. She pressed the glass into his hand, watching as he took a long, desperate swig. "Talk to me, Blake," she urged softly, perching beside him, her hand finding his in a gesture of silent support.

Blake took a shuddering breath, his free hand running through his disheveled hair. "We were on the terrace. The gunman . . . in the bushes. I couldn't shield her." His voice trailed off, lost in the echo of gunshots. "I managed to fire back and take him down, but Sabrina . . . I couldn't save her, Angela. She died in my arms."

The dam broke. Blake's body shook with sobs, raw and primal. He turned to Angela, burying his face in her shoulder, his tears soaking through her blouse. "She was my best friend," he choked out between gasps. "All my life, she was there. Her life had been so unhappy with Raymond. She deserved better."

"I know," Angela murmured, her own eyes brimming with tears as she held him tightly, rocking gently back and forth. "I know you loved her, Blake. I'm so sorry she's gone." Her words seemed inadequate in the face of such grief, but she repeated them like a mantra, a lifeline for Blake to cling to.

For long minutes, they sat in silence, the only sound Blake's ragged breathing as he fought to regain control. When he finally pulled away, his eyes were red-rimmed and swollen, his face etched with lines of grief and exhaustion.

"Blake, can you take some time off to grieve?" she asked, her eyes searching his.

Blake took a few deep, shuddering breaths. "I think I'll need it," he admitted, his voice hoarse. "But not yet. I've got to report to Jack Blair." His expression hardened slightly, a glimpse of the detective emerging from behind the veil of grief. "David Smith is officially heading up the investigation, but frankly, Angela, I don't have confidence in him."

Angela's brow furrowed at the mention of David Smith, filing away the information for later scrutiny. For now, she focused on the immediate needs. "Alright," she said, standing and gently pulling Blake to his feet. "Why don't you take a shower and wash up? I'll call the tailor shop and get you a clean shirt."

Blake nodded, gratitude flickering in his eyes. "Good idea," he murmured. Then, almost hesitantly, "Can you come with me to report to Blair?"

"Of course," Angela replied without hesitation, giving his hand a reassuring squeeze.

As Blake made his way to the bathroom, his steps unsteady, his body and soul visibly aching, Angela watched him go, her heart breaking for his loss. Once the bathroom door closed, she allowed herself a moment to process, the stress and trauma Blake had shared washing over her in waves.

Taking a deep breath, Angela steeled herself, pushing aside her own turmoil. Blake needed her strength now, her unwavering support and clear-headed thinking. Her resolve solidified. Whatever lay ahead – grief, danger, or both – she would stand by Blake's side. In this storm of loss and betrayal, they would be each other's anchor.

As she waited, Angela's gaze fell on the scattered documents on the floor. She knelt, gathering them up, her eyes scanning the pages out of habit. Suddenly, she froze, her breath catching in her throat. There, buried in the legalese and financial jargon, was a name she recognized – one that had no business being there.

The sound of running water from the bathroom mingled with the faint sounds of the city beyond the hotel windows. Angela's mind raced, connecting this new piece of information with what Blake had told her about Sabrina's documents. A picture was forming, one that sent a chill down her spine.

A knock at the door startled her from her thoughts. The concierge, with the clean shirt for Blake. Angela thanked him, closing the door and leaning against it for a moment, her heart pounding. She looked at the documents in her hand, then at the closed bathroom door where Blake was showering.

Not now, she decided. Blake wasn't ready for this. Not when the wound of Sabrina's loss was still so raw. She would keep this to herself, for now, and investigate quietly. Blake needed time to grieve, to process what had happened. But Angela knew that soon, very soon, they would need to confront the dangerous web that seemed to be closing in around them.

The bathroom door opened, and Blake emerged, a towel wrapped around his waist, his hair damp and tousled. The shower had washed away the blood, but not the haunted look in his eyes.

"Here," Angela said softly, handing him the fresh shirt. "Feel any better?"

Blake managed a weak smile that didn't reach his eyes. "Cleaner, at least," he said, his voice still rough with emotion. He dressed quickly, wincing slightly as the movement pulled at his injured arm.

"Let me look at that," Angela said, gently examining the graze on his arm. It wasn't deep, but it looked angry and painful. She applied a fresh bandage, her touch gentle and caring.

As she worked, Blake spoke softly, almost to himself. "I keep seeing her face, Angela. The moment she . . . " He trailed off, swallowing hard. "I should have protected her. I should have been faster, smarter."

Angela cupped his face in her hands, forcing him to meet her gaze. "This is not your fault, Blake," she said firmly. "You did everything you could. She trusted you with this information because she knew you'd do the right thing with it."

Blake nodded slowly, covering one of Angela's hands with his own. "You're right," he said, his voice gaining a hint of its usual strength. "And I will. I'll make sure her death wasn't in vain. I'll find out who's behind this, Angela. I swear it."

Angela saw the familiar determination returning to Blake's eyes, pushing back against the grief. It was a start, a small step towards healing. But she knew the road ahead would be long and fraught with danger.

"We'll find the truth," she said, emphasizing the 'we'. "Together, Blake. You're not alone in this."

Blake pulled her into a tight embrace, burying his face in her hair. "Thank you," he whispered, his voice thick with emotion. "I don't know what I'd do without you."

As they stood there, holding each other in the quiet hotel room, Angela's mind returned to the documents she'd seen, to the name that shouldn't have been there. She knew that soon, she'd have to share this information with Blake. Soon, they'd have to dive into the dangerous waters that had claimed Sabrina's life.

But for now, in this moment, all that mattered was being there for Blake, helping him navigate the overwhelming tide of grief and loss. Whatever challenges lay ahead, whatever dangers they might face, they would face them together.

Blake pulled back slightly, his eyes meeting Angela's. "We should go," he said softly. "Blair will be waiting."

Angela nodded, reaching for her coat. As they moved towards the door, she cast one last glance at the stack of documents on the table. A storm was coming, she knew. But for now, they had each other. And sometimes, that was enough to weather any storm.

Chapter 26

Suspicion

The Hong Kong night pulsed with an electric urgency as Blake and Angela wove through the city's serpentine streets. Twenty minutes felt like an eternity, each second weighted with the gravity of recent events. Their destination loomed ahead – the monolithic structure of police headquarters, a fortress of justice that seemed to touch the very sky.

As they strode through the stark corridors, their footsteps echoing off cold, unforgiving walls, Blake felt the weight of Sabrina's loss anew. Each step was a battle against the tide of grief threatening to overwhelm him. Angela, sensing his inner turmoil, placed a steadying hand on his arm, her touch a silent anchor in the storm of his emotions.

The door to Commissioner Jack Blair's office stood before them, an imposing barrier between the chaos of the outside world and the order within. As they entered, the atmosphere shifted, charged with an almost palpable tension.

Blair's face was a canvas of concern, deep furrows etched into his brow. His eyes, bloodshot from sleepless nights, scanned them both with an intensity that spoke volumes. In a gesture that caught Blake off guard, Blair stepped forward and embraced Blake tightly, his usually stoic demeanor cracking.

"I'm so sorry about Sabrina's death, Blake," Blair's voice was rough with emotion. "I know you had a close lifelong friendship."

The unexpected display of empathy hit Blake like a physical blow. He struggled to swallow past the lump in his throat. "Thank you, Chief," he managed, his voice barely above a whisper.

As Blair stepped back, composing himself, Blake saw a flicker of something in the older man's eyes – a mixture of sorrow and determination that mirrored his own inner conflict.

"Are you alright?" Blair asked, genuine concern coloring his tone. "Dennis said you were wounded. But I'm more worried about your emotional state, Blake. Losing Sabrina . . . it's got to be tearing you apart."

Blake instinctively straightened, pushing aside for a moment the pain in his arm. "A minor flesh wound Chief," he replied, his voice steadier now. "Nothing that won't heal quickly." Blair knew instinctively that Blake was not alright emotionally. He could see the pain and sorrow in his eyes.

Blair's eyes narrowed, his mind clearly racing. "Do you suspect the attack was aimed at Sabrina, or was it you they were after?" The question cut through the room like a knife, laying bare the heart of the matter.

Blake leaned in, a strategic mind at work as he pieced together the intricate puzzle. "The crosshairs seemed trained on both, but my instincts lean towards Sabrina. She's been delving into the shadowy dealings of Samuel and Raymond Fung. Confronting Raymond with evidence of her name falsely listed on a shipment to Mexico. It's no coincidence that her demise followed shortly after," he elaborated, his analysis painting a picture of intrigue and betrayal.

Blair absorbed their words, his gaze intense as he examined the document Blake had brought. "Is this the original piece of evidence?"

"No, that's with Raymond. Sabrina managed to secure a copy before her untimely death," Blake clarified, setting the stage for what was to come.

Blair, decisive and unwavering, laid out their next steps with a command that brooked no argument. "This is sufficient grounds to question Raymond Fung again and charge him if you think it warranted. The tangled web of his shipping empire must be unraveled."

I'd like to request that I interrogate Raymond alone, without David Smith's involvement, at his home rather than here at HQ." Blake replied, "I think his hands are busy investigating the deaths of Simon Chang, Samuel Fung and now Sabrina."

Blair's brow furrowed, the weight of past and present corruption heavy in his eyes. "David's got a full team, Blake, but I'll agree to your request. Your instincts have never led us astray."

"If you have no objection, I'd like Agent Torres to present while I question Raymond," Blake added, "to record the conversation."

Blair rubbed his chin. "It's not the usual protocol, but Agent Torres has official status, and if it facilitates Raymond being more agreeable to answering questions, go ahead. I don't need to add that there should be an official interrogation recording. Are you agreeable Agent Torres?"

"I'd be glad to help, Commissioner," Angela said willingly.

Yet, there's something else, isn't there?" Blair asked pointedly.

The tension in Blair's office was palpable as Blake leaned forward, his voice low and urgent. "Chief, can what I'm about to say be off the record."

Blair's eyes narrowed, his hand stroking his chin thoughtfully. The weight of potential implications hung heavy in the air. "Alright," he said after a moment.

Angela nodded, unsurprised. The dance of confidentiality was one she knew well. "Of course," she said, her tone professional as she quietly exited, closing the door behind her with a soft click.

Once alone, Blake's posture tensed, his words carefully measured. "As you're aware, David was investigated a few years ago for allegedly taking bribes from at least one Triad. Internal Affairs cleared him, but..." He paused, weighing his next words. "My gut instinct suggests he isn't free of them."

Blair's gaze sharpened. "Do you have proof, Blake?"

"No, not yet, but I believe I can get it," Blake admitted, "have you noticed how quick-tempered and critical he is about my involvement in his investigations?"

Silence fell between them, heavy with unspoken concerns. Blair's eyes unfocused slightly, lost in thought. Blake waited, knowing the Commissioner's penchant for reflection.

Finally, Blair spoke, his voice grave. "I've relied on your intuition before, Blake. You've never been wrong." He leaned back, his chair creaking softly. "As a first step, complete your investigation, but I must have hard evidence. For now, this stays between us."

"Understood," Blake nodded, relief and determination mingling in his expression.

Blair's face darkened, the weight of history settling on his shoulders. "If David is dirty, Blake, it would be a black mark on the force. You're keenly aware of how our force was once corrupt, with members working hand-in-hand with Triads, fueled by bribes."

The spectre of past corruption hung between them, a shared history that had shaped both their careers. Blake's mind drifted back to darker days, his voice tinged with old anger. "Yes, Chief. I remember the '50s and '60s when syndicated criminals paid regular bribes to staff sergeants. Triads operated with impunity." His fists clenched unconsciously. "By the '70s, corruption had peaked. That enforcement-evasion arrangement, Triads infiltrating the force... And then the scandal with your predecessor, Peter Godber."

Blair nodded grimly. "Overseas bank accounts stuffed with hundreds of thousands from Triad collusion. It hurt us badly when he fled prosecution."

"That led to the Independent Commission Against Corruption in '74," Blake recalled, a hint of pride creeping into his voice. "You were recruited to head it, and you brought me on board."

A ghost of a smile crossed Blair's face, softening the worry lines. "Those clean-up campaigns and undercover work we initiated made a real difference. Godber's and Superintendent Hunt's convictions were turning points."

Blake leaned forward, his voice passionate. "Your leadership dealt with the police corruption of the '70s, Jack. It seems like only yesterday we were arresting and prosecuting corrupt officers."

Blair's expression hardened. "Having you head up the Triad Society Bureau in '78, independent of Smith's Crime Division, was crucial. But there's pressure to subsume your division into his." He locked eyes with Blake. "My greatest fear is that corruption is still there, under the surface. I need to know if David Smith can be trusted!"

Blake nodded, determination etched in every line of his face. "Smith would love nothing more than to have me under his thumb. I'll do everything I can, Chief. I only ask that you allow me to act without David's interference."

"You've got it, in spades," Blair said firmly. His gaze flicked to the door. "It looks like you've got a smart colleague to rely on as well. You have my permission to give her access to your work." He nodded toward the door. "You can call her back in now."

"Thank you, Chief." Blake stood, feeling the weight of responsibility settle on his shoulders as he moved to let Angela back in. The hunt for truth was on, and the stakes had never been higher.

As Angela re-entered, Blair's voice cut through the tension-filled office, his words sharp and authoritative. "Here's the plan. David Smith will continue investigating the murders of Simon Chang, Samuel Fung, and Sabrina." His eyes locked onto Blake, a silent understanding passing between them. "Blake, you'll pursue Raymond

Fung and the family businesses. Keep digging into the Triad-Mexican Cartel connection with Agent Torres. Resources are yours if you need them." A pregnant pause. "And that other matter we discussed . . . handle it discreetly."

Angela's eyebrows rose slightly. "That's quite the plateful," she remarked, her tone a mixture of admiration and concern.

Blake's jaw tightened. "On the surface, yes. But I'm convinced they're all connected." The weight of his suspicions hung heavy in the air.

"Commissioner, with your permission, I'd like to report a development that has some relevance. Senator Connor's scheduled a public hearing on CIA misconduct. He wants us to testify again in Washington." She glanced at Blair. "You'll likely get an official request."

Blair's sigh spoke volumes. "Fine by me if it's helpful to us."

As Blake and Angela left, the atmosphere shifted. The bustling office felt oppressive, hiding secrets in every shadow. They paused at Dennis Wang's desk, his fingers flying over his keyboard.

Blake leaned in, his voice low. "Dennis, any new leads?"

Wang's eyes lit up, a stark contrast to the somber mood. "My Kowloon Walled City informant says the Min Wo Triad took out Simon Chang. They're making power moves, Blake. Big ones."

Blake's mind raced. "Any names?"

Wang shook his head. "The Dragon Head, Robert Lee. But there's talk of internal power struggles."

Throughout the exchange, Angela watched, her analytical mind piecing together the puzzle. Her eyes met Blake's, a silent question forming.

Blake nodded, almost imperceptibly. "Let's take this outside."

In the relative privacy of the street, Blake's facade cracked slightly. "Dennis, am I imagining things, or is Smith gunning for me?"

Wang's expression darkened. "He's been on edge since that Internal Affairs investigation. But with you? It's personal, Blake. He's keeping you in the dark deliberately."

Blake's fists clenched at his sides. "The Commissioner's given me *carte blanche* on anything associated with the Triads and Raymond Fung. I'll need your help, Dennis."

Wang's loyalty shone in his eyes. "You've got it. No questions asked."

"I'd like you to discover as much as you can about what's transpiring in the Min Wo Triad and Smith's other investigations surreptitiously. I'll check in with you later. Angela and I will be interrogating Raymond Fung again at his home, with more pointed questions." Dennis acknowledged with a nod.

Angela's mind was racing ahead. The unspoken question of how Raymond would react to her presence hung between them, adding another layer of tension to their already fraught situation. She placed a comforting hand on Blake's arm, a gesture of support in the face of overwhelming odds.

As they drove back to the Peninsula Hotel, the weight of their mission pressed down upon them. The city's skyline cast long shadows, a visual representation of the dark undercurrents they were about to navigate. Yet, in the midst of this growing darkness, their unwavering commitment to justice and truth was bright – a beacon of hope illuminating their path through the treacherous waters ahead.

Blake's mind whirled with the day's revelations, his grief for Sabrina intertwining with the determination to uncover the truth. As they pulled up to the hotel, he turned to Angela, his voice low and resolute. "I need to rest and recuperate tonight. The next few days will put us under the gun. This web of corruption and murder . . . we need to start connecting the dots."

Angela nodded, her eyes reflecting the same mix of determination and concern. "I'm with you, Blake. Whatever it takes."

As they stepped out of the car, the bustling Hong Kong night enveloped them – a city of secrets, where every shadow could hide a potential ally or enemy. The hunt for truth was on, and the stakes had never been higher.

Chapter 27

Unholy Alliance

The Mexican sun hung like a molten coin in the cloudless sky, its relentless heat turning the air into a shimmering veil above the opulent terrace. Raul Ramirez reclined in his custom-made deck chair, its supple leather creaking softly with each subtle shift of his body. To the casual observer, he might have appeared the picture of relaxation – a man of wealth and power enjoying his hard-earned paradise. But beneath the veneer of calm, Ramirez's mind churned like a tempest, each thought a calculation, each breath a measured act in the endless performance of survival.

His eyes, shielded behind polarized designer sunglasses, scanned the breathtaking panorama before him. The infinite blue of the Pacific stretched to the horizon, a deceptive façade of tranquility that belied the turbulent undercurrents of his world. The pool, a feat of architectural bravado, seemed to defy gravity as it cantilevered over the cliff's edge. Its still surface mirrored the sky, creating an illusion of endless space – a fitting metaphor, Ramirez mused, for the limitless reach of his ambition.

The air was heavy with competing scents: the salt of the sea, the sweet perfume of bougainvillea cascading down the stark white walls, and underneath it all, the faint metallic tang of danger that never quite dissipated. Vibrant red petals drifted on the gentle breeze, nature's blood-red confetti in this theater of power and peril.

Armed guards patrolled the perimeter with practiced nonchalance, their casual attire a carefully orchestrated deception. Ramirez knew each man by name, knew their families, their weaknesses, their ambitions. It was a chess game of loyalty bought with fear and favor, each guard a pawn in his grand strategy of survival.

Across from Ramirez, Raphael Salinez sat with the poise of a man balancing on a knife's edge. His pristine white linen suit was a masterpiece of tailoring, each crease and fold a silent testament to the precision with which he approached every aspect of his life. Salinez's handsome features were schooled into a mask of calm, but his eyes – sharp, hungry, ever-assessing – betrayed the ambition that simmered beneath the surface.

Ramirez studied his cousin covertly, a mixture of pride and wariness coloring his thoughts. Salinez was capable, ruthlessly efficient, and unquestioningly loyal – or so it seemed. But in their world, loyalty was a currency more volatile than any stock market, and Ramirez had not climbed to the summit of his blood-soaked empire by trusting blindly.

The third player in this dangerous triumvirate was Jack Cross, the CIA's Deputy Director of Special Covert Operations. His presence here, on this sun-drenched terrace overlooking a Cartel stronghold, was a stark reminder of the strange bedfellows created by geopolitics and greed. Cross's guayabera shirt, a nod to local custom, fluttered gently in the sea breeze. The casual attire did nothing to soften the hard edges of the man beneath – this was a predator dressed as prey, a wolf in tourist's clothing.

Cross sipped his mojito, the ice cubes clinking against the glass like tiny warning bells. His eyes, the pale blue of arctic ice, never stopped moving, cataloguing every detail of his surroundings. He was a man who dealt in secrets and shadows, for whom paranoia was not just a survival trait but a way of life.

The heat doesn't get to you?" Cross inquired, his tone light but his gaze penetrating. It was a probing question, a test wrapped in small talk.

Ramirez's laugh was as dry and biting as the desert wind. "Jack, when you're born into it, this is nothing." His dismissive wave encompassed more than just the climate – it was a reminder of the harsh crucible that had forged him, the trials he'd endured to reach this pinnacle. "It gets hotter—much hotter. A man born here stops noticing after a while." The words hung in the air, laden with unspoken threats and shared history, and a light jab at Cross' masculinity.

"And why the personal visit, Jack?" Ramirez's voice was a blend of amusement and veiled menace, each word carefully chosen to maintain the delicate balance of their alliance. "Wouldn't a call suffice?" He leaned forward slightly, the movement casual but calculated to assert dominance in this dangerous dance.

Cross's gaze swept over Salinez, assessing, calculating. The younger man met his look unflinchingly, a silent challenge that made Ramirez's nerves prickle with unease.

"Too important for phones," Cross replied, his words clipped and precise. "I need to know your progress with the Unified Socialist Party (PSUM) of Mexico. We're concerned about their growing support." The air seemed to thicken with tension as he continued, outlining the CIA's concerns about the PSUM's growing influence and anti-American stance. Each word was laden with unspoken consequences, a reminder of the Sword of Damocles that hung over their partnership.

Ramirez leaned forward, his posture deliberately casual but his eyes burning with an intensity that belied his relaxed demeanor. "We've infiltrated the PSUM," he began, his voice smooth as silk but edged with steel. "Their leader, Gonzalez will have an unfortunate accident. Very tragic, very believable." A shark-like smile played at the corners of his mouth, a brief flash of teeth that was more threat than mirth. "His replacement is more amenable to our interests. The anti-American rhetoric will die down, I assure you."

He paused, allowing the weight of his words to settle before continuing. "But the DEA, they're becoming a problem. That last raid in Manzanillo was a disaster. It's making our Hong Kong partners nervous." His tone hardened, a hint of genuine concern bleeding through his carefully maintained facade. "Especially that Agent Torres. She's becoming quite the thorn in our side."

Salinez, sensing an opportunity to assert himself, leaned in eagerly. "She's incorruptible," he interjected, his words rushing out like water from a broken dam. "Unlike her Mexican counterparts. We can't buy her, can't threaten her. She's a real problem."

The glare Ramirez shot at his cousin could have melted steel. Salinez visibly wilted under the intensity of that look, realizing too late he'd overstepped his bounds. In that moment, the power dynamic between the two men crystallized – Ramirez the unquestioned leader, Salinez the ambitious lieutenant forever striving to prove his worth.

Cross's voice cut through the tension like a knife through silk. "Let's cut to the chase, Raul." His words were clipped, aggressive, the façade of civility slipping to reveal the ruthless operative beneath. "Our deal stands – you handle the PSUM, we handle the rest. Including Torres." The threat in his voice was unmistakable, a promise of dark deeds lurking just beneath the surface of diplomacy. "Thirty percent cut, no paperwork. Everything through Nugan-Hand Bank in Hong Kong. Untraceable, as always."

Ramirez nodded, his face a mask of compliance hiding a maelstrom of calculations and contingencies. "The deal stands, Jack. We're on top of it." His tone was conciliatory yet firm, a reminder that while they might be partners, they were far from friends.

As Cross stood to leave, the air seemed to crackle with unspoken tensions and veiled threats. His departure was marked by curt nods and thinly veiled warnings, each man fully aware of the precarious nature of their alliance.

Once Cross had disappeared beyond the bougainvillea-draped walls, Ramirez turned to Salinez, his face darkening like a gathering storm. The mask of civility dropped, revealing the ruthless Cartel leader beneath. "Never overstep again," he hissed, each word dripping with menace. "Are we clear? You handle the PSUM issue—personally. Understand?"

Salinez's reply was meek, a far cry from his earlier eagerness. "Yes, understood. I was just trying to help." The words sounded hollow even to his own ears, and he knew he'd have to work hard to regain his cousin's trust.

Left alone on the terrace, Ramirez' gaze drifted to the horizon, where the sun was beginning its slow descent, painting the sky in shades of gold and crimson. But his mind was far from the beauty before him, instead whirling with plots and counterplots.

As he sipped his mojito, Ramirez reflected on the current situation. *"Cross is a dangerous ally, a viper we need but can never truly trust. The CIA's involvement is a double-edged sword – protection and peril intertwined. And Salinez..."* Ramirez's eyes narrowed as he contemplated his cousin. *"Ambitious, capable, but perhaps too eager."*

Ramirez's fingers tightened on his glass as he mentally reviewed his next moves. *"I have an empire to protect, shipments to arrange with Raymond Fung, and a cousin to watch. The DEA was closing in, with Agent Torres leading the charge. And somewhere in the shadows, other Cartels waited to pounce on me, hungry for any sign of weakness. And I know from experience that I can trust Cross only as long as I am useful to the CIA."*

Ramirez stood as the sun dipped lower, casting long shadows across the terrace. The coming darkness would bring no respite, only new challenges to face, new enemies to outmaneuver. But for men like Raul Ramirez, that was the only game worth playing. In this world of shadows and blood, of shifting alliances and sudden betrayals, one misstep could mean the end of everything he'd built.

Chapter 28

Securing Loyalties

The muffled thuds of Jack Cross's Italian leather shoes against the plush Persian rug echoed like a ticking time bomb in Benjamin Cranston's office. Cross moved with barely contained energy, his lean frame coiled tight with tension; there were no remnants of jet lag from his trip to confer with Raul Ramirez. His sharp jawline clenched and unclenched, a physical manifestation of the thoughts churning behind his intense, calculating eyes.

Cranston, the CIA's Director of Covert Operations, sat behind his massive mahogany desk, a monolith of authority in the dimly lit room. His weathered face, etched with the lines of countless covert decisions, remained impassive. But beneath his stoic exterior, a storm of concern and irritation brewed. His fingers, steepled before him, trembled almost imperceptibly – a rare sign of unease from a man accustomed to making life-or-death decisions.

"Sit down, Jack," Cranston growled, his gravelly voice cutting through the tension like a knife. "Your restlessness is making my damn ulcer act up."

Cross complied, sinking into the leather chair across from Cranston. He leaned forward, elbows on knees, his body language screaming barely contained aggression. "Ben, we need to talk about these hearings. The DEA, the Senate Intelligence Committee – they're breathing down our necks about Mexico. There seems to be no appreciation for the need for us to weaken and, if necessary, destroy the Communist groups in Mexico, which pose a clear threat to American interests."

Cranston's eyes narrowed. "When I gave you the green light to initiate covert activity in Mexico, I didn't appreciate the degree to which you would be working directly with the drug Cartels there and a Triad in Hong Kong, Jack."

Cross's face darkened, a shadow passing over his features. His voice dropped to a dangerous whisper, "It's not just an operation, Ben. It's a necessity. Those Cartels have their tentacles in every level of the Mexican government. They're our perfect proxy to root out the Commie threat. And let's not forget – their drug money is filling our coffers when Congress keeps tightening our purse strings."

Cranston looked up at a photo on the wall, in a wistful manner, of General William "Wild Bill" Donovan, legendary head of the Office of Strategic Services (OSS). This organization preceded the CIA, hoping for Donovan to say the CIA had wandered from its original mission of collecting intelligence to a modern focus on covert activities. The silence stretched between them, broken only by the ominous ticking of an antique clock.

"But Jack, let's stop and think for a moment. The CIA is now working with criminals and aiding drug trafficking—and even profiting from it. Is that a legitimate strategy?" his voice heavy with the weight of moral compromise.

Cross leaned in, his eyes glittering with a zealot's conviction. "We do what's necessary, Ben. Always have, always will. Or have you forgotten your time in Laos? The Hmong? Air America? Your hands aren't exactly clean either."

Cranston flinched as if struck, the memories of past transgressions flashing across his face. He looked down at the dossier on his desk, unable to meet Cross's piercing gaze. When he spoke again, his voice was barely above a whisper, "Proceed with Mexico, Jack. But so help me God, if this blows up in our faces . . . ."

The threat hung unfinished in the air. Cross nodded, a predatory smile playing at the corners of his mouth. "There are a couple more things, Ben. The Senate investigation – it needs to disappear. And that

DEA agent, Torres? She's digging too deep. Her and that Hong Kong cop, Blake Morgan."

Cranston's head snapped up, alarm evident in his eyes. "What are you suggesting, Jack?"

Cross stood, looming over the desk. His voice was cold, devoid of emotion. "I'm suggesting we do whatever it takes to protect our interests. By any means necessary."

"Does that mean what I think it does, Jack? Because if it does, I want no part of it," Cranston said with a sigh of resignation, "and this conversation never took place."

Cross paused at the door, throwing a chilling smile over his shoulder. "Of course not, Ben. It never does."

The door closed behind Cross with a soft click, leaving Cranston alone in the gathering darkness. He reached for the bottle of scotch in his bottom drawer, his hand shaking. As he poured a generous measure, he couldn't shake the feeling that he had just made a deal with the devil – and the price would be steep. He had to admit to himself, he didn't know the details of most of Cross' operations, having satisfied himself with the broad strokes. Now that decision may be leading to some dangerous consequences.

Outside, Cross strode down the hallway, his mind already racing with plans. Cranston's reluctance was a problem, but not an insurmountable one. He had contingencies in place for such eventualities. As for Senator Connor, Agent Torres, and Inspector Morgan – well, they would soon learn the price of meddling in affairs beyond their understanding.

It was time to call Raymond Fung in Hong Kong. The board was set, and Cross was ready to make his move. In this game of shadows and secrets, there could be only one winner – and Jack Cross had no intention of losing.

Chapter 29

Silencing the Chairman

The heavy oak doors of the White House closed behind Senator Bryce Connor, Chairman of the Senate Intelligence Committee, with a sound like a judge's gavel, final and foreboding. He stood for a moment on the top step, the warm Washington air thick with humidity and the weight of unspoken threats after his unsettling conversation he'd had with the National Security Council (NSC). His face, usually composed and diplomatic, now betrayed a storm of emotions – frustration, anger, and a gnawing fear that clawed at his insides.

Despite being a member of the opposition party, Connor felt duty-bound to present his committee's interim report, given the grave nature of the evidence regarding CIA corruption. The Council however, had responded with a staunch defence of the CIA and a subtle insistence that the investigation be quietly shelved. They had suggested, without outright ordering, that the CIA director should handle the matter internally. It was a political dance, a masterclass in plausible deniability, but it left Connor frustrated and deeply troubled.

As he approached the White House gates, the Senator's fists clenched and relaxed rhythmically. He took a deep breath, trying to clear his mind. *"Throughout my years of service in the military and politics, I've been guided by an unwavering commitment to ethical and moral behavior,"* he muttered to himself. *"The Council's obsessive fear of Communism, and their relentless efforts to obliterate even a hint of its existence, is tarnishing our nation's claim to be a moral leader in the world."*

Connor was an adept and savvy politician, easily re-elected twice in his California district. His years of service had earned him a reputation for integrity and an unwavering commitment to the truth.

Elected in a predominantly Democratic, liberal district in San Francisco, where anti-administration attitudes were strong, Connor was under significant pressure to champion oversight and accountability of the intelligence agencies, particularly the CIA.

He paused at the gate, turning to look back at the imposing structure of the White House. A sense of foreboding washed over him. The battle he was fighting was not just political; it was moral. And the stakes were higher than ever.

"Senator, are you alright?" Martin Foster, his long-time aide, interrupted his thoughts. Foster had been with Connor for over a decade, sharing his commitment to uncovering the truth. His presence was a steadying force, a reminder that Connor was not alone in this fight.

"Yes, Martin, I'm fine," Connor replied, forcing a smile. "Let's head back."

As they walked towards the parking lot, Connor's mind raced. The evidence his committee had uncovered was damning – CIA operatives colluding with drug Cartels, assassinations disguised as accidents, a web of lies and deceit that stretched from Mexico to Hong Kong. And yet, the NSC's response had been nothing short of dismissive.

They made their way to Connor's sedan parked in the secure lot. Connor took the wheel, preferring to drive himself home to Rosemont, a quiet, affluent neighborhood in Alexandria, DC. The familiar route wound through the capital's bustling streets, across the Potomac River, and into the serene suburbs. Their shared tension was palpable as they cruised down the George Washington Parkway.

"Martin," Connor said as they pulled out of the parking lot, his voice tight with suppressed emotion, "I've spent my entire career fighting for truth and justice. I've faced down enemies on the battlefield and in the Senate chambers. But this . . . this feels different."

Foster nodded, his own face a mask of concern. "The stakes are certainly higher, Senator. The CIA's activities in Mexico and Hong Kong . . . if even half of what we've uncovered is verifiable, it's unprecedented."

Connor's knuckles whitened in frustration on the steering wheel as they merged onto the George Washington Parkway. The Potomac River glittered to their right, a stark contrast to the darkness that seemed to be closing in around them.

"It's not just about the CIA anymore, Martin," Connor said, his voice barely above a whisper. "It's about the very soul of our nation. We claim to be a beacon of democracy, a shining city on a hill. But how can we hold that mantle when we're no better than the enemies we claim to fight?"

Connor's hands gripped the steering wheel like he was choking someone. "My gut tells me Cross may be freelancing. Cranston looked a bit uncomfortable when I presented the evidence we have," Connor replied, his eyes focused on the road ahead.

The traffic slowed on a downhill slope and Connor shifted his foot to the brake pedal. Suddenly, he felt it go soft under his foot. He pressed harder, but the car failed to slow down. Panic flashed in his eyes as he realized the brakes were not responding. The sedan hurtled down the parkway at an alarming speed, weaving dangerously between lanes. Grasping the dashboard, Foster shouted at Connor to pull over, but it was useless. The car careened out of control, the speedometer climbing higher with each passing second.

Connor's mind raced as he struggled to regain control. The guardrails and trees blurred past in a dizzying whirl. The inevitable happened as they approached a sharp curve near a secluded stretch of the road. The car veered off the pavement, ploughing through the guardrail and crashing into a thick stand of trees. The impact was catastrophic. The sound of metal crunching and glass shattering echoed through the night.

Emergency services arrived quickly on the scene, but it was too late. Bryce Connor, the fearless guardian of national integrity, lay lifeless amidst the wreckage. His loyal assistant, Martin Foster, had met a similar fate.

Connor's death, initially deemed an accident because of brake failure, would soon be shrouded in suspicion as whispers of foul play emerged. For those like Blake Morgan, Angela Torres, and his supportive colleagues in the Senate, it was clear that Connor had been silenced, a casualty in the murky war of shadows and secrets. The quest for truth had suffered a great blow, threatening the entire Senate investigation of the CIA.

As dawn broke over the Potomac, casting a blood-red glow across the sky, the wreckage of Connor's car stood as a grim monument to the price of challenging the status quo. In the coming days, weeks, and months, the battle for the soul of America would rage on, but it would do so without one of its fiercest warriors.

The shadows had claimed another victory, but in doing so, they had sown the seeds of their own eventual downfall. For in silencing Bryce Connor, they had created a martyr – and martyrs, as history has shown, have a way of inspiring others to take up the fight.

Chapter 30

Narco Warfare

Tijuana's night had descended like a velvet curtain, casting a kaleidoscope of neon lights and shadows over the bustling city. The streets thrummed with the symphony of nightlife: the distant roar of traffic, the sudden booming blast of music from passing cars, and the ceaseless murmur of voices. *Avenida Revolución*, the pulsating heart of Tijuana's nightlife, overflowed with tourists and locals alike, spilling out of lively cantinas and taquerias, blissfully unaware of the storm brewing beneath the surface.

Once a honky-tonk town of bars and brothels serving San Diego's naval station, Tijuana, Mexico, with a population of two million, had become one of the fastest-growing cities in the world. Huge shantytowns with shacks built from cardboard and shipping pallets lined dirty streets and sprawled down the slopes of desert mesas below the *maliquadoros*, the American border factories. The migration of thousands of people north to the border, looking for work and the creation of new elites from the enormous economies of drugs, had marred the efforts to build a viable economic and social structure. In a place where anything was for sale, the price of human life is on a razor's edge.

A handful of bars and clubs in Tijuana, such as the Chicago Club and the Adelita Bar were choked with people that evening. Half a dozen streetwalkers from the *Zona Norte* had wandered down from *Calle 1A* to look for customers. The sound of blaring music and the laughter of drunken men accosting young women filled the air.

Amid this vibrant chaos stood *La Cantina del Diablo*, a well-known bar frequented by locals and tourists seeking an authentic experience. Its walls were adorned with colorful murals depicting scenes of old Mexico, a stark contrast to the dark reality that was about to unfold.

The air inside was thick with the scent of grilled meat and the tang of tequila as patrons crowded around tables, their laughter and chatter creating a deceptive veil of normalcy.

Outside, the narrow alleyways that crisscrossed behind the main strip needed to be more inviting. Dimly lit and lined with crumbling buildings, these backstreets were the domain of the city's darker elements. Here, the neon glow faded into a murky twilight, and the air grew heavy with the anticipation of violence.

In a dimly lit corner booth of *La Cantina del Diablo*, Raul Ramirez, the leader of the Tijuana Cartel, sat with his trusted lieutenant, Raphael Salinez. They kept their watch on the Cantina's entrances, waiting for a corrupt member of the Mexican police whom Ramirez had seduced to work for his Cartel. He had new information for them about Mexican police and DEA activities.

"Necesitamos empujar más fuerte, " (We need to push harder), Raul," Salinez said, his voice low but urgent. The two men interspersed their conversation in both Spanish and English. *"Los de Sinaloa se están volviendo más atrevidos. Nuestras líneas de suministro están en riesgo. Ellos todavía están enfocados en la cocaína, la marihuana y la heroína, pero pronto verán un enorme mercado para la metanfetamina y el fentanilo. Verán cómo les hemos tomado la delantera con el fentanilo* (they are still focused on cocaine, marijuana, and heroin, but they'll soon see a huge market for methamphetamine and fentanyl. They'll see how we've got the jump on them with fentanyl)."

Ramirez took a slow sip of his tequila; his eyes fixed on the swirling liquid as if it held the answers. "I know," he replied, his voice a deep rumble. "But we can't rush this. Fentanyl is too valuable. One mistake, and we lose everything. We have to choose and protect our trafficking routes carefully."

Salinez nodded, though his impatience was evident. ""*Y la nueva ruta por Mexicali? Es menos vigilada, menos ojos"* (what about the new route through Mexicali? It's less guarded, fewer eyes)?"

Ramirez considered this momentarily, tapping his fingers on the wooden table. "It's risky, but it might work. We need to make sure our men are ready. No room for error."

Salinez leaned in closer, his voice dropping to a whisper. "And the DEA? They were backup on the Mazanillo bust, and their assets here seek reliable informants. We need to keep them off our trail."

Ramirez's eyes flicked up, sharp and alert. "The CIA is committed to provide protection from the DEA as long as we're aggressive in infiltrating the Socialist and Communist political groups here. They'll feed us any intel we need. But we need to be smart, move carefully. The other Cartels won't hesitate to exploit any weakness."

A black SUV with dark tinted windows pulled up in front of the Cantina. The car windows rolled down, an automatic rifle stuck out and fired on Ramirez' and Salinez. As soon as the assault began, they capsized their table and took cover behind it.

The assailants continued to fire their automatic weapons from the vehicle, bullets spraying wildly around the Cantina. Several patrons drinking at tables in the bar were struck by strays. Then Salinez went down, struck by a bullet that had penetrated the table and hit him in the upper chest.

Ramirez was enraged and, grabbing Salinez's gun and his own, stood up and charged the SUV, firing both the Glock 20s wildly. The vehicle did not have bulletproof glass, and his bullets penetrated the windows and struck the man who was firing the automatic weapon in the head, and he went down.

The driver of the SUV, wounded by one of Ramirez's bullets, jammed his foot on the accelerator, and the vehicle sped away down the street, sideswiping several cars.

Ramirez rushed back into the Cantina, where wounded innocent bystanders were being attended to. He found Salinez in the same spot he had fallen.

"Raphael!" Ramirez called out, but there was no response. He dropped to his knees beside his fallen cousin and lieutenant, a torrent of emotions washing over him. The bond they had forged over years of loyalty and hardship had been shattered instantly. He embraced Raphael, sobbing.

Grief quickly turned to survival instinct as the sound of approaching sirens grew louder. Ramirez knew he had to escape. He grabbed his guns, tucking them into his waistband, and ducked out the back door.

A competing Cartel had put Ramirez on notice that it was coming after him. Blood stained the sidewalk outside the cantina, a grim testament to the violence that had taken place. As the survivors slipped away into the night, the city of Tijuana continued its restless dance, the neon lights and vibrant nightlife masking the brutal reality of the drug war that raged just beneath the surface. Raul Ramirez, with the weight of Salinez's death heavy on his shoulders, slipped into the shadows, determined to exact retribution and become the most powerful Cartel in Mexico. *"There will be blood,"* Ramirez promised himself.

Chapter 31

Targeted But Unbroken

Angela and Blake had flown back Washington from Hong Kong to testify for Senator Connor's committee in an open public hearing. He had told Angela he had new important new evidence regarding CIA that he wanted to share in person with her and Blake. Upon their arrival they received the news that Senator Connor and his assistant had been killed in a car crash.

The Angela's car purred to a stop in front of her inherited mansion, its tires crunching softly on the gravel driveway. As Angela and Blake stepped out, the cool evening air carried the scent of jasmine from the manicured gardens. The opulent façade loomed before them, its grandeur a stark contrast to the dark underbelly of the world they'd been navigating.

Angela's fingers trembled slightly as she reached for her briefcase. The weight of Senator Connor's death pressed heavily on her chest, a constant, suffocating presence. "I can't believe he's gone," she whispered, her voice catching. "All that evidence he wanted to share. It feels like we're losing this battle before it's even begun."

Blake's hand found her shoulder, a comforting warmth in the chill of uncertainty. "We'll find the truth, Blake. We owe it to Connor, to ourselves, and to every person whose life has been destroyed by this corruption. I'm optimistic that Connor's replacement on the Senate Committee will keep the investigation alive." Her voice was low, intense. "This isn't just about the CIA anymore. It's about the question of whether the rule of law is still alive in America."

The luxury of her mansion, a majestic structure adorned with antiques and artworks passed down through generations, stood in stark contrast to the grim nature of her revelations—ties between the CIA, Hong Kong Triads and the Mexican Drug Cartels.

As they approached the grand oak and glass door, Angela's hand hovered over the ornate brass knob. Her personal assistant Sally was away on a short vacation. She noticed looking through the side window that Sally had not left the usual night lights on. An alarm shiver ran down her spine, goosebumps prickling her skin. "Blake," she murmured, tension knotting her brows, "something feels off. It's too quiet. Even the cicadas have gone silent." She grabbed his arm and pulled him back to the car, and opened the trunk. Inside was a sleek black case. She opened it, revealing two handguns and ammunition. "Precautions," she said, handing him one. They both then loaded the guns and went back to the entrance.

Blake, ever the protector, tightened his grip on his concealed weapon. His only response was a small, reassuring nod. The door swung open to the familiar warmth of Angela's home, yet the air was charged with an unsettling stillness.

Blake and Angela stepped gingerly along the foyer, hugging the walls into the large living room.

They had barely taken three steps when the silence shattered. Two dark figures materialized from the shadows, their movements fluid and predatory. The assassins, clad in black tactical gear, seemed to absorb the dim light, their intentions as clear as they were lethal. They began firing their handguns at Angela and Blake, missing them in the darkness.

Angela's training kicked in instantly. She dove to the side, rolling behind a luxurious antique sofa. Blake moved over to the cover of a large credenza so that he and Angela were not close targets. The air crackled with the tension of the impending confrontation; the only sounds now were the muffled thuds of bodies in motion and the faint creak of the mansion's old wooden flooring.

"Blake!" she called out, her voice tight with concern.

"I'm okay," came his reply from behind a large credenza. "Two targets. Heavily armed. This isn't a random hit, Angela. They knew we were coming."

Their eyes met briefly across the room, a silent communication born of trust and shared peril. The air crackled with tension, the only sounds the muffled thuds of bodies in motion and the faint creak of the mansion's old wooden flooring.

Another shot from the assailants came like a thunderclap, shattering the crystal vase on the side table near Angela's head. She flinched as a glass fragment rained down, a sharp sting on her cheek telling her she hadn't entirely escaped. "Damn it!" she hissed, feeling warm blood trickle down her face.

The room erupted into a maelstrom of gunfire and splintering wood. Angela's training took over, her movements automatic as she returned fire. The Glock bucked in her hands, the acrid smell of cordite filling her nostrils. "Blake, I'm pinned down!" she shouted over the cacophony.

Across the room, Blake was a blur of motion, his own weapon barking in response to the threat. "I'll draw their fire!" he called back. "Be ready to move!"

Blake suddenly broke cover, firing rapidly as he sprinted across the room. The assassins' attention shifted, giving Angela the opening she needed.

One of the assassins, emboldened or desperate, broke cover in a bid to flank Angela. Time seemed to slow as she tracked his movement, her breath steady despite the hammering of her heart. "Not today, you bastard," she muttered, squeezing the trigger in rapid succession.

The shots echoed like cannon fire in the confined space. The assassin's momentum carried him forward even as the bullets found their mark in his face and neck, blood blossoming on his chest. He crashed to the floor in a spray of crimson, his weapon clattering across the polished hardwood.

"One down!" Angela called out.

Blake, seizing the moment of distraction, had circled behind the remaining assailant. His voice rang out, steady and authoritative: "Police! Drop your weapon, lie face down, and place your hands on your head. This is your only warning!"

The response was immediate and violent. The assassin whirled, his weapon spitting fire, hitting the wall beside Blake's head. He returned fire, striking the assailant in the chest and head. The assailant dropped heavily to the floor and lay motionless.

Angela and Blake checked the assailants' vital signs and shook their heads. They removed the Balaclava-style head coverings to examine their faces, and Blake checked their clothing for any signs of identity. He found none.

"God, Blake," Angela whispered, her voice muffled against his chest. "I thought . . . for a moment there . . . I thought I'd lost you."

Blake's arms tightened around her, his cheek resting on the top of her head. "I know," he murmured. "But we made it. We're okay. You were incredible, Angela. I've never seen shooting like."

"And you," Blake returned the embrace warmly and kissed her forehead.

"You're bleeding," Blake said softly, gently touching the cut on her cheek.

Angela winced slightly. "It's nothing. Just a small sliver of glass."

"I'm going to check outside to see if there's anyone else or a vehicle," Blake said.

"Be careful, Blake. I'll call the police and report this," Angela replied.

Blake returned shortly, indicating no sign of a vehicle or anyone else.

"Angela, this changes everything. They came for us in your home. This isn't just an investigation anymore. It's personal."

"I know," Angela replied, her voice tight. "We need to call this in, get forensics here. But Blake, who do we trust now? If they knew we were here?"

Blake's expression hardened. "We trust each other. And we find out who's behind this, no matter where it leads. Connor died trying to get us information. We owe it to him to see this through? Where's your closest first aid supplies?"

"Kitchen, top left-hand cabinet."

Blake returned with some antiseptic and a small band aid. Blake quickly cleaned up the surface wound in Angela's cheek, ensuring there were no remaining glass fragments.

"I don't think this will spoil your beautiful face," Blake said, brushing the hair off her forehead.

"Ha!" Angela retorted, thanking Blake for bringing some levity into the situation to relieve the tension.

Blake poured two small shooters of Scotch, which Angela took and placed on the coffee table. "First, we need this," she said, embracing Blake and holding him tight. "I'm a strong and resilient woman, but I must be honest with you, Blake, this whole affair is rattling me somewhat. I've never experienced the target criminals coming after me. They're usually figuring out ways to escape me."

Blake kissed Angela's hand. "You're right. Even the Triads we've investigated and convicted in Hong Kong reacted with evasion. It feels now like I'm being stalked. The big question in my mind is why. Who is targeting us, and why? We know these men were not ordinary thieves. They had a chance to steal some valuable things before we arrived."

Angela took a sip of her drink and handed Blake his. "That question ran through my mind as well, Blake. The likely suspects are the Mexican drug Cartel or the Hong Kong Triad. No one else makes any sense . . . unless it's the CIA that wants our investigations terminated, and God help us if it's them."

"Or it points to collusion among them. Getting rid of us as well as Senator Connor solves all their problems."

The doorbell alerted them that the police had arrived very quickly. Angela got up to open the door and let them in, along with a team of detectives and crime scene support personnel.

After identifying themselves, Angela and Blake spent most of the next hour answering police questions.

For the balance of the evening, Angela and Blake talked more about the attack on them and what steps to take next. Both felt a dark cloud descending, intent on finding the light, finding the right next moves. They both felt that the answers to their questions lay back in Hong Kong. Angela made arrangements for them to return as soon as possible.

"I forgot to mention to you. Just before we got here, I got a message that Raymond is holding a funeral service for Sabrina. I want to be there and would be honored if you could attend with me," Blake said sadly.

Angela embraced him. "Of course I'll be there with you."

Chapter 32

The Last Goodbye

The late summer sun cast long shadows across Chiu Yuen Cemetery, its golden rays a stark contrast to the somber mood that hung heavy in the air. Blake and Angela descended the winding path, the looming silhouette of Mount Davis above them seeming to mirror the weight of grief pressing down on Blake's shoulders. The delicate scent of bauhinias mingled with the salty tang of Victoria Harbor, creating a bittersweet perfume that seemed to mock the tragedy that had brought them here.

Blake's chest constricted with each step, a dull ache that had taken up residence since he'd heard the news of Sabrina's murder. His mind raced, cycling through memories of their shared childhood, their unbreakable bond forged in the crucible of Stanley Internment Camp, and the brilliant, compassionate woman she had become - now forever silenced. The loss felt like a physical wound, raw and bleeding.

Angela's voice, tinged with concern and a hint of suspicion, cut through his reverie. "Don't you find it unusual for the funeral to be held so soon?" Her hazel eyes, sharp and observant, searched Blake's face for a reaction, a silent promise of support in their depths.

Blake nodded, his jaw tightening as a flicker of suspicion ignited in his chest. "Raymond wants to move things along as soon as her will was read. And he never consulted me." The words came out clipped, barely concealing the storm of emotions brewing beneath his stoic exterior.

"He must have been shocked, let alone surprised I'm sure to find out that Sabrina had left her entire considerable estate to you and not him," Angela added.

"It was a shock to me as well," Blake admitted, his voice low. "But I wouldn't be surprised if he contests it."

Angela's hand found his, squeezing gently. "From what I know about estates, he'll fail. But if he does contest, ensure you get the best lawyer money can buy."

"After questioning Raymond about Sabrina's death," Blake said, his voice barely above a whisper, "I doubt we will be on friendly terms ever again," unwittingly forecasting the future.

Angela stopped, turning to face him fully. Her touch on his arm was gentle but firm, grounding him in the moment. "Blake," she said, her eyes filled with empathy and fierce protectiveness, "I've watched you hold yourself together, barricading your grief behind duty and resolve. I know how deeply you loved Sabrina and what her friendship meant to you." Her voice softened to a whisper with words meant for his ears alone. "And remember, I'm here. Whenever you need to let that wall down . . . I love you."

In that moment, Blake's carefully constructed defences faltered. He pulled Angela into an embrace that spoke volumes about their intimacy and the solace they had found in each other. As they parted from a tender kiss, a single tear escaped Blake's control, tracing a path down his weathered cheek. He quickly wiped it away, but not before Angela saw the raw emotion it represented.

As they approached the grave site, the atmosphere grew thick with tension. A small, somber assembly of mourners had gathered. Raymond Fung stood apart from them by himself.

When Blake approached, Raymond's handshake was perfunctory, his greeting minimal, bordering on rude. The coldness in his eyes fueled the Blake's growing suspicions.

Blake's grip was firm but devoid of warmth. "Sabrina's death is a great loss for both of us," he said, watching intently for any flicker of genuine emotion in Raymond's eyes. He found none.

Raymond's gaze dropped to the polished mahogany casket, lowered into the freshly dug earth. "The divorce was difficult enough, following on my father's death . . . and now this." His voice quivered slightly, but Blake couldn't shake the feeling that it was more performance than genuine grief. The lack of emotion in Raymond's words only deepened Blake's suspicions and intensified his own sorrow.

Choosing not to respond, Blake turned slightly. "Forgive my rudeness, I'd like to introduce Angela Torres from the US. She's been working with me on one of our cases."

Angela stepped forward, her eyes locking with Raymond's in a sympathetic and scrutinizing gaze. "I'm sorry for your loss, Mr. Fung," she said, her tone sincere despite the undercurrent of tension.

Thank you," Raymond replied, his mask of composure firmly back in place.

The funeral was stripped-down, devoid of the usual elaborate Chinese customs. Raymond had opted for simplicity—no priest, no traditional rites. Standing before a couple of mourners, he spoke briefly, his words echoing hollowly in the cemetery's hushed atmosphere. Blake was surprised that Raymond had not invited Sabrina's many friends and close business associates.

"Sabrina Fung was an incredibly beautiful and intelligent woman with a mind of her own. That's why I married her. She left an indelible mark on our family and Hong Kong, and she will be missed," Raymond said emotionless. With that, Raymond grabbed a handful of earth, letting it fall onto the casket with a soft patter.

The brevity of Raymond's words left an uncomfortable silence hanging in the air. Blake felt a surge of anger rising within him, barely contained beneath his professional exterior.

"Raymond," he said, his voice steady despite the emotion roiling beneath the surface. "do you mind if I say a few words?"

Raymond nodded. "If you must."

When Blake stepped forward to speak, his voice trembled with raw emotion. "I knew Sabrina since we were just children, two families imprisoned by the Japanese in Stanley Camp for four brutal years. She was like a sister to me, and we were inseparable for much of our lives." His voice cracked, a physical manifestation of the loss that threatened to overwhelm him. "Her courage, intelligence, strength, unfailing optimism and compassion for others were the hallmarks of her indomitable spirit. There will be a hole in my heart with her passing, and she will never be far from my thoughts."

Blake stepped away from the grave and rejoined Angela.

He felt Angela's hand slip into his. Her touch was a lifeline, anchoring him in the storm of his grief. Her eyes, when he met them, were filled with love and fierce protectiveness, silently promising that she would be his rock through this ordeal.

The other mourners quickly departed, only a few offering condolences to Raymond.

Blake regained his composure. He called Raymond to step over to join him. Blake's voice hardened as he turned back to Raymond, grief giving way to steely determination. "And one more thing, Raymond. I swear to you that I'll find out who killed her, and they will meet justice." The words hung in the air, a solemn vow and a thinly veiled challenge.

A flicker of something – alarm? Guilt? – passed across Raymond's face before he regained his icy composure. "Of course, Blake," he said, his voice dripping with false sincerity.

Blake took a deep breath as the other mourners began to disperse, offering final condolences. The time for grief was passing; the investigation would begin in earnest. He turned to Raymond, his demeanor shifting from mourner to detective in the blind of an eye.

"Raymond, Commissioner Blair has asked me to question anyone who had connections with Sabrina, including you."

Raymond's face darkened, his carefully maintained façade cracking to reveal a flash of anger and perhaps . . . fear? "You're not intimating that I might have something to do with her death?" he sneered, his rudeness now on full display.

"I'm saying I'm obligated to question you," Blake replied, his voice hard as steel. "I suggest we do it back at your home in familiar surroundings. And because it's an official proceeding, I've arranged for Angela to officially record our conversation."

Raymond's jaw tightened, but he nodded. "Fine, I'll see you back in my library at home."

As Raymond stormed away, Blake felt the full weight of the day crash down upon him. His shoulders sagged, and he let out a shuddering breath. In an instant, Angela was there, wrapping her arms around him, offering silent comfort and unwavering support.

"I thought you handled that well," she murmured, her voice a soothing balm to his raw emotions. "Especially your words about Sabrina. They touched my heart."

Blake leaned into her embrace, drawing strength from her presence. "There are so many emotions mixing right now," he admitted. "I need to be focused during my interrogation of Raymond."

"You will be," Angela assured him, her eyes blazing with determination and love. "I'll be right there with you every step of the way. We'll find the truth, Blake. For Sabrina."

Together, they made their way back to Blake's car, hands clasped tightly. The sun was setting over Victoria Harbor, painting the sky in hues of orange and purple. As they drove away from Chiu Yuen Cemetery towards Raymond Fung residence, Blake felt a mixture of grief, suspicion, and resolve settle over him. With Angela by his side, he was ready to face whatever challenges lay ahead in their pursuit of justice for Sabrina.

The mahogany double doors of Raymond Fung's library swung open with an ominous creak, revealing a sanctuary of old-world opulence that seemed to exist in defiance of the bustling modernity of Hong Kong beyond its walls. Blake hesitated for a fraction of a second before stepping over the threshold, the soles of his worn leather shoes sinking into the plush Oriental rug. At his side Angela moved with practiced ease, her sharp eyes taking in every detail of their lavish surroundings.

Angela, ever the professional, masked her curiosity and wariness behind a calm facade as she discreetly checked her recording device, ensuring it was ready for the interview.

The air hung heavy with the mingled scents of polished wood, aging paper, and something else—a cloying sweetness that Blake couldn't quite place. Sandalwood, perhaps? Or was it the lingering ghost of Sabrina's favorite perfume? The thought of his murdered friend sent a jolt of pain through Blake's chest, quickly followed by a surge of determination. He was here for her, to uncover the truth that Raymond Fung seemed so desperate to hide.

Raymond strode into the library with a brisk step. "Blake, Agent Torres," Raymond's voice was smooth as silk and just as slippery. "Please, make yourselves comfortable. Can I offer you a drink? Some of my father's prized scotch, perhaps?"

Blake shook his head, noting how Raymond's eyes hardened at the mention of his father. "No thank you. We're here on official business."

A flicker of something—annoyance? amusement? — passed over Raymond's face before it settled back into its mask of polite indifference. "Of course, of course. Though I must say, Blake, this cloak-and-dagger routine is growing rather tiresome. Surely by now you've realized I had nothing to do with my Sabrina's death?"

Blake settled into one of the armchairs, feeling the leather cool against his back. He kept his face carefully neutral as he replied, "Until we can identify who murdered Sabrina, we'll question whoever can help us find out, and that includes you."

At the mention of his ex-wife's name, Raymond's composure slipped for just a moment. His left eye twitched, and his hands, resting on the arms of his chair, clenched ever so slightly. Blake filed away the reaction, another piece in the puzzle he was slowly assembling.

"Before we begin," Raymond said, his voice tight, "I want to know if there's been any progress in finding my father's killers. It's been weeks, Blake. Weeks of silence and platitudes from the police."

Blake exchanged a quick glance with Angela, who had positioned herself slightly to the side, her stance relaxed but alert. "The investigation is ongoing, Raymond. These things take time."

"Time?" Raymond cut him off, his carefully cultivated accent slipping to reveal a harder edge. "While you and your incompetent colleagues waste time, the trail grows cold. There are other ways to get results, you know. More efficient ways."

"Raymond, don't go off and do something you'll regret later," Blake warned, the alarm clear as he caught Angela's eye. She blinked slowly, a silent show of agreement with Blake's caution, her own mind racing with the implications of Raymond's words.

Raymond shifted in his chair, seemingly agitated but resigned. "Alright, let's proceed with the interview," he conceded. Blake nodded to Angela, who clicked her recorder on, feeling the tension between the three of them intensify.

"September 15, 1987, 4 pm at Raymond Fung's residence. The interview officer is Inspector Blake Morgan. U.S. DEA Special Agent Angela Torres is recording the interview on a standard police recorder."

"Do you consent to this interview without your attorney present, Mr. Fung?" Blake asked, his voice steady but laced with an underlying tension.

Raymond nodded. "Yes, I do," he answered confidently, yet there was a flicker of uncertainty in his eyes.

"In what capacity are you familiar with the deceased, Sabrina Fung?"

"For the past three years, she has been my wife. We just finalized our divorce. Before we got married, we were acquainted for a couple of years." Raymond's voice was measured, but Blake detected a subtle crack, a hint of vulnerability that he quickly masked.

"And what was the reason for your divorce?" Blake watched Raymond carefully, noting how his fingers drummed a restless rhythm on the arm of his chair.

"Irreconcilable differences," Raymond said, his voice flat. "It's a common enough story, Inspector. Two people grow apart, realize they want different things from life. Surely even you can understand that?"

Blake let the condescension slide off him, focusing instead on the slight tremor in Raymond's left hand. "Did you or Sabrina initiate the divorce proceedings?"

A pause, just a heartbeat too long. "I did," Raymond admitted. "But Sabrina was agreeable to it. In the end, we both knew it was for the best."

"How would you describe your relationship with Sabrina during your marriage?"

Raymond looked surprised at the question, his mask slipping to reveal a flash of genuine emotion. "I believe we loved each other, at least at first. Sabrina was extraordinary. Brilliant, ambitious, beautiful. But we saw life differently. She was always pushing, always wanting more. She wasn't content to just be Mrs. Fung, my wife."

"It was my understanding talking to her work colleagues and business associates that she was an extremely thoughtful and successful business genius, but took her time and was strategic in her decisions. Besides, she inherited a massive fortune from her parents, and didn't need to keep pushing for more success. Or am I wrong about that?" Blake retorted.

"Well, we have different perspectives, Blake," Raymond replied.

"Were there any specific areas of conflict between you in recent times?" Blake pressed, sensing they were approaching something important.

Raymond's eyes hardened. "Sabrina's business ventures became all-consuming. I thought she was taking unnecessary risks, getting involved with people and operations that were . . . questionable. We argued about it, frequently."

Blake leaned forward, his instincts on high alert. "So, you're saying you had greater business insight than she did? What kind of risks are we talking about, Raymond? What kind of people?"

For a moment, it seemed Raymond might answer truthfully. But then the shutters came down, his face smoothing into an impassive mask. "I'm not privy to the details of Sabrina's business dealings, Inspector. Perhaps you should direct those questions to her associates."

Blake nodded, making a mental note to follow up on this lead. "Let's talk about the divorce settlement. What was the general outcome?"

Raymond's lips thinned. "Sabrina had a substantial estate. You must understand, Blake, Sabrina had substantially more wealth than I did when she married me. That must be apparent to you, given that she left you almost all her estate. And I'm putting you on notice, Blake, that I will be contesting Sabrina's will." Raymond's voice hardened, a clear attempt to assert control over the conversation.

Blake chose not to respond to Raymond's last comment. "And to your knowledge, have her businesses been successful?"

"Yes, very," Raymond answered curtly. "Sabrina had a talent for making money. And for making powerful friends."

"So, you're saying she didn't need your financial resources?"

"Yes."

"Did you in any way need hers?"

The question hung in the air between them, charged with implication. Raymond's face flushed with anger, his carefully maintained composure cracking. "What exactly are you implying, Blake? My father and I had more than adequate wealth to run our businesses. We didn't need anyone's help, least of all Sabrina's."

Blake held up a placating hand, even as his mind raced, filing away Raymond's reaction for later analysis. "I'm not implying anything, Raymond. I'm simply trying to establish the financial dynamics of your relationship with Sabrina. Now, did you involve her in any way in your businesses? Your shipping company, for example?"

Raymond paused for a moment as though he was searching for an answer. "No, she chose not to be involved in Fung businesses." Blake noticed the hesitation, the brief moment of uncertainty that slipped through Raymond's controlled exterior.

"And were you involved in any of your father's businesses?"

"He shared information about his various businesses, but I devoted my time to the Fung Shipping Company." Raymond's voice took on a defensive edge, his body language stiffening.

"But you knew everything he was involved in?"

"I said I did," Raymond snapped, his patience clearly wearing thin. "Is there a point to these questions, Inspector? Or are you simply fishing for something to justify your baseless suspicions?"

Blake paused, then stood. "If it's okay with you, Raymond, I need to take a bathroom break. Too much coffee this morning. We'll continue when I return." He exchanged a covert glance with Angela, but she did not turn off the recorder. Angela's mind was racing, piecing together the fragments of the conversation, sensing the tension between Blake and Raymond.

Raymond pointed at the door. "The bathroom is down the hall, second door." Blake left the room, his mind buzzing with suspicion and doubt, leaving Angela and Raymond alone in the library.

The air in Raymond Fung's opulent study crackled with tension, thick enough to cut with a knife. Raymond's eyes focused Angela, his fingers drumming an erratic rhythm on the polished mahogany desk. The ticking of an antique grandfather clock in the corner seemed to echo the mounting pressure in the room.

"How long have you and Blake been working together, Angela?" Raymond's attempt at casual conversation was betrayed by the slight tremor in his voice. Beads of sweat had begun to form on his upper lip, glistening in the warm light of the crystal chandelier overhead.

Angela leaned back in her chair, her posture relaxed but her eyes sharp as a hawk's. "About six months now," she replied, her tone deceptively light. "It's a pleasure to work with such an accomplished professional." The words hung in the air, laden with unspoken implications.

Raymond swallowed hard, his Adam's apple bobbing visibly. "And what's the focus of your investigations?" he pressed, desperation seeping into his voice.

Angela's lips curved into a smile. "I can't give you details, but it involves drug trafficking." She watched Raymond closely, noting how his left eye twitched at the word 'drug'.

"Here in Hong Kong, or in the U.S.?" Raymond's voice had risen an octave, his composure slipping further with each passing second.

"It involves drug trafficking," Angela repeated, her voice now carrying a razor's edge. She leaned forward, her gaze boring into Raymond. "Why are you so interested, Mr. Fung? Something on your mind?"

Raymond cleared his throat nervously. "I... just curious as a matter of interest, that's all."

The door opened with a soft click, and Blake strode back in. His face was a mask of professional detachment, but his eyes glinted with barely suppressed intensity. The room seemed to shrink as he took his seat, the weight of his presence palpable.

"Let's continue, Raymond," Blake said, his voice low and measured. "Can you describe the nature of your shipping business to me? What is a typical manifest?"

Raymond's hands trembled slightly as he reached for a glass of water. "Fung Shipping transports various products on our ships from here and from Shenzhen," he said, his words coming out in a rush.

Blake's eyes narrowed. "What bank does your shipping company do business with?"

"The Nugan-Hand Bank of Hong Kong," Raymond replied, a hint of pride creeping back into his voice. "It's an Australian bank with branches worldwide."

At this, Angela let out a slight cough. Her eyes met Blake's, a silent message passing between them. Blake's jaw tightened imperceptibly, but his voice remained steady.

"I'd like to return to Sabrina for a moment," he said, leaning forward. The mention of her name sent a visible shudder through Raymond. "Was she involved in any way in your shipping business?"

Raymond's response was too quick, too rehearsed. "No, as I said already, she had no involvement in any of our businesses."

Blake stretched out his hand to Angela, who took a document from her briefcase and handed it to Blake. The tension in the air thickened as Blake's eyes scanned the page, his expression unreadable.

"Could you explain this then, Raymond?" Blake's voice was soft, but it cut through the silence like a knife. He slid the document across the desk. "This is a copy of a document Sabrina gave me just before she was killed. She said she gave you the original and queried you on it."

Raymond's face showed strain as he stared at the paper.

Blake continued, his words measured and relentless. "The document shows Sabrina being involved in your shipping business, which she denies, and you have already said here that she had no involvement in any of your businesses. She told me that when she confronted you about the document, you denied having any knowledge of it but would follow up with your accountant to find out. What did you find out?"

"I checked with our accountant; he maintains it was a clerical error."

"The document was heavily redacted, without a clear description of the manifest. The document refers to chemicals. What chemicals?"

"As I said, I'm not familiar with the document so I'd have to look into it," Raymond replied nervously.

"Well, I expect an answer to that question in twenty-four hours," Blake demanded.

"The accountant is old and gets confused at times. I have been worried about the quality of his work, he might have made a mistake. But I said I'll look into it." Raymond's voice wavered slightly, the cracks in his facade becoming more apparent.

"I'm giving you notice now that we want to see your business records for the shipping company. I assume you'll provide them voluntarily? Also, if you'd provide me with a list, we will interview select employees in your shipping company."

"My shipping business is private, not public, and you'll have to provide me with either a warrant or a subpoena," Raymond said, his tone petulant, a hint of desperation creeping in.

Angela handed Blake a document, who handed it to Raymond. "Here's a court order for you to submit those documents that I referred to. Are you satisfied?" Blake snapped.

Raymond stared at the document, rage boiling up inside him.

"Well, I think we're done for now, Raymond. We may want to talk to you again, though." Blake paused. "The interview with Raymond Fung terminated on September 15, 5:30 p.m." Blake motioned to Angela to turn off the recorder.

"Just to advise you, Blake. If you plan to interview me again, my attorney will accompany me."

"That's your right, Raymond. To be honest, your responses to my questions were evasive. I feel like you haven't been forthcoming to me."

Blake and Angela got up and walked to the door. "We're done for now. You'll be hearing from us again shortly," Blake said curtly.

Chapter 33

The Ends Justify the Means?

Blake and Angela left the Fung mansion, got into Blake's car, and returned to the Peninsula Hotel. Back in Angela's hotel room, Blake stormed, slamming his service revolver on the table and then paced back and forth, his emotions roiling.

"I think Raymond is dirty. I know he's involved in some way in fentanyl trafficking. And there will be nowhere he can hide from me if he was involved in Sabrina's death." Blake's voice was filled with anger, the lines between personal and professional blurring.

"He certainly was evasive and took a real interest in our fentanyl investigations when he talked to me," Angela replied. "But capable of murder?" Her mind raced with the implications, weighing the evidence and the man she had just interviewed.

"I think he's been leading a double life. I'm jumping ahead here, but if my fears are substantiated, and there are grounds to charge Raymond for Sabrina's death and possibly drug trafficking, I have a fear he could evade conviction because several of the prominent judges are personal friends. If those fears were realized, I can't trust our legal system to bring Raymond to justice." Blake's frustration was palpable, the sense of betrayal cutting deep.

Angela held Blake's hands, trying to steady him. "I can tell you're worried. I'm sure Commissioner Blair would ensure an impartial and 'clean judge' is picked if Raymond is indicted."

"Angela, I'm conflicted. I've devoted my life to enforcing the law and holding those who break it, accountable. Sabrina's death has raised some doubts about my confidence in the justice system being able to do that once we do catch and charge the criminals. It has raised the question of 'does the ends justify the means?'"

"My heart goes out to you, Blake, for Sabrina's death; I'm sure it's affected you deeply," Angela said sympathetically.

"When is it justified to take the law into your own hands and deliver justice?"

"You are referring to physically assaulting a suspect or killing them? We need to ensure our actions are always justified. The line between right and wrong in our job is razor thin."

"Look, we're up against brutal people here. The Cartels don't think twice about taking lives. Neither do the Triads. Sometimes, there's no time to think about ethics or morality, only survival. And sometimes, it's them or us."

"But if we start justifying every time we pull the trigger as 'just doing our job,' we become like them. In the DEA, we aim to neutralize the threat, but killing is always the last resort. The stakes are high, and in the field, sometimes decisions have to be made in split seconds. However, I train my team to use force only when necessary. We must uphold the law, not become its violators."

"The use of force is a continuum and depends on the situation. I won't hesitate to fire if it means protecting innocent lives or my partner's. I want to bring them to justice, not act as judge, jury, and executioner . . . but . . . ."

"But what?"

"I understand that, Angela, but there is a large grey zone in Hong Kong, and the Triads and corrupt police have learned to navigate this zone with impunity. In an ideal world, the perpetrators of a crime, particularly murder, meet justice. The man we're investigating, a long-time friend turned powerful figure, might never face justice. He has connections that could tilt the scales in his favor."

"I get that. But isn't it critical that we stick to our principles of morality and ethics and honor our oath to uphold the law?"

"Principles might not be enough this time. I've seen how these Triad and white-collar criminals leverage their influence. Both politicians and judges can be bought, not to mention police officers."

"But I would argue, Blake, that your justification is more about revenge than justice."

"I want to ensure no one else must feel the pain that I feel over Sabrina's death. If bending or even breaking the rules can achieve that end, then maybe it's worth it. Maybe in this broken world, that's the only kind of justice we can hope for. Isn't the ultimate aim of the law to protect us? And if the law fails in that duty, should we not do what's necessary to protect ourselves and others? The philosopher Niccolò Machiavelli once said that the ends justify the means for those who want to achieve something. This isn't just about revenge but rectifying a grievous wrong when all lawful paths have led to dead ends. If I step outside the law, it's not out of disregard for it but of necessity forced upon me by its shortcomings."

"Blake, your arguments are inconsistent with the man I know, the man with integrity, honesty, a solid foundation of ethics and morality and who knows intuitively what is right. That's the man I fell in love with and who demonstrates all that is best with law enforcement. That man would not take the law into his own hands and take someone's life rationalizing it as the 'ends justify the means. And remember, the ends justify the means is the argument that the CIA uses to justify its corrupt actions."

Blake sighed deeply, looking down at his hands realizing they were clenched. He took a deep breath and relaxed them and calmed himself. The words of Marcus Aurelias came to his thoughts: "*The best revenge is to be unlike him who performed the injury.*" Blake took a deep breath. "This is why I need you in my life. I can't thank you enough for having the courage to confront me on my rationalization. Your arguments are the ones I've been having with myself, and having you articulate them so clearly has helped me decide. I can't take the law into my own hands and act out of revenge. If I do that, I will surely lose myself and violate my oath as a law enforcement officer and my belief in doing the right thing, even in the most trying of circumstances." Blake reached over and embraced Angela and kissed her softly. "Thank you."

Angela returned his embrace and kissed with equal fervor. "I just said what you already knew in your heart. I'll help you in any way I can to find Sabrina's killer, even if it's Raymond."

Chapter 34
Blackmail and Betrayal

The door to Jack Cross' office burst open with a thunderous bang, startling his secretary outside. Benjamin Cranston, the CIA's formidable Director of Covert Operations, stormed in like a category-five hurricane. His normally impeccable silver hair was disheveled, and his face was flushed a violent shade of crimson that clashed spectacularly with his navy power suit.

"You damn lunatic!" Cranston shrieked, spittle flying from his quivering lips. "Senator Connor? A hit? On American soil?" His voice cracked, a mixture of fury and barely concealed terror. "Have you lost what's left of your mind, Jack?"

Cross, a statue carved from glacial ice, didn't even flinch. His arctic blue eyes, devoid of warmth or mercy, locked onto Cranston's unraveling form. A predatory smirk tugged at the corner of his mouth as he reclined in his chair, the leather creaking ominously in the charged silence.

"Ben, my old friend," Cross drawled, his voice dripping with condescension. "Accidents happen every day. Brake lines fail. It's tragic, really." His eyes glittered with malicious amusement. "But I won't shed a tear for that pinko-loving traitor. One less obstacle in our crusade to keep America pure and strong."

Cranston's legs wobbled, and he collapsed into a chair, his bravado evaporating like mist in the desert sun. "Come on, Jack," he whimpered. "The timing . . . Connor's committee . . . your Mexican mess . . . ."

Cross leaned forward, his grin now a shark's maw full of razors. "Impeccable timing, wasn't it?" he purred. "That meddling bastard and his bleeding-heart committee are worm food. Our allies will bury any real investigation deeper than Jimmy Hoffa. We'll weather a strongly worded memo, make a few empty promises, and continue our sacred duty." His voice dropped to a fanatical whisper. "The Reds are at the gates, Ben. Mexico is the first domino. We stop them there, or we'll be speaking Russian in Washington in a couple of years."

Cranston's shoulders slumped in defeat. "The National Security Council wants answers, Jack. Real ones."

Cross' eyes flashed with contempt. "Then feed them the pablum they crave, you spineless worm. Paint them a picture of communist guerrillas swarming across the Rio Grande, ready to plant the hammer and sickle on the White House lawn. Make them piss their pants at the thought of losing their precious positions to the Red Menace."

Cross leaned forward, his expression suddenly earnest. "Then let me help you give them some courage, Ben. I'll personally assure them our work in Mexico is vital to national security. After all, they wouldn't want to be caught with their pants down if those pesky communists gain a foothold, would they? Nothing motivates politicians quite like the threat of losing their cushy positions."

A heavy sigh escaped Cranston's lips, his shoulders sagging under an invisible weight. "I'm not convinced the communist threat in Mexico is as dire as you claim, Jack. Certainly not enough to justify our entanglements with the Cartels."

Cross' eyes narrowed dangerously. "Are you suggesting we abort the operation, Ben?"

"I'm saying we need to pause, reassess. I need to speak with my boss."

"I'd be more than happy to join that meeting," Cross interjected, a note of steel creeping into his voice.

"That won't be necessary," Cranston snapped.

Cross' expression hardened. "I had hoped to avoid this, old friend," he murmured, reaching into his desk drawer. Cross withdrew a thick manila envelope, sliding out a series of glossy photographs like a grim tarot reading. Cranston's face drained of all color, his eyes bulging in abject horror.

"I'm sure your wife wouldn't like to see these!"

"How did you ... you bastard," he whispered. "You've been spying on me?"

"I protect America by any means necessary," Cross growled, his voice thick with jingoistic fervor. "Even from weak-kneed traitors like you, Ben. There are no lines I won't cross, no depths I won't plumb to keep our nation safe and pure."

He slid the damning evidence back into the envelope, holding it out to Cranston like a poisoned chalice. "These are copies, of course."

Cranston snatched the envelope, his hand trembling almost imperceptibly. "You'll get your operation," he hissed through clenched teeth. "But mark my words, Jack – what goes around, comes around."

For the briefest moment, surprise flickered across Cross' face at Cranston's uncharacteristic vehemence. Then his mask of smug confidence slipped back into place. "My, my, Ben," he chuckled. "Where has this lion been hiding all these years? Do let me know if you'd like me to chat with the Director after all."

Cranston spun on his heel and stormed out, the door slamming behind him with enough force to rattle the framed CIA seal on the wall.

Cross leaned back, a self-satisfied smirk playing on his lips. He steepled his fingers, lost in thought. "*Well played, Jack,*" he mused to himself. "*Ben's far too smart to risk his family and reputation now. Still, loose ends have a nasty habit of unraveling. Time to tie things up nice and tight.*"

As Cranston fled, Cross reached for his secure line, a fanatical gleam in his eye. "Time to remind everyone what real patriotism looks like," he muttered. "For God and country . . . no matter the cost."

Chapter 35

Showdown in the Walled City

Blake stared out the window at the rain-soaked streets of Hong Kong. Tropical downpours were common, and tonight was no exception. Dennis Wang, his colleague, was driving their unmarked police car.

"Great work getting a witness on the Simon Chang and Samuel Fung assassinations," Blake said. "You sure he'll be here tonight?"

Dennis nodded. "Absolutely. He's a foot soldier for the Min Ho Triad. He was freelancing protection services for shopkeepers, and his beating of one shopkeeper who wouldn't pay ended in the shopkeeper's death. Inspector Smith said he'd probably be picked up tomorrow and charged. But he's willing to blow the whistle on the Chan and Fung murders in exchange for a reduced sentence."

"It's about time we caught a break," Blake replied, glancing out the window.

As they drove on, the bustling market gave way to shabby tenements and seedy bars. Pimps and toughs dealt "red chicken" heroin packed into yellow plastic straws. Street dealers expertly shot the straws into waiting hands in second and third-story windows. Anything could be bought here: drugs, prostitutes, even assassins. No questions asked.

They arrived at The Hot Whispers Bar-Disco, a popular two-level hangout for *gwai los* and Chinese businessmen. Dennis parked directly in front.

Blake and Dennis approached the entrance of The Hot Whispers Bar-Disco, where a hulking redhead with a vibrant tiger tattoo snaking down his arm stood guard. His pale skin, flushed from the humidity, marked him as one of the countless Western expats drawn to Hong Kong's intoxicating blend of opportunity and vice.

"Evening, gents," the bouncer drawled in a thick Australian accent, eyeing them suspiciously. Blake flashed his police ID, noting how the man's demeanor shifted instantly from confrontational to cooperative. It was a dance Blake had seen countless times – expats caught between their new lives in Hong Kong and the ingrained respect for law enforcement from their home countries.

Inside, the club was a sensory assault. The bass-driven disco music vibrated through the floor, rattling Blake's teeth and thrummed in his chest. Flashing strobe lights bounced off the shiny black bar, creating a dizzying kaleidoscope effect. Giant video screens flanking the dance floor displayed a mix of Western and Cantopop music videos, a visual representation of the cultural melting pot that was Hong Kong after dark.

As they made their way to the bar, Blake's gaze swept across the room. The crowd was a stark illustration of Hong Kong's expat scene – middle-aged Western businessmen in rumpled suits mingled with young English teachers still in their work attire, their faces flushed with alcohol and the excitement of being far from home, groups of Chinese businessmen looking for some stimulation before they head home.

At the bar's curve, Blake and Dennis found seats that offered a clear view of the room. A group of boisterous American businessmen occupied nearby stools, their loud laughter and exaggerated gestures betraying their inebriation. To their left, a cluster of exchange students, barely old enough to be in such an establishment, giggled nervously as they sipped colorful cocktails.

"Bloody hell, mate! Another round!" one of the Aussies bellowed, slapping the bar top with enthusiasm. The Chinese bartender nodded with a practiced smile, used to the antics of overexcited *gwailos*.

Blake ordered a scotch, neat, holding up two fingers to indicate drinks for both him and Dennis. As they waited, he observed a silver-haired British expatriate in an impeccably tailored suit being fawned over by two young Chinese women in cheongsams. The man's wedding ring glinted in the pulsing lights as he draped his arms around their shoulders, his laugh a little too loud, his smile a little too wide.

Blake scanned the bar. Middle-aged men in rumpled suits clung to the bar, while teenage hostesses slung their arms around them, cooing into their ears and massaging their necks. This would be an expensive night for some, Blake thought, but they'd boast of their conquests in the morning, real or imagined.

The thrum of the music faded to a dull roar as Dennis leaned in close, his eyes darting towards the entrance. Blake followed his partner's gaze, tension coiling in his gut as he spotted a young man in an athletic jacket and jeans slipping through the crowd. The newcomer's eyes flicked nervously around the room, his shoulders hunched as if expecting a blow.

"That's him," Dennis murmured." He motioned for the young man to join them. The man walked over, clearly anxious and nervous.

As the informant approached, Blake could almost taste the fear rolling off him in waves. Sweat beaded on the young man's forehead, glistening under the pulsating lights of the club.

"This is Wing Chun," Dennis said, his voice low and measured. "Wing, this is Inspector Blake Morgan."

Blake locked eyes with Chun, noting the slight tremor in the young man's hands as they exchanged nods. The air between them crackled with unspoken tension.

Dennis leaned forward, his voice barely audible above the thumping bass. "As I told you, in exchange for the information you give us about the Simon Chan and Samuel Fung murders, the police will consider offering you a plea deal regarding the charges you're facing." His words were carefully chosen, each one heavy with implications. "Prosecutors may reduce your charge to manslaughter, reducing your sentence from life imprisonment to five to ten years. It all depends on the reliability of your information. Understood?"

Blake's eyes never left Chun's face, searching for any flicker of deception. The young man's Adam's apple bobbed as he swallowed hard.

"Yes, I understand," Chun replied, his voice cracking slightly. He shifted in his seat, the leather creaking beneath him.

Dennis continued, his tone becoming more formal. "And do you give this information voluntarily without coercion, and are you willing to repeat it in a sworn written statement at police headquarters and on the witness stand in court?"

Chun's nod was almost imperceptible. "Yes," he whispered, the word hanging in the air between them.

Blake leaned in, his voice low and intense. "So, tell us what you know, and we will ask you questions."

As Chun began to speak, his words came out haltingly, each one seemingly dragged from the depths of his being. "The Min Ho Triad is in competition with Simon Chan's Triad, the Wo Chin Sing. They've attacked each other to control Hong Kong's drug trafficking. The Min Ho made the hit on Chan to send a message that they're taking over."

The air grew thick with tension as Blake and Dennis exchanged glances. Blake's next question cut through the atmosphere like a knife. "Who in Min Ho performed the assassination of Chan and got away?"

"Daniel Chow," Yang replied, his eyes darting between the two detectives.

"Who in Min Ho ordered Chow to do it?"

"The Dragon Head, Robert Lee."

"Did Robert Lee also order the hit on Samuel Fung?"

"Yes."

"Why was Fung killed?"

"Samuel was the Dragon Master for Min Ho for many years, and still was very powerful. He spoke out against Robert Lee's leadership, something that Lee would not tolerate."

"Other than your word, is there any other proof for your claim?"

"Robert Lee recorded all Triad activities in a journal he keeps."

"Who else has knowledge of and access to this journal?"

"The White Paper Fan. The financial and administrative officer."

"Who is that?"

"Raymond Fung."

When Yang dropped the bombshell about Raymond Fung, Blake's reaction was visceral. He half-rose from his seat, his voice a harsh whisper. "What? Raymond Fung? White Paper Fan!" The shock was palpable, crackling in the air between them. "Are you saying he approved of the hit on his father?"

Chun's response came out in a rush, words tumbling over each other. "He didn't know anything about it until it was done. Since then, Raymond Fung and Robert Lee have had a blood feud. I think Raymond plans to challenge Robert Lee to be the Dragon Head."

Blake turned to Dennis, their eyes meeting in a moment of shared disbelief. The implications of this revelation hung heavy in the air, threatening to upend their entire understanding of the case.

Blake paused and looked at Dennis Wang whose eyes were wide open at this point.

"Do you know anything about Sabrina Fung's murder?" Blake continued.

"No," Chun replied.

"Do you know where we can find this assassin who killed Fung?"

"He lives in the Walled City."

Dennis slid over a piece of paper and pen. "Write it down."

"Jimmy Sui," Dennis said, reading the scribble on the paper.

"What about Daniel Chow. Where does he live?" Blake continued.

"He left Hong Kong and has gone to Macau."

Blake motioned to Dennis to step away from the table for a moment. "I want you to take Yang to HQ and book him for official interrogation," Blake muttered, his words clipped and urgent. "I don't want him running around free after our chat, and frankly, I don't trust David Smith to handle it. I'm going into the Walled City to find our assassin."

"Why don't you wait for backup," Dennis asked.

"I want to move on this right away. I'll call if I need help," Blake replied.

They stepped back to the table.

"Wing, Detective Wang will be taking you to police HQ so you can make a written statement about everything you told us, and you'll be temporarily held in protective custody for your protection," Blake said.

"And you'll keep your end of the bargain?" Chun asked.

"Yes, that's the least of your worries."

"Dennis, I'm close to the Walled City, I'll walk over. Call in for a car to pick you up, and leave your car for me."

"Alright," Dennis replied. He stood up and motioned to Chun to follow him out of the bar.

Blake ordered another Scotch and reflected on what just happened. He could understand the warring Triads over turf and control. Still, he was hit like a sledgehammer about Chun's incrimination of Raymond Fung. Blake's uneasy feelings about Raymond were becoming more concrete. It was clear to him now that Raymond was deeply embedded in a criminal Triad. A possible suspicion about Raymond's involvement in Sabrina's murder was now becoming a probable suspicion.

He took another sip of his Scotch, his thoughts still rolling in his head. "Now Raymond's involvement in the fentanyl drug trafficking makes more sense. But that leaves Sabrina's murder still a big question mark. But it's a question I'll not give up finding the answer to. In the meantime, it's time to bring things to a head."

Blake walked over to the phone booth in the corner and called Angela. "Dennis and I just met with an informer who has blown open the Chan and Fung murders. Dennis has taken the informer in because he's facing other charges but will be a star witness. I'm heading over to the Walled City to arrest the accused Min Ho Triad assassin. I'll check in with you from police HQ shortly. How are you doing?"

"Blake, please be careful," Angela said, " I know you've got to go. Come back safe!"

"I will, I promise," Blake replied confidently."

Chapter 36

Into the Jungle

Blake stood at the threshold of Kowloon's Walled City, his heart pounding a staccato rhythm against his ribs. The neon glow of Hong Kong's streets faded behind him, replaced by an oppressive darkness that seemed to pulse with malevolent life. He took a deep breath, steeling himself for what lay ahead, the weight of his service revolver a cold comfort against his hip.

As he stepped into the maw of this urban anomaly, Blake felt as if he were being swallowed whole by a colossal, living organism. The Walled City loomed before him, a chaotic jumble of buildings stacked haphazardly upon one another, defying gravity and sanity in equal measure. Fourteen-story towers leaned precariously, their walls meeting at impossible angles, creating a nightmarish geometry that seemed to warp the very fabric of reality.

The transition was jarring, like passing through a portal into a world where a madman had shredded and reassembled the rules of civilized society. The air hit Blake like a physical force – thick, fetid, and alive with a thousand intermingling scents. The stench of rotting garbage mingled with the acrid bite of industrial chemicals, overlaid with the greasy aroma of frying food and the sickly-sweet undertones of opium smoke. Each breath felt like a assault on his lungs, and Blake fought the urge to gag.

Dim, flickering fluorescent lights cast an eerie, jaundiced glow over the cramped corridors, creating a disorienting dance of shadows that seemed to move with a life of their own. The illumination was barely enough to navigate by, and Blake found his other senses heightening to compensate. His ears strained to catch every sound, from the constant drip of leaking pipes to the scurrying of rats in the darkness.

Blake's boots squelched on the grimy floor as he ventured deeper into the labyrinth, a treacherous film of leaked water, grease, and unidentifiable substances making each step a potential hazard. The walkways were narrow, forcing him to turn sideways at times to squeeze through, his back scraping against rough concrete walls slick with moisture and grime.

Above him, the sky was a distant memory, obscured by a dense canopy of rusting pipes, tangled electrical wires, and makeshift bridges. These precarious connections formed a web between the buildings, a twisted nervous system for this concrete behemoth. Water dripped constantly from this metallic foliage, a perverse imitation of rain in this man-made jungle, each drop a reminder of the decay that permeated every inch of the Walled City.

Blake's senses were assaulted at every turn as he navigated the warren-like passages. The click-clack of mahjong tiles mixed with the wail of a hungry infant and the rhythmic chopping of butchers' cleavers. In the distance, he could hear the metallic clanging of illegal factories, their machines running day and night in defiance of any labor laws. The acrid stench of chemicals from these clandestine operations mingled with the pungent aroma of traditional medicine shops, creating an olfactory cocktail that made his head spin.

He passed by unlicensed dentists operating in full view, their patients' screams blending seamlessly into the cacophony of the city. The sight of rusty dental tools and blood-spattered aprons made Blake's stomach churn. Food stalls lined the narrow alleys, their woks sizzling with a variety of meats – some recognizable, others disturbingly alien. The sweet scent of roasted chestnuts clashed with the gamey odor of hanging animal carcasses.

As he delved deeper into the heart of the Walled City, Blake felt a growing sense of unease, a primal fear clawing at the edges of his consciousness. Here, in these shadowy depths, the true nature of this urban nightmare revealed itself. Glassy-eyed addicts huddled in corners, their emaciated bodies contorted in poses of desperate ecstasy as they chased their next high. The constant clicks of lighters and the acrid smell of burning heroin hung in the air like a toxic fog.

Underage prostitutes, their faces a mask of premature world-weariness, beckoned from shadowy doorways. Their hollow eyes and forced smiles sent a chill down Blake's spine, a stark reminder of the human cost of this lawless enclave. He averted his gaze, guilt and anger warring within him at his inability to help these lost souls.

A system of self-governance, held together by the watchful regulation of the Triads, was the rule of law in the Walled City. Not answering to one body of authority, everyone played a role in keeping the community in check. There were no taxes, no regulation of businesses or production, no public health care, and no centralized planning system.

As Blake was keenly aware, the police presence was rare, making it easy for open habits of drugs, prostitution and criminal activity. Many convicts on the run found an escape by slithering their way behind the concrete dungeon of the Walled City to avoid the metal bars of jail time.

This was an urban wilderness beyond the reach of the law. The Triads became the city's de-facto enforcers and rulers, running a protection racket, illegal businesses, and the drug trade. Beginning in the 1950s, Triad groups such as the 14K and Sun Yee On gained a stranglehold on the walled city's numerous brothels, gaming parlors, and opium dens.

Blake learned early on the force that the police would rarely enter the city. This was an anarchist society, self-regulating and self-determining. It was a colony within a colony, a city within a city, a tiny block of territory the locals called *"Hak Nam"* — the City of Darkness.

Blake's target, the assassin Jimmy Tsui, supposedly resided on the fourth floor of a particularly decrepit building. As he approached the structure, Blake's trained eye took in the details. The building seemed to sway slightly in the stagnant air, its foundation eroded by years of neglect and the constant seepage of water and waste. Makeshift iron balconies clung precariously to the exterior, laden with drying laundry and improvised gardens in rusting tin cans.

The stairwell was a twisted path of broken concrete and exposed rebar, each step a potential deathtrap. As Blake climbed, the melancholic strains of a Cantonese opera filtered through the paper-thin walls, an incongruous soundtrack to his grim mission. The sorrowful melody seemed to echo the despair that permeated the very air of the Walled City.

With each floor he ascended, Blake felt the weight of isolation pressing down on him. In this vertical shantytown, he was cut off from backup, from the rule of law, from everything he knew and trusted. The familiar comfort of his police badge seemed laughably inadequate in the face of the Walled City's entrenched anarchy.

Outside Tsui's door, Blake paused, his heart thundering in his ears. Muffled voices seeped through the thin wood, speaking in rapid-fire Cantonese. His palms were slick with sweat as he gripped his service revolver, the metal warm against his skin. In this moment, poised on the brink of action, Blake felt a curious mix of fear and exhilaration. He was an intruder in this world, a representative of a law that held no sway here, about to confront a killer on his home turf.

Drawing a deep breath, tasting the city's miasma on his tongue, Blake made his decision. In one fluid motion, he kicked the flimsy door open, the crash echoing through the Walled City's twisted corridors like a gunshot.

The splintered door exploded inward with a resounding crack, showering the room with splinters and decades of accumulated grime. Blake surged through the opening, his senses on high alert, nostrils flaring at the assault of odors – stale sweat, rancid cooking oil, and the metallic tang of fear.

"Police officer!" Blake's voice boomed, filling the cramped space. "Don't move! Hands up over your head!"

The room swam into focus, illuminated by a single bare bulb swinging lazily from a frayed wire. Its sickly yellow light cast grotesque, elongated shadows across walls adorned with peeling posters – faded advertisements for cigarettes and girlie bars. In the corner, a battered TV flickered, bathing the room in an eerie, electric-blue glow. The floor was a minefield of discarded takeout containers and empty beer bottles, crunching underfoot with each step.

Jimmy Tsui, a wiry man with the sharp, hungry features of a cornered rat, sprang to his feet. His eyes, wide with panic, darted to a gun lying on a rickety table, its scratched metal surface gleaming dully in the dim light.

Time seemed to stretch like taffy. Blake felt his heart hammering against his ribs, each beat reverberating through his body. Adrenaline surged through his veins, sharpening his senses to a razor's edge. The acrid taste of fear coated his tongue, mixing with the metallic flavor of the city's polluted air. Every nerve ending screamed danger, his body coiled tight as a spring, ready to explode into action.

In that split second, Blake saw Tsui's muscles tense, tendons standing out like cords in his neck. The assassin's nostrils flared, reminding Blake of a bull about to charge. Time snapped back into normal speed as Tsui launched himself forward with the desperate fury of a trapped animal.

Tsui's arm whipped around in a vicious roundhouse, aimed squarely at Blake's temple. The air whistled as the fist cut through it, and Blake could smell the rank odor of stale cigarettes on Tsui's breath. Blake's training kicked in, his body moving on pure instinct honed by countless hours of practice. He ducked, feeling the whoosh of Tsui's fist grazing his hair, close enough to ruffle it.

As Tsui's momentum carried him forward, Blake pivoted on the ball of his foot, the floorboards creaking in protest beneath him. He drove a precise, devastating strike into the assassin's kidney. The impact sent shockwaves up Blake's arm, the solid connection oddly satisfying. Tsui's grunt of pain was guttural and raw, music to Blake's ears. But there was no time to savor the small victory.

The fight devolved into a chaotic dance of survival, a brutal ballet performed in a space barely larger than a closet. Every piece of ramshackle furniture became both obstacle and weapon. Blake's foot caught on a frayed rug, sending him stumbling. He caught himself on a rickety chair, which collapsed under his weight, splintering into makeshift weapons.

Tsui, recovering quickly, snatched a rusted pipe from a pile of debris. The metal was rough and pitted, flakes of rust coming off on his hands as he gripped it. He swung the improvised weapon in a wide arc, aiming for Blake's head.

Blake dove to the side, feeling the displacement of air as the pipe whistled past his ear. The near miss sent a jolt of electric fear down his spine, the cool kiss of mortality sharpening his focus to a laser point. As Tsui wound up for another swing, Blake saw his opening.

With fluid grace born from years of rigorous training, Blake stepped inside Tsui's guard. His hands moved in a blur, executing a textbook arm-bar. He grabbed Tsui's wrist with both hands, one at the base of the hand, the other at the elbow. In one smooth motion, he hyperextended the joint, applying pressure against the natural bend of the elbow.

Tsui's wrist twisted at an unnatural angle, tendons straining against skin. The pipe clattered to the floor, the metallic ring echoing in the small space. The assassin's howl of pain was primal and raw, cut short as Blake drove his knee into Tsui's solar plexus with a meaty thud.

But Tsui wasn't finished. As he doubled over, gasping for breath, his hand darted to his waistband. Blake's eyes widened as he saw the glint of a blade, the light catching its edge as it sliced through the air.

Time seemed to stretch again, each moment crystalline in its clarity. Blake could see every detail – the sheen of sweat on Tsui's face, the wild desperation in his eyes, the way the knife's blade reflected the room in its polished surface. He could hear his own heartbeat, loud in his ears, and smell the sharp tang of their mingled sweat and fear.

Blake's body moved on pure reflex, muscle memory taking over where conscious thought faltered. He spun, his hand shooting out to catch Tsui's wrist mid-thrust. The knife's edge gleamed inches from his face, so close he could see his own wide-eyed reflection in the steel. Tsui's manic eyes bore into him, filled with a mixture of hatred and terror. For a heartbeat, they were locked in a deadly embrace, a tableau of violence frozen in time.

Then Blake twisted, hard. Bone ground against bone, the sickening sound audible even over their ragged breathing. Tsui's fingers spasmed open, tendons standing out like cords. The knife fell, embedding itself with a solid *thunk* in the rotting floorboards, quivering from the impact.

Blake didn't hesitate. His elbow smashed into Tsui's nose with a sickening crunch, cartilage giving way under the force of the blow. Hot blood sprayed, spattering Blake's shirt and adding to the room's already pungent odors. He followed up with a devastating palm strike to the assassin's temple, the impact reverberating up his arm.

Tsui crumpled like a marionette with cut strings, sprawling across the grimy floor. Blood and saliva bubbled from his lips as he gasped for air, each breath a wet, rattling sound. His eyes rolled wildly, unfocused and glassy.

Blake stood over him, chest heaving, every muscle quivering with residual adrenaline. The room spun slightly, the aftermath of combat leaving him light-headed and nauseous. He tasted copper in his mouth and realized he'd bitten his cheek during the scuffle. His knuckles stung, skin split and bleeding from the force of his blows.

"Police," Blake panted, fumbling for his handcuffs. The metal felt cool against his overheated skin as he pulled them free. "Stay down. Jimmy Tsui, you're under arrest for the murders of Samuel Fung and Simon Chan." The words came automatically, drilled into him by years on the force. "You have the right to remain silent. Anything you say can and will be used against you in a court of law."

Tsui's laugh was a wet, gurgling sound that made Blake's skin crawl. He spat a glob of blood and saliva onto the floor, the red stark against the grimy linoleum. His eyes, though unfocused, still gleamed with defiance. "I don't know what you're talking about," he slurred, blood bubbling at the corners of his mouth. "I didn't kill anyone."

Blake felt a complex surge of emotions – disgust at Tsui's actions, pity for his current state, and a grim satisfaction at having brought him down. He hauled Tsui to his feet, noting how small and pathetic the killer looked now, broken and bleeding. "Save it for the judge and jury, Jimmy," Blake muttered, securing the cuffs with perhaps more force than necessary. The metal bit into Tsui's wrists, eliciting a hiss of pain.

As Blake half-dragged Tsui through the labyrinthine corridors of the Walled City, he felt the weight of every eye upon them. The residents, ghost-like figures in the shadows, watched in eerie silence. Children peeked out from behind their mothers' skirts, eyes wide with a mixture of fear and fascination. Old men playing mahjong paused their game, the click of tiles giving way to hushed whispers.

The narrow passageways seemed to close in around them, the damp walls almost pulsing with hidden life. The constant drip of water from rusted pipes provided a steady backdrop to their labored breathing. Rats scurried away from their approach, disappearing into cracks and crevices with alarming speed.

Blake's skin crawled with the sensation of being watched, judged, marked. In this lawless enclave, he was the intruder, dragging one of their own away. The hostility was palpable, hanging in the air like a physical presence.

By the time they reached Dennis' police car, parked at the edge of the Walled City, Blake was drenched in sweat, his shirt clinging to his back like a second skin. The night air, though thick with pollution, felt blessedly cool after the stifling confines of the urban labyrinth. He sucked in deep breaths, trying to clear the stench of the Walled City from his lungs.

He handcuffed Tsui to the security bar in the backseat, noting with grim satisfaction the assassin's subdued demeanor. Tsui slumped against the seat, all fight gone out of him, looking small and broken in the harsh light of the streetlamps.

As Blake slid behind the wheel, a wave of exhaustion washed over him. The adrenaline crash hit hard, leaving him feeling hollow and slightly shaky. His hands trembled as he gripped the steering wheel, knuckles white with the effort of maintaining control. Every muscle ached, the exertion of the fight making itself known now that the danger had passed.

But underneath the fatigue, a small spark of triumph glowed. He'd walked into the belly of the beast – the infamous Walled City – and emerged victorious, with a key player in custody. It was a significant step forward in the case, one that could potentially break it wide open.

The engine roared to life, the vibrations traveling up through the seat and into Blake's battered body. He pointed the car towards police HQ, eager to get Tsui into a cell and start the formal interrogation process. As the Walled City receded in the rearview mirror, its towering, chaotic silhouette slowly swallowed by the night, Blake allowed himself a small, grim smile.

One more piece of the puzzle was in place. But he knew, deep in his bones, that this was just the beginning of a much larger, more dangerous game. The real challenge lay ahead – unraveling the web of corruption and violence that had led to this moment. As he drove through the neon-lit streets of Hong Kong, Blake steeled himself for the battles to come.

Chapter 37

A Deadly Choice

The night hung heavy over Hong Kong, an oppressive blanket that seemed to muffle all sound save for Inspector David Smith's ragged breathing as he approached the Fung mansion. The sprawling estate loomed before him, a monolithic testament to wealth and power that seemed to devour the scant moonlight. David's shoes crunched on the gravel driveway, each step feeling like another nail in his own coffin.

As the wrought iron gates creaked open, their ominous groan setting David's teeth on edge, he couldn't help but reflect on the choices that had led him to this moment. There was no noble cause, no greater good that had driven him down this path of corruption. It had started small – a overlooked infraction here, a conveniently misplaced piece of evidence there. Each compromise had seemed so inconsequential at the time, each bribe a harmless boost to his modest police salary. But now, years later, David found himself drowning in a sea of his own making, with no shore in sight.

The mansion's façade loomed over him, its windows dark and accusing. David tugged at his collar, feeling the weight of his service weapon against his side – a reminder of the oath he had long since betrayed. The manicured gardens, usually a point of pride, now seemed like a mockery of order in David's chaotic world.

Raymond Fung opened the door himself, his tailored suit a stark contrast to the turmoil in David's mind. Raymond's eyes, cold and calculating, swept over David's disheveled appearance. "Inspector," he said, his voice smooth as silk hiding steel. "Do come in."

As they ascended the grand staircase, their footsteps echoing off the marble, David felt each step like a physical blow. The opulence surrounding him – the gleaming banisters, the priceless artworks adorning the walls – only served to remind him of the world he had sold his soul to join, and how far he still was from truly belonging.

The air in Raymond's office, now cleaned and cleared from his father's murder, was heavy with the scent of aged wood, expensive cigars, and the cloying stench of David's own fear. The massive rosewood and jade desk dominated the room, a physical manifestation of the power imbalance between them. David's eyes were drawn to the portrait of Samuel Fung above the ornamental fireplace, the elder Fung's stern gaze a silent accusation.

As David sank into the leather chair across from Raymond, he felt the last vestiges of his self-respect crumble away. He was no longer an officer of the law, but a pawn in a game far beyond his control. Raymond, in contrast, exuded confidence, lounging in his seat like a predator toying with its prey.

"What's the status of your investigations?" Raymond's question cut through the silence like a knife.

David's mind raced, searching for the right words to appease his master. He could feel sweat forming on his brow as he delivered the news about Jimmy Tsui's arrest, each word tasting like ash in his mouth. "Blake Morgan received an informant's tip. They identified one of Min Ho's foot soldiers, Jimmy Tsui, in the Walled City, as the killer of Simon Chan. And he said Lee ordered the hit on Fung for challenging his authority. Tsui is in custody now."

Raymond's fist slammed down on the desk with a resounding crack, causing a nearby crystal decanter to rattle. "David, you were supposed to control the investigation and arrange to plant and eliminate a suspect of your choice who meets an accident, someone who has no connection to the Min Ho Triad. Why is Blake running around free to interfere with your investigation?"

David swallowed hard, feeling the sweat trickle down his back. "Blake managed to get Commissioner Blair's approval to conduct his investigation, and we were supposed to collaborate. He acted on his own without my knowledge."

"It sounds like Blake doesn't trust you," Raymond sneered. "Tsui is a good foot soldier, but I don't know what he'll do under interrogation. He's sworn an oath of obedience and secrecy upon death by the Min Ho, but facing life imprisonment or the death penalty can change a man."

David's mind raced, trying to find a solution to appease Raymond. "There's not much I can do now. He's in custody. I'd have to arrange to be the only one interrogating him, with no witnesses, and figure out how to release him. That's not going to be easy."

Raymond's eyes narrowed, his voice a deadly whisper. "What's your alternative, David? Have you forgotten about our arrangement? You provide me and the Min Ho with protection, and in return, I've been putting a substantial amount of money in your overseas bank account. Are you saying you want to cancel the arrangement?"

More sweat trickled down David's cheeks as he struggled to maintain his composure. "I've provided good service to your father and you over the years, at some risk to me. But maybe it's time for me to retire from the force and our arrangement."

Raymond stood abruptly, his chair scraping against the floor as he came around the desk to stand before David, his face inches from David's. The scent of his cologne was overpowering, a mix of sandalwood and something darker, more menacing. "You don't seem to understand. People don't quit me unless I want them to, and I don't want you to quit—yet. So, suck up your fears and do what's necessary. If you think you can't control the interrogation, arrange for Tsui to have an accident in his cell. Report he was distraught and decided to kill himself. Figure out the best method that won't raise suspicion."

David stood, trying to muster a semblance of confidence. "Alright, but remember this: if I go down, you'll go with me. I will start making plans for my exit from the police force after I've done what you ask and move overseas to a country with no extradition."

Raymond's jaw clenched, his eyes boring into David's. "I'll assume you didn't threaten me, which would be a fatal mistake. Take care of the Tsui matter, and I'll consider releasing you from our arrangement. Fail me, and you won't be traveling anywhere—and neither will your family!" He paused, the silence in the room becoming palpable. "And when you've finished that, we'll chat about the best way to eliminate Blake Morgan. His meddling in my affairs has got to stop."

David's heart skipped a beat at the cold declaration. He nodded silently, the gravity of Raymond's threat sinking in. He left the office quickly, the weight of his predicament pressing down on him like a physical burden. As he descended the grand staircase, he could feel Raymond's eyes on his back, already plotting his next move should David fail.

The night air was cool as David stepped outside, but it did little to ease the tension within him. The moon had disappeared behind a bank of clouds, casting the mansion and its grounds in near-total darkness. David hurried to his car, his mind a whirlwind of fear and determination. He knew that his next steps would determine his fate and everyone he cared about.

There was no noble way out, no path to redemption that David could see or even wanted. His only concern now was survival – his own, and that of the family whose comfort he had prioritized over his honor. As Hong Kong's neon-lit streets blurred past his car window, Inspector David Smith steeled himself for the challenges ahead. He was a man who had willingly stepped off the edge of integrity, and now found himself in free fall, grasping at any chance to save himself from the consequences of his own actions.

Chapter 38

Unmasking the Betrayal

The atmosphere in Jack Blair's office was thick with unspoken tension, the air heavy with the weight of impending revelations. Dim light filtered through the blinds, casting long shadows across the room and accentuating the deep furrows etched into Blair's weathered face. His tall, imposing figure cast an even longer shadow as he paced back and forth, each step a deliberate, muffled thud against the worn wooden floorboards.

Blair paused before a framed photograph on his bookshelf, his stern facade cracking for just a moment as his gaze softened, tracing the outline of his daughter's smiling face. The innocence captured in that frozen moment stood in stark contrast to the grim reality he now faced. With a deep, shuddering breath that seemed to carry the weight of his years of service, he turned to face Blake.

Blake leaned forward, his voice steady but urgent. "We have a photos and audio recording of David Smith receiving an envelope containing ten thousand dollars in cash from a Min Ho man two weeks ago," he said, his tone leaving no room for doubt.

Dennis, a seasoned detective with a sharp intellect, stepped in. "We arrested the Min Ho man shortly after Inspector Smith and have charged him with attempting to bribe a police officer. He confessed the amount and revealed that Inspector Smith was a recipient of regular payouts in return for not interfering with Min Ho operations," Dennis explained, his words clipped and precise.

Blake's eyes flickered with a mix of determination and frustration. "That's not all, Chief," he continued. "Following your instructions to investigate David thoroughly, I obtained a court order to access his bank account information. We discovered regular large cash deposits which were transferred to foreign banks for the past three years."

Blair's expression darkened, his lips thinning into a tight line. "Anything else?" he asked, his voice a low growl.

"Yes," Blake said, leaning in closer. "For two weeks, we tailed David. He frequented several locations known as Triad hangouts and met with their men. On multiple occasions, he received similar envelopes from known Triad members."

"My first impulse, Blake," Blair began, a gravelly whisper filled with restrained fury, "is to throw the book at David. The tape recordings and eyewitness accounts you've provided about David's collusion with Raymond Fung, his Triad and the Mexican Cartel are damning. We could lock him up for the rest of his life."

Blake's jaw clenched and his eyes burning with determination, rose from his chair. He joined Blair by the bookshelf, staring at the family photo, feeling the weight of Blair's burden of office. "And he must be held accountable for his betrayals. But we have an opportunity here to dismantle a major Triad operation and get crucial intel on the fentanyl conspiracy involving the Tijuana Cartel and the CIA. We need to convince David it's in his best interest to spill everything he knows in exchange for a plea deal."

Blair walked over to the window, the cityscape stretching out below him, a sprawling maze of neon lights and shadows. He watched the ceaseless flow of traffic, the heartbeat of a city unaware of the dark conspiracy festering in its underbelly. "I'll need approval from the Chief Executive and the Security Bureau, but I'm confident they'll give us the green light. This has to be handled with extreme caution, Blake. David might deny everything, refuse to cooperate."

Blake's eyes flashed with intensity. "We've got to be convincing and make him an offer he can't refuse. There are two ways to do this. The official route with a plea deal and formal charges, or a more unorthodox approach: no charges and a free ticket for him and his family to leave Hong Kong, but only after we've brought Raymond Fung and his cronies to justice."

"David was once a good policeman and a good man. I believe deep down that man still exists. I want to give him the chance to redeem himself. His family deserves it, and this city deserves it," Blair replied, his voice filled with conviction. "If he agrees, he can't remain in Hong Kong. He'll have a target on his back, and maybe his family too."

"I agree, Chief. Although I have had my differences with David, there was a time when I saw him as a good policeman," Blake admitted, a hint of nostalgia in his voice.

Blair nodded, his face grim. "We need David onboard quickly. I'll call him in, confront him with the evidence, and offer a plea deal once I get the green light from my boss. How soon can you be ready?"

Blake's voice was resolute. "I'll have the tapes and witness affidavits ready by the end of the day."

Blair's expression softened, a rare glimpse of the man beneath the uniform. "Before you go, I haven't properly express my condolences for your loss of Sabrina. I know she meant a lot to you. How are you holding up?"

Blair reached out and put his arm around Blake. "Thank you, Jack," Blake said, his voice thick. Losing Sabrina has been like a knife to the heart. She had a difficult life; she deserved better."

"If you need time off . . ." Blair said empathetically.

"At some point Jack, thank you, but not now."

"So let's get moving on gathering all the evidence. Then I will arrange a meeting with David, and I'd like you two to be present," Blair said, his voice brooking no argument.

"Right, Chief," Blake answered, and he and Dennis left Blair's office quickly.

Once inside Blake's office, Blake turned to Dennis. "If you compile all the photos, audio, and witness testimony, I will get the necessary bank records. I've got the court order already. We will have everything ready for Jack," he instructed.

"Right, Blake. Are you confident David will take the deal?" Dennis asked, his voice tinged with concern.

"While I'm generally not in favor of plea deals that go easy on criminals, David's testimony regarding the fentanyl conspiracy could be invaluable for us and worth the concession," Blake responded thoughtfully.

With their plan set in motion, Blake and Dennis left police HQ. Blake, driving through the neon-lit streets, decided to make a detour to the hotel where Angela Torres, the sharp-witted DEA agent, was staying. As was now his habit, he sought her insight and wisdom on this latest development.

The city's vibrant energy mirrored the chaos swirling within Blake's mind. This case wasn't just a professional hurdle; it was a deeply personal test of loyalty and integrity. As he parked his car and approached Angela's suite, Blake knew the days ahead would be pivotal in uncovering the betrayal that had infiltrated their ranks.

"I think we've got a break in our investigation," Blake announced with a mix of optimism and urgency as he entered Angela's hotel suite and dropped onto the sofa. "But I need your thoughts before we move forward."

Angela, radiant in an orange summer dress, set aside the document she had been studying and sat beside him. "What's happened, Blake?" she asked, her eyes reflecting curiosity and concern.

"As you know, I've suspected David Smith from the beginning. His behavior has been obstructionist and downright hostile towards me. With Jack Blair's approval, we've gathered video, audio, and documented evidence proving David's been on the take from several Triads, offering them protection against prosecution. And the kicker? He's been taking bribes from Raymond Fung, who he identifies as the Dragon Head of the Min Ho Triad, now that the previous Dragon Head, Robert Lee, is dead."

Angela's eyes widened, and she kissed Blake enthusiastically. "You've hit the jackpot!"

"We're not done yet," Blake cautioned. "We need to present our ironclad evidence to David and make him spill everything he knows, especially about Raymond. Jack Blair has agreed to offer David a plea bargain. Our plan is to have David set up a meeting with Raymond, Jack Cross, and Ramirez, and wear a wire to get them on record."

"Oh, that's ambitious, but you sound confident."

"Semi-confident. I'd like your input. Is there anything we might have overlooked?"

"Overall, it sounds solid. The key will be to thoroughly prepare David. Go over every detail of the meeting, rehearse what he needs to say, and make sure he sticks to the script."

"Good advice. Thank you, Angela. Would you help with that?"

"You don't need to ask twice. Of course."

Blake stood up, determination in his eyes. "I'm heading to David's bank now to get his records showing the Triad bribes. I'll call you when we're ready to bring him in. And by the way, has anything new developed in Mexico or back in the U.S.?"

"Yes, on both fronts. In Mexico, Cartel warfare is heating up. A rival Cartel attacked Ramirez and his lieutenant Salinez in Tijuana. Salinez was killed, and Ramirez took out one of the attackers. He'll be desperate to keep the fentanyl pipeline flowing to build his private army. Back in the U.S., with Senator Connor's death, the Intelligence Committee has paused any further CIA investigation. They likely won't replace Connor with someone as dedicated to holding the CIA accountable, or they might suspend the investigation all together. So, the timing of your plan is crucial."

"Let's cross our fingers that it works!" Blake kissed Angela, feeling a surge of hope and resolve, and left the hotel, heading for David Smith's bank with a court order in hand.

Chapter 39

The Plea Deal

The dimly lit conference room in Hong Kong Police Headquarters was filled with oppressive tension. A video camera was mounted on the wall and an audio recorder was placed in the middle of the table and a TV and video recorder were placed on a cart by the table. Jack Blair and Blake Morgan were prepared to confront David Smith about his crimes.

The evidence they had gathered against Smith was irrefutable: wiretaps, documents, and damning audio-visual recordings. Today would be the day they put an end to his betrayal.

The door opened and Smith walked in, his confident demeanor masking any hint of guilt. His pristine uniform, a sharp contrast to the grime he had accumulated on his soul, only added to the bitter irony. He looked at Blake, wondering what Commissioner Blair had asked him to meet here rather than in Blair's office.

Blair motioned to Smith to take a seat at the table. Smith looked intently at the audio recording device and glanced up at the video camera on the wall.

"What's this about?" Smith inquired in a tense tone.

"David, I must tell you that our conversation is being recorded. Do you object?"

Smith shifted nervously in his seat. "How can I object when I don't know what this is about."

"Is there anything you need to hide or avoid answering David?"

"No, no, of course not."

Do you consent, David?" Blair insisted.

"Yes, go ahead," Smith snapped.

Blair nodded at Blake.

Blake switched on the audio recorder and then opened the folder on the table, revealing a series of documents and photographs. "These are financial records showing unexplained transactions in your bank accounts. Large sums of money that we can identify having been given you by several Triads and Raymond Fung. Here are photographs of you meeting with known Triad members, and recordings of your conversations." Then Blake showed Smith photos of Smith meeting with Triad members and Raymond, taking envelopes filled with cash and discussing the fentanyl drug trafficking alliance.

The color drained from Smith's face as he listened and watched to the incontrovertible evidence of his guilt. The audio played like a grim symphony, each word a note in the orchestration of his downfall.

"We also have wiretap recordings of your phone calls," Blake continued, this evidence clearly shows you were part of a drug trafficking conspiracy, offering protection and police information to the other members of the conspiracy in return for money. And it appears as though you've been taking bribes from several Triads for several years."

Smith's bravado suddenly crumbled, replaced by a look of desperation. "I was coerced," he stammered. "They threatened my family."

Blair leaned forward, his gaze piercing. "That may be true, but your actions have endangered countless lives and compromised our operations. Do you deny any of the evidence we have presented to you?"

Completely defeated, and yet almost relieved, Smith slumped in his seat, looking defeated. "No . . . no. In a way I knew this day would come."

However, we are willing to offer you a deal, David," Blair continued.

Smith looked up, a flicker of hope in his eyes. "What kind of deal?"

Blair crossed his arms, his expression unyielding. "You will turn government witness. In exchange for no charges for your criminal behavior, you will help us bring down the Triads and their associates."

Smith looked panicked. "I don't know if I can do this. What if they are suspicious or don't agree to the meeting?"

"Here is your opportunity to be convincing as though your life depends on it. In a way, it does, as you have known it," Blake retorted. "What's the alternative? A long jail sentence? Even in prison, they can exact revenge. Also, your family is not safe here."

"What's the deal you offer me," Smith asked, gaining some of his composure.

"In return for your cooperation, I am authorized to offer to relocate you and your family to another country under assumed names. If you stay here, you know they will kill you and your family," Blair said.

The room fell silent as Smith wrestled with his conscience. Finally, he nodded, resigned to his fate. "I'll do it."

"Your first task is to contact Jack Cross from a public telephone and ask him to come to the meeting you're setting up, explaining it has to be in person and that you've got critical information about police activities you need to share that might threaten their operation. We'll provide a recording device you can attach to the phone. Then, invite Cross, Raymond and Ramirez to the meeting here in Hong Kong. We need visual and audio recordings of everything. We'll set up the meeting place with remote visual and audio recording devices, because they may check you for a wire," Blair said.

"What if they don't agree to the meeting?" Smith asked, sweat forming on his upper lip.

"You'll have to be convincing David," Blake retorted. "Remind yourself that your life and your family's may depend on it."

Blair chimed in. "Once they have agreed to meet, we'll set up a meeting location for you with a hidden police presence. You will have a conversation where you get them to incriminate themselves."

"We'll coach you through what to say and rehearse until you've got it down pat," Blake added.

"Alright, alright. I agree to it. But I want a written guarantee of the plea deal," Smith replied.

"Done," Blair replied confidently. "Blake, I want you and Dennis to work with David and rehearse the phone call and meeting setup. Let me know when you're ready to go, and we'll make all the arrangements for a meeting place and a backup team for you."

"Understood," Blake said, feeling apprehensive of David's commitment, but more optimistic about breaking this case open than he had for quite a while.

Blair stood, signaling the end of the meeting. "Remember, David, this is your chance to redeem yourself and protect your family. Don't squander it."

Blake nodded, determined to see this through. The battle against the Triads was far from over, but with Smith's cooperation, they had a fighting chance. The next steps would be critical, and Blake knew they had to plan meticulously.

As they watched Smith's slowly leave Blair's office, Blake couldn't help but reflect on the complexity of human nature. Here was a man who had once stood for justice, now reduced to a pawn in a deadly game. But redemption was within reach, and Blake was determined to guide him through the perilous path ahead.

"We'll need to be ready," Blake said aloud, voicing his thoughts to Blair. "I don't fully trust him to keep his word. We should have a team in place, ready to move at a moment's notice."

Blair nodded in agreement. "I have already arranged for a team to be on standby. You'll lead the operation, Blake. Make sure everything goes according to plan."

Blake felt relief knowing that his DEA colleague, Angela Torres, would be part of the team. Angela's expertise and unflinching determination made her an invaluable ally in this dangerous game. The real war was beginning, and with every step, they edged closer to dismantling the criminal empire that threatened to engulf them all.

Chapter 40

The Invitation

The neon signs of Kowloon cast an eerie glow on Inspector David Smith's face as he stood before the weathered door of the Golden Dragon Bar. His hand hovered over the tarnished brass handle, trembling slightly. The weight of the wire beneath his shirt felt like a ticking bomb against his skin.

"You can do this, David," he muttered to himself, drawing in a deep breath that reeked of exhaust fumes and rotting garbage. With a final steadying inhale, he pushed open the door.

The interior of the Golden Dragon was a time capsule of vice and desperation. Smoke hung in thick curtains, illuminated by flickering neon beer signs. The clack of mahjong tiles mixed with the low murmur of hushed conversations in Cantonese and broken English. In a corner, an ancient jukebox crooned a melancholic Canto-pop ballad.

Smith's eyes swept the room, cataloging faces and potential threats out of habit. He recognized a few low-level Triad soldiers nursing beers at a corner table. They pointedly avoided his gaze. His reputation as a dirty cop still held weight, even as he worked to dismantle it.

He approached the bar, where a man who seemed as ancient and immovable as the hills of Hong Kong stood polishing a glass with a dingy rag. The bartender's eyes, sharp despite the deep wrinkles surrounding them, met Smith's in silent question.

Smith placed a red *lai see* envelope on the counter, sliding it forward with two fingers. The movement was smooth, practiced – a dance of corruption he'd performed countless times before. But never with stakes this high.

"I need to use your phone," Smith murmured, his voice barely audible above the ambient noise. He jerked his head towards a battered phone booth in the corner. "And I was never here."

The bartender's gnarled hand moved with surprising speed, making the envelope disappear. He gave a single, curt nod towards the booth. Message received.

Smith's shoes stuck slightly to the floor with each step as he made his way to the phone booth. The acrid stench of stale beer and decades of spilled drinks assaulted his nostrils. He slipped inside the booth, grimacing at the graffiti-covered walls and the lingering odor of cheap cologne and desperation.

With practiced ease, he attached a state-of-the-art recording device to the receiver. It was smaller than a pack of cigarettes, a marvel of technology that could potentially bring down an international criminal conspiracy. Smith's hands shook slightly as he dialed the number he'd memorized months ago, praying he hadn't forgotten a single digit.

One ring. Two. Smith's heart pounded so loudly he was sure the device would pick it up.

"Cross." The voice on the other end was curt, impatient.

Smith swallowed hard, forcing a tremor into his voice that wasn't entirely feigned. "Mr. Cross, this is David Smith in Hong Kong."

There was a sharp intake of breath on the other end of the line. When Cross spoke again, his voice was low and dangerous. "Smith? Have you lost your goddamn mind? You know better than to call me directly."

"I'm not at HQ," Smith snapped back, letting genuine frustration seep into his tone. He'd rehearsed this part extensively with Commissioner Blair, finding the right balance of fear and defiance. "I'm at a public phone in the ass-end of Kowloon. Things have gone completely FUBAR here, and I need to update you before it all goes to hell."

A beat of silence. Then, "You have two minutes. Make them count."

Smith took a deep breath, mentally reviewing the script he'd gone over a hundred times. "Blake Morgan's gotten his hands on intel about the fentanyl shipments. Raymond Fung's wife, Sabrina – she talked before Raymond had her taken care of. Morgan and his DEA partner, Torres, they're not just sniffing around anymore. They're right on top of the whole operation."

"How much do they know?" Cross's voice was tight, controlled, but Smith could hear the undercurrent of panic.

"Too much," Smith said, ramping up the fear in his voice. "They're connecting dots we didn't even know existed. Morgan's like a pit bull with a bone – he's not letting go. I've tried everything to throw him off, but... Cross, they' plan to expose the Agency's involvement."

"Damn it!" Cross exploded. Smith could almost see him, pacing in his wood-paneled office, thousands of miles away. "How the hell did this happen? You were supposed to keep a lid on things!"

"I've been trying!" Smith protested, his free hand clenching into a fist. "But Morgan's got that DEA agent Torres helping him and some credible informers. He's been two steps ahead at every turn. And now with Sabrina Fung's murder, he's out for vengeance. Cross, this is spiraling. Fast."

There was a long pause. Smith could hear Cross's heavy breathing, could almost feel the gears turning in the CIA man's head. When Cross spoke again, his voice was low, measured. "What's Raymond suggesting?"

This was it. The moment of truth. Smith's mouth went dry.

"He wants a meeting," Smith said, careful to keep his voice steady. "All of us. You, him, Ramirez. Here in Hong Kong. Face to face, where we can figure out how to contain this mess before it blows up in all our faces. He says he won't discuss it over the phone. I agree it's necessary."

The silence that followed seemed to stretch for an eternity. Smith's palm was slick with sweat against the grimy receiver. He could hear the blood rushing in his ears, drowning out the muffled sounds of the bar beyond the booth.

Cross replied after a moment of silence. "I'll be in touch with Raymond to confirm our conversation, and I suggest you arrange the meeting as soon as you can. In the meantime, do everything you can to slow down Morgan in his investigations."

Smith felt a surge of triumph, quickly tempered by the cold reality of what was to come. "Understood. I'll coordinate with Raymond on the details."

"And Smith?" Cross's voice had taken on a dangerous edge. "Make damn sure Morgan and Torres don't make any more progress before I get there. Whatever it takes. Are we clear?"

A chill ran down Smith's spine. "Crystal clear."

The line went dead. Smith slowly lowered the receiver, his hand shaking. He'd done it. Cross had taken the bait. But the real danger was just beginning.

He quickly pocketed the recording device and slipped out of the booth. As he made his way to the exit, he felt the weight of a dozen eyes on him. The Triad soldiers in the corner. The world-weary working girls by the jukebox. The ancient bartender, still polishing that same glass. They all knew a man walking a knife's edge when they saw one.

The humid Hong Kong night hit Smith like a wall as he stepped outside. He loosened his tie, gulping in air that tasted of exhaust and fried food from nearby *dai pai dongs*. His feet carried him automatically around the corner into the alley way where Blake, Jack Blair and

Angela were waiting in a van with electronic listening devices. Smith climbed up into the van.

"It's done," Smith said, his voice hoarse. He pulled out the recording device, handling it as if it were a live grenade. "Cross took the bait. He's coming to Hong Kong. And Ramirez has already agreed."

Blair accepted the device with a nod. "Good work, David. I know this wasn't easy."

"You've done the right thing," Angela added, her voice softening slightly. "This could save a lot of lives."

Blake, however, leaned forward, his face inches from Smith's. "Remember, David. There's no backing out now. We'll be watching your every move until Raymond, Ramirez and Cross are behind bars. One hint that you're playing both sides, and you'll wish the Triads had gotten to you first."

Smith met Blake's gaze unflinchingly, even as he felt a bead of sweat trickle down his spine. "I know what's at stake, Blake. For my family's sake."

A moment of truth passed between the two men. Blake leaned back, giving an understanding nod.

As the van pulled out of the alley and headed back to police HQ, for the first time in years, as David thought of the lives destroyed by the very operation he'd once protected, he felt something close to peace. Whatever happened in the coming days, he was finally on the right side of history.

In Washington, Jack Cross sat at his polished mahogany desk, his mind racing. *I can't afford to let the investigation continue. If Morgan and Torres succeed, not only would Raymond and Ramirez go down, but it could also spark wider Congressional and Administration probes into the Agency's covert activities. That was a risk I can't take. Everyone involved—Raymond, Ramirez, and Smith—is expendable. I'll go to Hong Kong and press*

Raymond, Smith and Ramirez to finish the botched job on Morgan and Torres first."

Cross slammed his fist on the desk, a gesture of steely resolve. He rose from his chair with aggressive confidence and strode out of his office, already planning his next move. The fate of his operation, and perhaps his career, depended on the next steps he would take. And he wasn't about to leave anything to chance.

Chapter 41

Showdown

The glittering tapestry of Hong Kong sprawled beneath Blake Morgan's feet, a pulsing network of light and shadow that seemed to mirror the conflicting emotions churning within him. From his vantage point atop Victoria Peak, the city's frenetic energy reached even these secluded heights, transforming the bustling harbor below into a shimmering mirage that starkly contrasted with the verdant tranquility surrounding him.

Blake's steely gaze swept over the park, his sharp mind cataloging every detail of the carefully chosen rendezvous point. By 10:00 PM, the Peak Tram would cease its relentless climb, leaving only the whisper of leaves and the distant hum of the metropolis below. It was the perfect stage for this clandestine meeting.

Unseen sentinels lined the winding roads leading to the park – Blake's carefully positioned officers in unmarked cars, their eyes peeled for the arrivals of Jack Cross and Raul Ramirez. The tension in the air was palpable, a living thing that seemed to writhe and coil around them all.

Victoria Peak, or simply "The Peak" to locals, wore many faces. By day, it was a haven of manicured gardens and riotous blooms, a lush escape from the city's frenetic pace. But as darkness fell, it became something else entirely – a place of secrets and shadows, where the panoramic views served as a reminder of how small even the mightiest could be.

In a nearby pavilion, its Victorian colonnades casting ghostly echoes of Hong Kong's colonial past, Blake and Angela huddled with his team. David Smith shifted nervously, his eyes darting like a trapped animal as he rehearsed the dangerous performance he was about to give. Two police snipers took their positions on the hill above, their scopes trained on the meeting point. Dennis Wang melted into the shadows of the surrounding foliage, his sharp eyes scanning for any sign of movement.

"Customs confirmed it," David said, replacing his walkie-talkie back in his coat jacket pocket. Cross and Ramirez are already enroute."

Blake nodded, his intense gaze never leaving David's face. "You've done well so far. Remember, we need them talking. Get them to confirm their involvement, reveal the details. Our recorders need to catch their admitted guilt."

David's hand reflexively touched his chest, feeling the weight of the hidden microphone. "And if they clam up?"

"Persistence, David. Patience. And if they ask you to cross a line – even if it involves me or Angela – you agree. Push for specifics. We need it all on tape."

A crackle from David's radio shattered the moment. "They're close," he hissed. "And Raymond just pulled in below."

"Places, everyone," Blake ordered. He and Angela disappeared into the foliage at a forty-five-degree shooting position from Dennis should they need them.

David stood alone in the pavilion, bathed in moonlight, as footsteps approached. Raymond materialized from the shadows, his eyes glinting with suspicion.

"This had better be worth my time, Smith," he growled.

"Jack Cross and Raul Ramirez should be here soon. They left the airport by taxi about twenty minutes ago," David replied calmly.

Raymond looked around suspiciously, his eyes scanning the pavilion and surrounding bushes, now only partially illuminated by a few lights. "You came alone, no one knows you're here?"

"You needn't worry," David replied, injecting a note of confidence he didn't feel. "I was due a few extra days off. As far as Commissioner Blair and Blake Morgan are concerned, I'm on a mini vacation."

The air seemed to thicken as Cross and Ramirez appeared, their silhouettes emerging from the shadows to join Raymond and Smith. The four men stood in tense silence, the weight of their collective crimes hanging heavy between them.

"This had better be good, Smith," Cross said, his voice low and dangerous. Ramirez nodded in silent agreement, his hand resting casually near the bulge of a concealed weapon.

David waited until they were all standing together before he spoke. "Blake Morgan has assembled evidence that incriminates the three of you in fentanyl drug trafficking. And he claims he has evidence, Raymond, that implicates the Min Ho in Sabrina's murder and Robert Lee's assassination."

"What kind of evidence?" Raymond replied, unperturbed.

"Eyewitness testimony, video and audio recordings, and documents," David replied, fighting to keep his voice steady.

Raymond scoffed, a cruel smile playing at his lips. "If anything, it's weak evidence. Morgan already told me he has proof of fentanyl being shipped on one of my vessels. He can't prove it wasn't planted. Nothing he can charge me with."

David pressed on, his palms sweating. "Blake says he has more. Testimony from your accountant and the ship's captain, who will testify you gave direct orders regarding the fentanyl. Also, he says he has eyewitness evidence to show your active involvement in the Min Ho Triad."

"I don't believe it," Raymond retorted. "I told the captain to make up a story if anyone investigated. He's loyal to me. And the accountant? He might have an accident any day now."

Cross leaned in, his voice dropping to a dangerous whisper. "And what has he got on Raymond that can prove he got rid of his wife?"

David swallowed hard, feeling the weight of Blake and Angela's hidden gazes. "She had confronted Raymond about her name appearing on a fentanyl manifest document. He claimed clerical error, but then she shared the information and more documents with Morgan. Apparently, she had done some investigation on her own."

Raymond's facade cracked, just for a moment, rage and fear flashing in his eyes. "I couldn't afford to let her live," he hissed. "Besides, the bitch had left her entire large estate to Morgan and cut me out."

David's heart raced, knowing they were close to the admission they needed. "One other thing, Raymond. Blake has eyewitness testimony identifying you talking to Ramirez about fentanyl in the Hong Kong Club."

Raymond waved a dismissive hand. "That's true, but I'll deny it. My word against his. Besides, Raul could prove he was in Mexico."

"Easy to do," Ramirez agreed.

"There's more, Raul. Angela Torres told us the Mexican Federal Police agent heading the bust on your Manzanillo operation, Jimmy Candelero, now has eyewitness testimony that it's your operation. He has a sympathetic prosecutor and judge ready to come after you," Smith added. "And, Jack, he has a judge who will testify your man along with a State Department accomplice extradited the AERCO pilot."

"In Mexico, buying off prosecutors and judges and eliminating witnesses is standard practice. They'll never get me for my fentanyl operation or any others before it," Ramirez said.

"Torres said Candelero managed to kick the issue upstairs and has the Federal prosecutors—someone named Gonzalez—prepared to come after you," Smith said.

"*Mierda!* Gonzalez is trouble." Ramirez exclaimed.

"And Morgan's collaborator, DEA Agent Angela Torres, says she now has proof the CIA, under your orders Jack, was collaborating with Raul's Cartel. And she claims she has evidence connecting you to Senator Connor's death," Smith continued.

Cross's laughter was chilling. "I don't care if she's got proof of my collaboration. The National Security Council won't do anything about it. And the Senate investigation is dead, just like Connor."

"But my estimation of Special Agent Torres is that she's persistent and won't give up," Smith said.

"Is there anything else, Smith?" Cross asked, somewhat annoyed. "I don't think this required my trip to Hong Kong."

"Earth-shattering or not," Raymond asserted, his voice dropping to a menacing growl, "we can't afford to let things stand as they are. Raul and I don't want anything to interfere with our fentanyl operation."

"It's clear that both Jack and I can't have Torres meddling in our operations anymore," Ramirez said. "She's got to go."

"It's Best to make the hit on her here in Hong Kong; it's too risky now to do it in the U.S.," Cross said matter-of-factly.

"Smith, what are they planning to do?" Ramirez asked.

Fighting to keep his voice steady, David replied, "My understanding is they are putting together all the evidence to make arrests any day now."

"Well, there's a simple solution. Eliminate Blake and Torres, and the problem goes away," Raymond said with finality.

"And I know the perfect person to do that," Cross said, looking intently at David.

"You want me to kill Blake and Torres?" Smith asked incredulously. "I'm no killer."

"You have the easiest access and can arrange to meet alone. The alternative is us seeing you as a loose end, David," Ramirez said with a grin, "and we don't like loose ends."

"If you need something to strengthen your spine David. I can get a reliable asset in Macao to help you," Cross said.

"David, I would like to be personally involved in eliminating Morgan. He's been a thorn in my side for too long," Raymond said.

"Alright, that's more than enough firepower than you need, David. Work out the logistics of when and where, and do it soon," Cross said. "And unless there's something else, I'm going to eat and rest, and head back to Washington in the morning. And one final word of warning. Do your job. Nobody and nothing are beyond my reach."

The tension in the air was electric as the men started to disperse. Suddenly, the night exploded into chaos as Blake and Angela burst from the bushes, guns drawn. "Stay where you are!" Blake's voice thundered across the park. "Hands in the air, you too, David. You're all under arrest!"

David's hands shot up immediately, his face a mask of feigned shock. Cross slowly raised his hands, a smirk playing at the corners of his mouth. Raymond and Ramirez, however, reacted with lightning speed, their hands diving for their concealed weapons.

Time seemed to slow as Blake watched Raymond's hand emerge with a gleaming forty-give caliber pistol.

The peaceful night air was shattered by a deafening cacophony of gunfire from the police snipers, Dennis, Blake and Angela, returning fire from Raymond and Ramirez. Blake and Angela dropped to the ground, making themselves smaller targets as bullets whizzed overhead. Raymond's shots went wide, missing Blake by inches.

Raymond's chest erupted in a spray of crimson as multiple rounds struck him, sending him crashing to the ground with a sickening thud.

Ramirez managed to squeeze off a shot that grazed Angela's leg, eliciting a sharp cry of pain. But even as she fell, Angela's training took over. Her gun never wavered as she returned fire, her bullet finding its mark with deadly accuracy. Ramirez's head snapped back, a look of surprise frozen on his face as he toppled backward, his body riddled with additional sniper rounds.

In the sudden lull that followed Ramirez's fall, a new sound cut through the night – a strangled cry of pain and shock. Blake's head whipped around to see David Smith stumbling backward, a crimson stain blossoming on his chest. In the chaos of the firefight, an errant bullet – likely from one of the snipers – had found an unintended target. David's eyes were wide with confusion and betrayal as he collapsed, dead before he hit the ground.

The echoes of gunfire faded, replaced by an eerie silence broken only by the ringing in Blake's ears and the distant wail of approaching sirens. Smoke hung in the air, the acrid smell of cordite mingling with the metallic scent of blood.

Blake's eyes darted around the battlefield that had once been a peaceful park. Raymond lay motionless, a pool of blood spreading beneath him.

Ramirez was sprawled awkwardly by the pavilion, his unseeing eyes staring at the star-filled sky.

Only one man remained standing amidst the carnage. Jack Cross stood with his hands raised, that infuriating smirk still plastered on his face, as if the bloodshed around him was little more than an inconvenience.

Dennis Wang emerged from the bushes, his gun trained unwaveringly on Cross. His usual calm demeanor was shaken, his eyes wide as he took in the scene of devastation.

"Dennis, watch Cross," Blake ordered, his voice hoarse but steady. Adrenaline still coursed through his veins as he moved swiftly to Angela's side, his heart in his throat as he assessed her wound.

"I'm alright, Blake," Angela said through clenched teeth. "It's a shallow flesh wound in my thigh. No major damage."

Blake's hands shook slightly as he tore a strip from his shirt, pressing it firmly against Angela's wound. "Here, apply pressure until the medics arrive. I need to check on the others." His eyes met hers for a moment, volumes of unspoken emotion passing between them.

Rising to his feet, Blake turned to face Cross, who stood with his hands raised, an infuriating smirk still plastered on his face. "Turn around and put your hands behind your back."

"Wait, Blake, wait!" Angela called out. "This will be my pleasure." She hobbled over, took Blake's handcuffs and cuffed Cross. "I guess we won't be having that lunch together after all, Jack," Angela said sarcastically. She not so gently pushed him in the back, so that he stumbled a few steps.

As Dennis read Cross his rights, the CIA operative's smile never faltered. "This has been most entertaining, but I'll be on a flight back to Washington in the morning."

Angela spun Cross around and placed her face close to Cross' and poked her finger in his chest. "You are such an arrogant bastard. You think you and the CIA are omnipotent and untouchable. History will show how corrupt and incompetent you both really are! "

Blake walked over to check on David Smith. His fingers sought a pulse, finding nothing. A wave of pity for Smith washed over him as he looked down at the man who had, in his final act, helped bring down a criminal empire.

Next, he knelt beside Raymond, who lay gasping on the ground, blood pooling beneath him. "Medics are on their way."

Raymond's eyes blazed with hatred. "I . . . don't need your pity, Blake," he choked out. "Don't . . . think you've won . . . we're too powerful and ruthless . . . you've just . . . signed . . . your death warrant." With a final, rattling breath, Raymond's eyes glazed over, staring sightlessly at the star-filled sky above.

Blake closed Raymond's eyes, a complex mix of emotions washing over him. He checked Ramirez briefly, confirming what he already knew. The Cartel leader was dead, his reign of terror finally at an end.

The wail of approaching sirens filled the air as Blake returned to Angela's side. He took her hand, squeezing it gently. "Backup and medics are here. They'll probably want to take you to the hospital to ensure proper treatment. I'll meet you there after we secure Cross at police HQ." He leaned in, pressing a soft kiss to her forehead.

"I'll be fine, Blake," Angela reassured him, her voice stronger now. "We did it. It's over."

But as Blake held her hand, waiting for the medics to arrive, he couldn't shake the feeling that this was far from over. His eyes met Cross's across the blood-soaked pavilion, and a chill ran down his spine. The smug confidence in the CIA operative's gaze told Blake that their battle was just beginning.

As the park erupted into a flurry of activity – medics rushing in, officers securing the scene – Blake felt the weight of what they'd accomplished. But mixed with the relief was a gnawing sense of unease. They had struck a blow against a powerful criminal network, but at what cost? And what repercussions would they face in the days to come?

Chapter 42

Escape from Consequences

The late afternoon shadows filtered through the tall windows of Jack Blair's office at police headquarters, casting a warm, golden hue across the room. Papers, files, and maps cluttered the large oak desk, while the walls bore the weight of countless photographs and case evidence. The scent of old leather and the faint aroma of coffee permeated the air, blending with the hum of distant chatter and ringing phones from the bustling precinct outside.

Commissioner Jack Blair, stood at the head of the table, his presence commanding yet approachable. He leaned forward, his face illuminated by the soft glow of the setting sun. "First, I want to congratulate and express my thanks for your success in cracking this case wide open, Blake, Angela, and Dennis," Blair said enthusiastically, his voice resonating with pride and relief. "This has sent a strong signal to the criminal community in Hong Kong that we're coming after them."

Blake Morgan, his eyes steely with determination yet softened by exhaustion, nodded appreciatively. "Thank you, Chief. It was a team effort," he replied, his voice steady. "We can only hope the same success occurs in Mexico and Washington."

Angela Torres, her face framed by dark, flowing hair leaned on her cane for support. "I'm optimistic that my counterpart in Mexico, Jimmy Candelero, will bring legal and police superiors onside and help him go after all the Cartels there, not just the Tijuana Cartel," she added, her tone resolute. "I'm also hopeful a dedicated and aggressive Senator takes over from Senator Connor for the Senate Intelligence Committee. They need to continue to hold the CIA's feet to the fire."

Blair nodded, his eyes narrowing in thought. "Is there anything else we need to add to our files on this case, Blake?"

Blake's expression darkened. "It turns out that Raymond was a bigger wolf in sheep's clothing than I had guessed. We have evidence now that he ordered the hit on Robert Lee, the Dragon Head of the Min Ho Triad, and Sabrina Fung. We've been able to break up the Min Ho, and their remaining members have scattered," he replied, the weight of his words hanging heavy in the room.

"I want to say a few words about David Smith. Once, a long time ago, David was a good, honest policeman who brought credit to our profession. At some point, he lost his way, and was seduced by the lure of money. In his final day on this earth, he restored his career, although not entirely, willingly. But let's remember him for his final act," Blair said.

"I agree, Jack. David put himself at great risk to help us crack this case wide open. For that we can honor him," Blake said.

"And I'm going to keep my promise regarding protecting his family. As we speak, his family are on their way to Vietnam with new identities. It's one of the countries where you can get lost easily, and nobody asks questions."

Blake's brow furrowed. "And what's the status of Jack Cross?"

Blair's shoulders slumped, a look of resignation on his face. "You won't like this. Cross was traveling here on what is known as 'Official Cover,' which means he was assigned a position in the U.S. Embassy here and held a diplomatic passport. He enjoyed the same diplomatic immunity as other diplomats under the Vienna Convention of Diplomatic Relations, which includes immunity from arrest, detention, and prosecution by the host country's authorities. He's been released and is on his way home."

Blake's jaw tightened, a flash of anger crossing his face. "Damn it! That explains his nonchalant attitude when we arrested him. He was covering his ass and knew we couldn't arrest and charge him."

Angela's eyes blazed with frustration. "Can you at least provide all the evidence we collected to the U.S. State Department to follow up on?"

Blair nodded, though his expression was skeptical. "We'll do that, but I wouldn't hold my breath hoping they'll do something about it."

Dennis interjected, "Now that Ramirez is dead, won't Cross' collaboration with a Cartel fall apart?"

Angela shook her head, her gaze steely. "One thing I've learned about the Mexican Cartels is that when one leader goes down, another one takes his place. Although Ramirez and his right-hand man, Salinez, are dead, someone else will take over. Cross doesn't care who, as long as they do what he wants."

Blair placed a reassuring hand on Blake's shoulder. "Blake, I want you to take a couple of weeks off. You deserve it. We can talk when you get back about what's next for you. I'm sure Angela could probably arrange some more time off herself," he said, glancing pointedly at Angela's leg.

Blake managed a weary smile. "You don't have to ask me twice."

The meeting concluded, and as Blake and Angela left the dimly lit office, the weight of their recent battles seemed to lift slightly. They walked slowly, Angela leaning on her cane, the pain in her leg a constant reminder of the dangers they had faced. The air outside was cool, the city alive with the sounds of evening.

They headed towards Sabrina's family home, now Blake's by her will. The mansion stood tall and silent, a stark contrast to the chaos they had just left behind. As they approached, Blake squeezed Angela's hand, their silent bond a testament to the battles fought and the ones still to come.

Chapter 43

A New Purpose

Blake found Angela resting on a chaise lounge just a few feet from the water surface in the Indian Ocean. They had come here on their planned vacation break to the St. Regis Vommuli Resort in the Maldives, their luxury villa on stilts in the crystal-clear blue water.

Blake sat down beside her, handed her a tall cold drink, and gently ran his fingers over the scar of the bullet wound she had sustained in their gun battle with Raymond Fung and Raul Ramirez.

"It's so beautiful and calm here, so far from the chaos that has filled our lives in the past year," Angela said. "I beginning to wonder if I want to go back to it."

They had faced down one of the most intricate webs of crime imaginable, a conspiracy that spanned continents and involved some of the most powerful players in the underworld. They had disrupted it, but at a great cost. The Triads, the Mexican Cartel, and the rogue elements within the CIA had all suffered blows, but the war was far from over.

"While you were out for a swim I received more bad news, but in a way, I'm not surprised, just saddened. Jimmy Candelero in Mexico said that all charges against the remaining members of the Tijuana Cartel have been dropped, as Raul and Salinez are both dead. And wait for this, the Senate Intelligence Committee hearings about CIA corruption have been put on hold indefinitely," Angela said.

Blake squinted as though he was trying to see something far out to sea. "In a way, I have expected this, but, held out hope it wouldn't happen."

Angela's voice was soft but tinged with the weight of their shared experiences. "Blake, do you ever wonder if we're just patching up a sinking ship?"

Blake turned to her, his eyes searching hers. "Every day, Angela. Every damn day. We've made a difference, but sometimes it feels like we're fighting an endless tide."

She nodded, taking sip of her drink. "The more we dig, the more we uncover the depth of the corruption. It's not just the criminals. It's the politicians, the bankers, the corporations . . . . They all have a hand in it."

Blake sighed, running a hand through his hair. "And they're the ones with the real power. We've cut off a few heads, but the beast just keeps growing new ones."

"I'm beginning to believe that the idea of the war on drugs is not just fruitless, it's making the problem worse."

"What do you mean?"

"The research experts I've consulted have come to these conclusions," Angela began, her voice tinged with frustration. "Despite billions spent on enforcement, drug use rates have not significantly decreased in America. One study found that drug prices have generally decreased while purity and availability have increased over time."

Blake nodded, his eyes dark with worry. "Go on."

"The war on drugs has led to a dramatic increase in incarceration rates, disproportionately affecting minorities and reinforcing the problem of inequality. Criminalizing drug use has deterred many people from seeking treatment and promoted riskier drug use practices," Angela continued, her voice growing more passionate.

Blake reached out, taking her hand in his. "It's more than frustrating. It's disheartening."

Angela squeezed his hand. "The financial burden of enforcement and incarceration has been immense. As it stands now, the U.S. spends over fifty billion dollars annually on the war on drugs. And as we've experienced, this war has created a lucrative black market, empowering drug Cartels and criminal networks, sometimes destabilizing entire countries."

Blake sighed deeply. "As usual, Angela, you're right on target. I want to add to that my perspective on the business aspect of the war on drugs. Criminalizing drugs has actually increased the profitability of drug trafficking. As legal risks increase, so do potential profits, attracting more criminal elements. The data I looked at suggests that profit margins can be three hundred percent or more, compared to five to ten percent in many legal businesses."

""The enormous profits from drug trafficking have allowed Cartels to amass huge resources," Angela responded, her voice heavy with disillusionment. "They regularly use this wealth to corrupt government officials, purchase sophisticated weapons, and establish parallel power structures rivaling governments. In fact, some Cartels have budgets rivaling those of small countries."

Blake nodded, his grip on her hand tightening. "And the competition for control of drug routes and markets has led to violence among criminal organizations, often spilling over into civilian casualties. To combat these violent drug trafficking organizations, law enforcement has increasingly resorted to more violence themselves."

"As drug trafficking organizations have grown more powerful," Angela continued, "they've branched out into other criminal enterprises such as human trafficking and arms smuggling, making them more resilient to law enforcement efforts focused solely on drugs."

Blake looked into her eyes, sharing her disillusionment. "In many countries, particularly in drug-producing and transit nations, the power of drug Cartels has grown to rival that of the central government. Ironically, they may even provide services and employment in areas where the government is absent, thereby gaining local citizens' support."

"And finally," Angela said, her voice tinged with sadness, "the profitability of the drug trade has allowed criminal organizations to expand beyond their borders to global operations. They've developed sophisticated international networks for production, transportation, and distribution, aided by legitimate big businesses and banks, making them increasingly difficult to combat."

Angela turned to face him fully. "So, what do we do? Keep fighting—fighting a war that can't be won? Do we walk away while we still can?"

Blake reached out, taking her hand in his. The warmth of her touch was a reminder of everything they had gained—and everything they had to lose. "You're right. The war on drugs isn't just a fight against criminals. It's a fight for the kind of world we want to live in."

Angela looked to the sky as though she was searching for something. "A thought came to me in the night. What has made the CIA almost untouchable?"

"The legal framework, protection by the White House and Congress, little or no accountability," Blake said matter-of-factly.

"And their massive off the books black-ops operations! What if I could convince the DEA to create a parallel structure strictly mandated to go after the people at the top of the drug trafficking world—the politicians, powerful business interests, corrupt banks?" Angela asked enthusiastically. The DEA has been losing the turf war with the CIA for some time now. Time is ripe to balance the scales."

"It almost sounds like a movie plot!"

"Maybe it does. Think about it. Increasingly, the Pentagon is using contract soldiers or mercenaries to do some of the dirty work for them overseas to reduce official American casualties. In many cases we have little knowledge about their activities. Why not build a parallel structure?"

"I like the idea, Angela, but would the powerbrokers in the DEA, FBI, State Department and White House go for it?"

"What's the alternative Blake? Being content with a drug bust here and there with little or no effect on the trafficking empires? I think it's worth a try, and I'm happy to carry the flag. I can't stay on for the status quo. And the other thing we can do support this strategy is to use our considerable financial resources to provide campaign contributions to those politicians in Congress and both political parties who agree with us, so that we have allies in our fight."

Blake nodded.

"And I know of some corporate leaders and investors with deep pockets who might be interested in getting onboard with us," Angela said with gusto.

"You've convinced me. And we both know, money talks. Sign me on. And I'm thinking I might be able to get the government in Hong Kong to collaborate."

Angela embraced Blake enthusiastically. "We now have a purpose Blake that I can pursue with passion—with you. Our fight is not over, it's just begun. And I can promise you, Jack Cross hasn't seen the end of me."

"Whatever we do, we'll do it together. I want you in my life forever."

Blake kissed her passionately. "You don't have to ask twice!" They embraced, looking out to the setting sun on the golden waves.

Afterword

I hope that this novel goes beyond sheer entertainment and enjoyment for readers. I wanted also to draw attention to how drug trafficking has become a global enterprise involving not just drug Cartels and crime syndicates, but also corrupt police, politicians, government officials, businesspeople and financial institutions.

Unfortunately, the popular public perception about drug trafficking is often depicted in movies and TV shows law enforcement pursuing the criminals at the bottom of trafficking organizations and sensationalizing drug busts by showing pictures or videos of tables covered in drugs or money. Rarely do we see the politicians, government officials, corporate leaders and power brokers at the top of drug trafficking enterprises.

The appearance of fentanyl in the drug world has created a deadly new menace to combat, along with the infrastructure that creates and supports it.

It's clear the war on drugs has failed according to multiple research studies. It's time to look at the problem from a different perspective and pursue smarter and more viable solutions.

Another step forward is to declare drug addiction a public health issue rather than a law enforcement issue.

Although this is a work of fiction, it contains many factual references, which are readily available in the public record.

About the Author

Ray Williams has had a lifelong career as an executive, leadership trainer, and executive coach and has written several books on leadership, the workplace, and personal growth. He has undergraduate and graduate education in History, English, Psychology and Management, and certification as a Master Executive Coach and Hypnotherapist.

He has written extensively about the workplace, organizations, personal development, and social issues. He also wrote a novel and screenplay and been interviewed or written articles for national publications and the media such as *The National Post, The Financial Post, The Washington Post, Entrepreneur,The Globe and Mail,* the *Vancouver Sun, USA Today* and *Inc.,* and online media such as *Psychology Today, Medium and Sivana East.*

His previous books are:

The Leadership Edge: Strategies to Transform School Systems.
Eye of the Storm: How Mindful Leaders Can Transform Chaotic Workplaces.
Toxic Bosses: Practical Wisdom for Developing Wise, Ethical and Moral Leaders.
Macho Men: How Toxic Masculinity Harms Us All and What To Do About It.
I Know Myself and Neither Do You: Why Charisma, Confidence and Pedigree Won't Take You Where You Want to Go.
Virtuous Leadership: The Character Secrets of Great Leaders.
The Journey to Self-Mastery: Unlocking the Secrets to Personal Transformation.
Dragon Tamer

Beyond his professional training and experience, he also brings insights into human behavior. He was born and raised in Hong Kong, where his family was imprisoned for four years by the Japanese in

WWII. This experience allows him a unique perspective on resilience, overcoming adversity, and sustaining a positive outlook.